JOHN SMOLENS

Angel's Head

J O H N   S M O L E N S

Angel's Head

A Foul Play Press Book

The Countryman Press
Woodstock, Vermont

Library of Congress Cataloging-in-Publication Data
Smolens, John.
    Angel's Head : a novel of suspense / John Smolens.
        p.   cm.
    "A Foul Play Press Book."
    ISBN 0-88150-297-9
    1. Police--Massachusetts--Cape Cod--Fiction. 2. Cape Cod (Mass)--Fiction. I. Title.
    PS3569.M646A83 1994
    813'.54--dc20   94-6641
                                        CIP

Text design by Chelsea Dippel

A Foul Play Press Book
The Countryman Press, Inc.
Woodstock, Vermont 05091-0175

Printed in the United States of America
by Quebecor Printing Book Press Inc

Acknowledgments

*Many thanks to my mother,
my brothers Peter and Michael,
and my sister Elizabeth;
and to Philip Spitzer.*

For Reesha

Author's Note

Readers familiar with Cape Cod's Pleasant Bay will know that none of its islands is named Angel's Head, and that the most recent breach in Nauset actually took place several miles south of where it is situated in this book.

If a man be gracious and courteous to strangers, it shows he is a citizen of the world, and that his heart is no island cut off from other islands, but a continent that joins to them.

—Francis Bacon

One

THE ISLAND LIES IN PLEASANT BAY ON THE ELBOW OF CAPE Cod. From the steep bluffs above the beaches it's easy to read the bay water by its changing colors—in sunlight the jade green shallows fan out to foaming rip currents, which mark the sudden drop to an ink blue channel. Powerful tides and the perpetual migration of sand shaped the island like a comma, its pointed southern tip beginning at Plummer's Marsh; curling northeast, the island widens and rises above the water, until it concludes at the round cove that appears to be a clean bite taken out of its northern end. The small village embracing the cove has been inhabited by generations of fishermen, clammers, and scallopers, though in recent decades a tourist trade has developed and summer cottages have been built wherever there is a view of the water. The island was first named after one of the local tribes— Titicut—but early in the seventeenth century the English explorer Bartholomew Gosnold renamed it Angel's Head because the cove lies below two elongated hummocks that appear to sweep upward from the water like wings, and on summer evenings the sun sets in the notch, presenting a crude image of an angel. Countless seamen have been thankful to reach the small, protected harbor, but were usually more thankful to make their departure. During Emerson Flood's lifetime of seventy-three years, it has ordinarily been a quiet place.

A fresh sea breeze blew across his porch, a relief after the day's heat, as he watched his granddaughter Rachel climb the path to his cottage, bearing a green bottle in one hand and the mail under her arm. Beyond her lay the inn and its cluster of outbuildings, the harbor and, two miles to the east, Nauset Beach, the narrow strip of sand that protects Pleasant Bay from the open Atlantic. The inn was built by his grandfather just over a century ago, in the late 1880s.

Rachel was fifteen and in the past year had undergone a dramatic transformation: her face suddenly sprouted an occasional blemish, and her developing hips and breasts caused her at times to move awkwardly and with shyness, but now she easily bounded up the steps to the porch. She leaned down, kissed his cheek, and laid the mail in his lap. As she sat in the other wicker chair she placed the beer bottle on the floor between them. Most summer evenings he questioned her about the events of the day at the inn, but tonight they both just stared out at the bay. He drank the beer from the green bottle—Rachel's mother Anne had him on what she considered to be daily rationing.

"Grapes, the detectives arrived on the five o'clock ferry." She had her grandmother's blue eyes, which is one reason she was so dear to him. Since she was a baby she'd called him Grapes, a mispronunciation of Gramps— though in the last year or so it had taken on a new meaning for her, since she made the connection between grapes and alcohol.

"'Detectives,'" he said. "A peculiar term, when you think about it."

"That's what they're called on TV."

"I suppose."

"Or dicks."

Television. It was one of the few concessions made to Rachel's generation. Access—that's what television provided—and Emerson couldn't help think that it only made the isolation here on the island more difficult. Television's constant parade of automobiles, cosmetics, rock videos, appliances—though the mainland was less than a mile away across water, a child of her age, in the last years of the twentieth century, must feel irrevocably, unjustly cut off. Still, she continued to face the ocean, her back defiantly to the mainland.

"Mom says for you to do it." Rachel hesitated, her finger probing a spot on her chin. "She's busy in the kitchen. She thinks you should deal with them instead of Cyrus."

"They'll want to talk to him eventually. They'll want to talk to everybody."

"And no one's seen Randall all afternoon."

"Just as well." His beer was half finished and, as usual, the ocean seemed a richer hue. To the east, above the horizon, high pink cumulus darkened toward purple. Laying the papers on the porch floor, he said, "Thirty-eight." Rachel looked at him. He knew they all debated how far gone he was, if he had, as Rachel would say, lost it. "The hurricane of thirty-eight," he said, getting to his feet slowly. "Totally unexpected: no predictions, no weather channel like nowadays. Except your grandmother Sarah said she could feel

14

something in her knees, and sure enough we watched that barometer drop like a stone. It was horrifying. The island was devastated, and the inn was nearly destroyed—it was so bad we considered selling the place."

Rachel continued to pick at the blemish on her chin. She did not seem wholly convinced: their family and this island were so closely entwined, she probably could not imagine one without the other. She gazed down upon the cove, where the boats were turning on the tide while Emerson drank his beer. There was one schooner, long and sleek in the tight cove, sitting on the glassine water with the poise and delicacy of a swan.

"This tiny island has been my vessel," he said after his beer was finished, "constantly battered by the waves, by the tides. Her beaches are my bow, her dunes my quarterdeck. Though my voyage has been stationary, it has not been an idle one. All these years I have watched and waited. Ships come and go from Angel's Head. Sometimes I think this island lures them." He looked at Rachel, and in her profile could see both his wife Sarah and their daughter Anne. "I imagine that one day you'll leave the island," he said.

Rachel continued to stare down at the cove, but she whispered, "Everything is an island."

They walked down the hill, raising cardinals from the bushes, and being careful not to damage the roses that leaned in their way. When they reached the fork in the path Rachel headed toward the Boat House, where she worked during the summer tourist season. Before she reached the shingled building above the harbor Emerson saw her pause a moment to gaze once again at the schooner. Here at the bottom of the hill the boat seemed larger, her masts dominating the cove.

Emerson continued on to the inn. It was late July, the busiest part of their season. By Thanksgiving the guests were few; from January to March the inn was not officially open, though they'd never turned away anyone who'd knocked at the door on a cold winter's night. Since Sarah died a decade ago, Emerson had little to do with the daily operation of the establishment. He referred to himself as Innkeeper Emeritus. Rachel's mother Anne and her husband Cyrus ran the place with the assistance of Anne's brother Randall and the temporary employees who hired on for the summer.

Though the dining room was full, Emerson immediately noticed two men sitting at the table near a front window. They had to be the detectives—a large black man dressed like a tourist and a thin white man wearing a tan summer suit.

"Welcome to Angel's Head, gentlemen. Sorry to keep you waiting."

The black man looked up from his apple pie à la mode. He wore a blue sport shirt that stretched taut over his girth, and he had the hands of a pugilist. His nose was quite flat, causing Emerson to wonder if he had not at some time won a purse or two.

"You must be Emerson Flood," the other man said, who had only a cup of coffee before him. "I'm Wendell Page and this is James McNeil—Homicide Division, State Police." His hands, in contrast to his partner's, were delicate, thin, and decorous: he wore three rings. His black hair was heavily oiled, and a wide-brimmed straw hat rested on the windowsill beside him.

"I gather you'd like to see what we've found," Emerson said, "but certainly it can wait until after you've finished your coffee and pie."

"This pie is excellent," McNeil said. "I never work on an empty stomach." McNeil smiled as though he were sharing a joke with Emerson, a joke that seemed to be at his partner's expense.

Page said, "I'm under the impression there isn't a body."

The dining room behind Emerson seemed now too quiet. "That is correct," he said softly.

"Well," McNeil said, pushing away his empty plate, "show us what you've got."

They walked through the dining room to the bar, which had been closed for the day.

"You were asked not to touch anything?" Page said.

"It sounded more like an instruction," Emerson said.

"We had a poor connection," McNeil said playfully.

"It seems we've had a bad connection with the mainland since the phone cable was laid during World War II." Emerson led them through the barroom to the back door. As they crossed the sand to the first outbuilding, he was flanked by the detectives. It was not the same as walking with guests; he didn't feel in control. However, he relied on some of his old banter to overcome what seemed to be a purposeful silence. Among other things, he was something of a local historian. "At some point several decades ago," he said, pulling the key ring from his windbreaker, "we realized the mainland was suffering from an ailment commonly referred to as progress. We decided to inoculate—or you might say isolate—ourselves as best we could, and we resisted changing the way we did things out here. Only year-round residents are allowed to have cars. The butter served in the dining room is churned, and tonight's catch was brought in by our own charter boat—caught by our guests. We've seen many a lean year, but

16

the fact is doing things the old way allows us to survive the vicissitudes of public taste. Lately, I suspect, people have come to appreciate visiting Angel's Head because of a growing disenchantment with progress." They arrived at the outbuilding door and he sorted through the key ring.

"But you have phones," Page said.

"Installed, as I said, during the war, when islanders kept a lookout for U-boats."

"And electricity," McNeil said.

"Yes, we've made certain concessions." Emerson unlocked the door and opened it, and, as if to prove his point, reached around the corner and switched on the light. "This island is determined to survive."

"Survive?" McNeil said. "The island?"

"Not all of them do, you know. Not the way things change in this bay. There used to be an island out here called Slut's Bush." He glanced at them briefly. "Can't find it on a map anymore."

"Currents shift," McNeil said.

"Yep. Salt water changes everything."

They stepped inside the building, which was really no more than a long, narrow shed. It had once served as a sail loft, but now the walls were lined with shelves full of canned goods.

Page looked up at the bare bulb suspended from the beam above them. "Was that on when you found it?"

"I'm not sure. You'll have to ask my son, Randall. He found it."

"And what time was that?"

"Shortly after lunch. About one o'clock."

"No one came in here before that?"

"I don't know."

At the back of the shed stood an old walk-in cooler; McNeil pulled on the handle and led them inside. The shelves were lined with tubs of butter, cartons of meat, and fish. It was in the corner next to a box marked sausage.

"Randall said he thought it was a piece of raw liver at first. He came for me."

"Where were you?"

"Back there in the barroom." They looked at him, expecting further explanation. "Randall and my son-in-law Cyrus do the manual labor around here, and Cy tends bar. I had just come into the bar where they were setting up for the evening rush. Cy sent Randall out here to get something, but he came back empty-handed. He seemed shaken, uncertain. Soon as I saw it I knew it was not just a cut of meat."

Leaning close to the shelf now, McNeil whispered, "It's a heart all right."

Page kept his distance. For a detective he seemed squeamish.

"Can you tell if it's human?" Emerson asked.

"We will take it to the mainland for tests," Page said.

"Oh it's human," McNeil said.

"How do you know?"

"You can always smell these things." McNeil found a box of Saran Wrap on a shelf just outside the cooler and tore off a large sheet. He carefully gathered up the organ and wrapped it.

"You said Cyrus sent Randall out here," Page said. "Where is your son?"

"We haven't seen him since." Both McNeil and Page watched Emerson. "Randall is the eldest of them, two years older than Anne and her husband. He had an accident years ago, a head injury. He's kind of a village stray, and it's not uncommon for us to not see him for a while."

"This head injury—"

"It affected his memory. He remembers things up to when he was in his early teens, but beyond that it comes and goes—"

"What kind of accident?" McNeil asked.

"A boating accident."

Page nodded. "All the guests, are they accounted for?"

"No one's been reported missing."

"And the rest of the island?"

"That's another story. There are maybe two hundred year-round residents, but this time of year there's three, four times that many. Then there are the daily tourists—"

"People come and go, I imagine," Page said.

"Every day the ferry's loaded with day-trippers."

"Who has a key to this shed?"

"Well, there's me, Randall, Cyrus, my daughter Anne—but there's a staff key that hangs on a nail in the kitchen."

McNeil took a small blue and white Igloo cooler from another shelf and placed the wrapped heart inside. He might have been handling something fragile and precious, like pastry warm from the oven.

Two

RACHEL MADE A FIST AND LOOKED AT IT CAREFULLY. A FIST: the detectives said it was about the size of a person's heart.

She placed her other hand inside her blouse, her fingertips pressing into the top of her left breast. Holding her breath, she could feel it—faintly at first. Then it became clear, not so much a beat as a double surge, the first one slightly more pronounced than the second. *ONE-two, ONE-two, ONE-two,* and she flexed her fist in time with the double surge in her breast. The rhythm was determined and persistent. It just kept coming. It beat of its own accord. How did it start in the first place?

"How do you know these things?" her mother asked. She was filleting haddock, her hands covered with scales that shone like flakes of glass. They worked at the old stove in the rear of the kitchen, their backs to the bustle of waiters, waitresses, busboys, the commands of cooks on the line.

"They were sitting on the porch," Rachel said, taking her hand out of her blouse. "They said a heart that large probably belonged to a man, though it could have been from a large woman. They're taking it back to the mainland to run tests."

"What tests?" Her mother was not a large woman, but quite tall. She had long dark brown hair, streaked with gray, which she said appeared within days of delivering Rachel. She never said this as though Rachel were responsible, though she more than once seemed to suggest that Rachel's father had been the culprit.

"Did Cy know my father?" Rachel asked.

She watched her mother pause, the boning knife still buried in the white flesh of the haddock. Then she continued to slice along the spine with a determined, wriggling motion. "No," she said, wiping hair from her brow with a wrist. "I met your father before Cy. I've told you this before." When she was finished cutting the haddock she looked at Rachel. "And

I've told you before: your father is not an issue. He hasn't been a part of your life, so there's no use trying to find out—"

"I was thinking about my heart," Rachel said. "About the exact moment when it started beating. Would my pulse have been synchronized with yours? Or would there be something in my father's sperm that set it off?"

Her mother took the fillet and laid it in the greased pan with the others. She was pouting her lips in a way that meant she was trying not to say the first thing that came to mind. When giving orders around the inn Anne Flood rarely hesitated, and no one—not the employees, not her husband Cyrus Martin, not Grapes—questioned, let alone contested, what she said. But now she was clearly in some debate with herself. "Synchronized. Sperm. What have you been reading lately?" she asked.

Rachel shrugged. "Something starts a heart beating, and then it just keeps on going. It's quite amazing, isn't it? You can't will it to stop—I tried. It's a life of its own inside you and you have no control over it. I suppose it's easier to stop someone else's heart." She picked up the boning knife on the cutting board. "I mean, cutting out someone's heart isn't that different from cleaning fish."

Her mother sighed, stared at the pan of fillets a long moment, then reached into the cupboard for the bread crumbs. "Bring me the eggs," she said evenly. "Killing a person is not the same as cleaning fish, Rachel."

"The one with the oil slick in his hair—"

"Page."

"Said something about a crime of passion. That's one of those phrases that means sex without saying it directly, right?"

"Wrong. The eggs."

Rachel got the carton of eggs from the refrigerator and began breaking them into a bowl. She liked eggs; she liked gathering them from the coop; she liked the feel of their shells in her hand; she liked the even consistency of the clear fluid and the perfectly formed raw yolks. When she had six eggs in the bowl, she began beating them with a fork.

"If Page and McNeil were talking on the porch," her mother asked, dipping the first fillet in the eggs, then rolling it in the plate of bread crumbs, "where were you that you could hear? Hmm?"

"Under the porch."

"Under the porch. Rachel—"

"I read there in the shade. I have all summer long—"

"You're a snoop and a voyeur."

"What's that?"

"You know—we've been through this before, you're peeking in windows and through cracks. Our guests' privacy—"

"I wasn't peeking, or voying. I was lying in the sand under the porch, reading. Then I must have dozed off until I heard their voices just above me. I couldn't see them at all Mom!"

"That's not the point. One day it'll get you in trouble."

"Not with them. They're taking the heart back on the evening ferry." Her mother looked at her now, eyes wide, demanding more, yet distressed that she should be taken in by her own daughter. Rachel thought she could actually feel her heart beating faster. "They determine the age of the heart by cutting it open and inspecting the arteries—old arteries are clogged. Then they test it for blood type, enzymes, amino acids, all sorts of stuff."

Her mother laid the last breaded fillet in the pan, then wiped her hands on a towel. She went over to the cabinet where the wine was kept, brought back an open bottle of red. She was forty and men still paid attention to her. Cyrus no longer slept in the same bedroom, but that was something else that she wouldn't discuss.

"I was born when you were, what, twenty-five? Was my father your first?"

There was a moment, a quickness in her mother's eyes, when Rachel thought she might actually hit her. But it passed, and a kind of sorrow and resignation settled in her face as she poured the wine into a skillet already simmering with garlic and onion. "That, Rachel, is none of your business."

"He was my father."

Her mother stopped pouring and regarded the remaining inch in the bottle. A slight smile crossed her lips, and some thought or recollection caused her eyes to become distant and less hard. Rachel wanted to know what she was thinking, what she was seeing exactly at that moment, but her mother only raised the bottle to her lips and drank the last of the wine.

Three

IT HAD BEEN MAY, DURING THE SEVENTH INNING OF A RED Sox–Tigers game, that Mark Emmons saw his life with such sudden clarity that he wondered if he was having one of those out-of-body experiences frequently reported in tabloids. He was sitting at the bar in Dagwood's in Lansing, Michigan, watching Roger Clemens work from the stretch, when he realized that he could hardly remember the latter half of the seventies, had missed the eighties, and now, in the spring of 1992, had little reason to look forward to the turn of the century. He emptied his pockets on the bar and with a swizzle stick sorted through the contents as if looking for a clue. His Michigan driver's license said he was 42, white, male, brown hair, brown eyes, five-foot-eleven. The photograph was disappointingly accurate. He didn't wear glasses, nor did he wear an earring or facial hair. There was twelve dollars and change, which had to hold him until his next check from *The Lansing State Times* at the end of the week. The keys allowed him access to a 1986 Chevy two-door, a yard-sale furnished $465 one-bedroom apartment, the editorial offices at the *State Times,* a friend's barn where his ex-girlfriend Leslie had stored some of her furniture after she moved to Seattle eight months earlier. Another key, small and rusted, was to his Aunt Mae's house on Angel's Head. He still kept that key, though it had been, what, fifteen years since he had lived in the small apartment above her garage.

He put down the swizzle stick and arrived at two simple conclusions: he was not young; he was a long way from home.

He remembered the envelope and took it from his back pocket. It had been in his mail at work this morning. No return address, but postmarked Angel's Head, Massachusetts. Inside, a clipping from the *Angel's Head Current:* "*NAUTICAL REGISTER—May 12. Schooner Northern Lady, Key West, moored in Angel's Head Harbor, Captain Eliot Bedrosian.*" There was no signature on the clipping, no note.

Eliot Bedrosian.

Eliot Bedrosian returned to Angel's Head.

Mark always believed he too would return to Angel's Head. All the years in the Midwest had only been a form of exile. Exile on the mainland. He would always have the heart of an islander.

It doesn't take long to leave a life. Especially once you begin to think of it as "a life." For years Mark Emmons had worked with and in and around quotes, and he was too old to start over at another paper, too young for an early buyout. The buzzword of the current presidential campaign was "change," and there were daily news stories about layoffs, closings, phase outs, restructuring, downsizing—thousands of American lives thrown into the cauldron of change. The *State Times* was not immune; Mark heeded the pressures, the hints, the silences that had put his life in quotes, and took an "extended leave without pay."

He returned to Angel's Head, and for several weeks early in the summer season he managed to go virtually unnoticed. He did so by walking the remote stretches of beach, by strolling the streets above the old harbor in the evenings when the tourists crowd the shops and restaurants. He avoided the streets where the aged, familiar faces—the islanders—had always taken refuge from the village establishments which have gone upscale. Hardly once in those first weeks did someone's eyes linger inquiringly upon his face, and he wished his return could remain indefinitely anonymous, un-fettered, and simple.

Sixteen years had changed the village only a little. The streets still had their essential crookedness, their rolling brick sidewalks polished smooth by generations of pedestrians; the row of old mansions at the top of North Street, built by wealthy sea captains and ship builders, still squared their shoulders to the annoyance of the twentieth century—even though Angel's Head was determined to remain "quaint," tourists brought boomboxes, rap music, skateboards, day-glo T-shirts. One thing couldn't be changed: the erosion of time. Every surface—wood, brick, paint, or stone—was weathered.

He felt relatively safe from detection because he was not in his old disguise. In his twenties he wore a full beard, hair down to his shoulders, bell-bottoms, and a faded army fatigue jacket. It was a uniform—it now seemed so obvious—worn during a period when there was such a determi-nation to express individuality. Now he was just a middle-aged man, a bit heavier though in reasonably good shape, his graying hair short—cut no different, really, than when he was in high school—and his face was clean shaven. He wore a tan jacket in the evening, and most of his shirts and pants were dark or neutral in color. He didn't have one distinguishing characteristic, again, he supposed, conforming to the trends of the period.

Except possibly his eyes. Not that they were unique or particularly memorable. But the eyes told so much more about someone—he truly believed that somewhere in his mind he registered every person he had ever looked in the eye so that if he encountered that person again, no matter how much later and how physically changed that person was, he would know that they had met before. Or, viewed another way: he always knew when he was looking a stranger in the eye. So he realized that others—long-standing residents of the island—might also see something not about but in his eyes that would instinctively tell them that they had met before. And because of this distinct possibility he did something he had always hated. He wore sunglasses. Day and night. The classic American wire-rimmed, reflecting sunglasses.

Eventually he found her. Found her by chance really. But it was inevitable: on an island the size of Angel's Head chance and inevitability are the same thing. Late afternoon he was walking slowly up Brick Kiln Street, which used to be the poorer end of the village. Now all the cramped houses were spiffed up and quaint. At the corner he saw her step out of Lesard's Package Store, a paper bag cradled in her arm. She walked around the truck, a small white pickup with a slight ding in the left bed-panel. She didn't notice him in the doorway across the intersection, apparently looking at cardigan sweaters imported from Ireland. Her face was a little broader, her dark hair shorter, thinner, more functionally cut than when they were young. The bones of her skull were more prominent now—it was the skull of her mother emerging. She was still a strikingly beautiful woman.

Over the next few weeks he saw her several times. The grocery, the apothecary, the stationer's, the post office, and twice more coming out of Lesard's Package Store. Her movements had a splendid clarity. They were orchestrated by someone who had lived on the island most of her life; they indicated an islander's knowledge of how to get through the ebb and flow of summer tourists.

He assumed that Anne was in charge of the inn now—now that her mother was dead. It required a full day of errands, of planning meals, of scheduling staff, of resolving guests' problems. Anne did all this. Not

Emerson, though he certainly would make himself both a nuisance and useful till the day he died. Not her husband Cyrus, though he would never really stop working. Not her brother Randall. And certainly not some manager, some Cornell School of Hotel Management graduate who would introduce an elaborate computer system and would refer to guests as units. No, not some hired off-islander. They—the college kids and the migratory chefs up for the season from Florida—would leave after Labor Day. He was sure it was Anne's inn now, and everybody knew it.

At night, though, her movements became somewhat indecipherable. The second week he was coming out of a bar, now called The Blue Anchor, when he saw her walking up Goode's Lane to a house, a typical white clapboard, black-shuttered house built in the middle 1800s, at the end of the first block. The fog was so thick it was raining under the trees and he stood next to the trunk of a maple getting soaked as he watched her knock on the side door until someone let her in—he could not tell whether it was a man or woman because that part of the house was dark. He stayed until he started to get a chill, then went and found a glass of brandy a couple doors down from The Blue Anchor.

The next night he went back to Goode's Lane, and, about the same time, a little after eleven, Anne entered the dark house again. The third night she didn't come—it was Friday, and the inn would be busy. She didn't return the whole weekend, nor Monday, the one day of the week when much of the operation of the inn throttles back to just what is essential to accommodate overnight guests. Traditionally the dining room at the inn is closed on Monday, and as a result it's not uncommon for guests to sit with or near inn employees in other establishments around the village. The best parties were always Monday nights. It was why they came to work on Angel's Head for the summer—they'd run their butts off six days, and though the tips weren't bad it never seemed possible to actually save what they earned, but there were the parties. All-nighters. Some were legendary.

Tuesday night Anne was back in Goode's Lane, and this time Mark waited about twenty minutes under the maple tree—no fog or rain now, just that soft southeasterly breeze that brings the smell of the Atlantic through the village—then approached the house. The first-floor windows were closed and the shades were drawn. He walked in the grass along the side of the house. Since he was a kid he had liked sneaking around in the dark. After ducking under a few windows, he stopped beneath one which was lit. There were voices from somewhere deep in the house, male and female, but otherwise indistinguishable. He raised his head up to the sill, but this shade was drawn too. There seemed to be three people in the room, a man, a woman, and a third voice that responded only occasionally and briefly, with a register that fell halfway between the other two. Man, woman, boy, or girl, he couldn't tell. He was sure that the woman's voice was Anne's; it seemed a bit deeper and maybe slower than he remembered, but the cadence was unmistakable. There had always been something straight and direct about her way of thinking that was evident in the way she spoke. Anne thought and spoke like a New Englander.

The man's voice had an urgency to it, as though he was trying to placate Anne. The third party's silence seemed to be the cause of friction. He didn't know this, but he felt it from the rhythm of their voices. They talked more rapidly, and louder, until finally the third person shouted *"No!"* Immediately there were footsteps that left the room, ran through the house, and concluded with a slam of the front door, which caused the storm window inches from Mark's nose to rattle in its frame. There were loud footsteps, which resounded on the porch stairs and then on the pavement of Goode's Lane until they faded away in the night. For minutes the entire house was silent.

He walked into the yard and stood next to the trunk of a willow tree. The back of the house was dark except for a light above the stove, visible through a sliding glass door. Suddenly there was a sound behind him and he turned quickly as a cat broke through the bushes lining the side of the garage. It brushed up against his legs; but when the kitchen door slid open it immediately sprinted up to the house. A man stood in the open door as the cat went inside—Mark couldn't see the man's face clearly in the dark. The man stared out into the yard for what seemed too long, then closed the door.

Mark's heart was pounding. Here he was standing in a stranger's backyard, and even though it was pitch dark he felt exposed: all the years in the Midwest had not diminished his need for this island, or for Anne Flood. He knew that he had long wanted to return to Angel's Head, but he suddenly realized that to do so was not only rejuvenating and foolish, but dangerous. He began walking quickly up the side of the house toward the street—but just before he reached the sidewalk, he sensed movement behind him. Turning, he saw someone step into the bushes next to the garage. Then he looked at the nearest window on the first floor of the house and noticed the curtain was being drawn back by a hand. The room was dark, a woman's hand, a man's hand, he couldn't be sure. And it disappeared so quickly that he was not only certain he'd been seen, but that he'd been recognized.

Four

EMERSON AND CYRUS TOOK THE *SERAPHIM*, ONE OF TWO charter boats operated by the inn, east across Pleasant Bay. Emerson waved to each boat he passed—fishermen and lobstermen returning from a day of working the shoals and channels. The familiar throb of the Chrysler diesel came up through the deck; he'd been running the *Seraphim* since the Truman administration, and when his hands were on the wheel it felt as though he was in touch with every inch of her 36-foot lapstrake hull.

"The detectives," he said, "they talk to you?"

"Yep."

"The shed, of all places."

"I told you ten years ago you should have let me tear it down. Build another one. Anything but leave it standing."

Cyrus Martin was a native, an Angelian. There'd been Martins fishing these waters for generations—though not as long as the Floods. In the social order of the island there were families that were said to remain at the waterline, while others moved up into the village, where they established a shop or a trade. Families that had risen above the waterline tended to look down upon those who still fished, a notion the Floods never subscribed to, having always managed to keep at least one foot wet. Cyrus was the distillation of generations of waterline pride and resentment; he said little, he labored constantly, and he knew the bay as well as anyone.

Yet Emerson never really considered him family. Cyrus didn't look much different from when he'd started working at the inn over twenty years earlier. His brown hair was thinner; his eyes seemed to have receded deeper into his lean face. Despite what his marriage to Anne had or had not become, he was as much a facet of the inn as any member of the Flood family. But he was not family, and by his actions it was clear that he understood this, accepted it. In fact, Emerson suspected he had come to prefer it.

Cyrus had the ability to anticipate, so that when Anne told him it was time to clean out the gutters or that the dining room doors were sticking from the humidity, he often said that he had done it yesterday. Washed it, replaced it, tightened it, planed it, painted it, fixed it. That a hinge, a lock, a lever, a switch worked properly was testimony of Cyrus Martin's worth.

"You didn't say anything about the shed?" Emerson asked.

Cy shook his head.

"Randall has been scarce."

"I've seen him around the cove and walking the beach, as usual. Ben Snow was looking for him—but I'm not paid to do police work."

"To cut out someone's heart." Emerson left it at that for a while, both of them staring ahead toward the beach. "Through the centuries we've been doing it to opponents," he said. "Sometimes if the defeated showed unusual strength or courage, the heart would be eaten so that the victor might obtain such qualities. I once read of a tribal king in Central America who had the hearts of twenty thousand opponents cut out. His general collapsed from exhaustion. Twenty thousand!"

"It's no different now," Cyrus said. "Only the tools are more efficient."

"I wonder if courage can still be found in the heart," Emerson said.

As the *Seraphim* neared the back side of Nauset Beach Emerson throttled down, and they entered a narrow inlet. A few hundred yards in they anchored, rowed the dinghy ashore, then began the trek across the dunes. For decades the inn had been under contract to supply provisions to the Rescue Station on Nauset, no matter what its function. When Emerson was young it was still an active Rescue Station, watching for and assisting ships in distress. It was equipped with long boats, line, life-preserving gear, and was staffed by a few men who for food, shelter, and a meager annual sum, watched and waited. Months could pass when no disaster occurred, but there would also be sudden storms that might wreck two ships on the same day. As a boy Emerson took a regular watch, usually spending a week at the station, then a week back at the inn. The station was decommissioned in the thirties—one of the last—and it stood unoccupied until the early fifties when it became a summer camp, first for children with polio, then for children who were handicapped. The station was closed again for several years until the mid-seventies, when it was purchased from the state for one dollar by Samuel Cross, who used to stand watch alongside Emerson eons ago when they would still spy the occasional tall ship on the horizon.

The shingled gables of the station came into view, rising sharply above the dunes. Samuel Cross led three of his "crew" out to greet them. His tanned face was deeply creased about the eyes, which were a bright, fierce blue. He wore a seaman's cap, and his great white beard covered much of his chest—Emerson had often been reminded of photographs of Walt Whitman. Ordinarily he sent the crew down to the inlet to unload supplies from the boat, but today there were only three of them and they all remained close behind him. The men were like a chorus waiting for their cue. Something was wrong. Samuel led everyone inside the station, where the air was cool and smelled of fresh paint. It was in Samuel's manner; the way he didn't look directly at Emerson. It was in the faces of his crew, an almost childish concern, as if they had done something bad.

Samuel's head and hands trembled permanently; they had done so for years. It gave him a vulnerability that could be deceiving: there was still roar and power in his voice. "We just called Doc Walter on the shortwave. He'll meet you back at the island."

"What's happened?" Cyrus asked.

"We have a guest." Samuel's voice also had a slight quiver. Guest was what they used to call anyone who washed up on the beach. Looking at his crew, he said, "You stay here." Then to Emerson and Cyrus: "Come."

Emerson was a year younger than Samuel, and it seemed that he'd spent much of his life trying to catch up to his cousin. Samuel led them up the narrow, winding stairs to the second floor, then beyond. It was quite dark in there and they all used the curved handrail to aid their ascent. Finally Samuel opened the door, admitting bright light, and they stepped out onto the watchtower, a small open platform next to the chimney. When Samuel was agitated, his tremors tended to quicken. Emerson thought this was the case now: his head bobbed even more rapidly, causing the cords at the side of his neck to strain noticeably. Leaning against the railing, he pointed down to the bayside beach, and said, "Washed up with the tide. They're bringing him up."

Emerson saw four of Samuel's crew walking up the beach with the body on a stretcher. It was covered by a khaki army blanket.

"The crew is very upset," Samuel said.

"Is this guest missing any organs?" Emerson asked.

"Let's find out."

Rachel sat with Ben Snow and the detectives while they waited for the last ferry to the mainland. Mr. McNeil, who at first seemed gruff, had offered her a stick of chewing gum. It was black and tasted like licorice.

"I never had this before," she said.

31

"Black Jack," McNeil said. "Used to chew it all the time when I was a kid—till my teeth started to turn black." He chuckled, looking directly at her in a way that made her feel somehow exposed. He spoke with a kind of reverence that she didn't ordinarily associate with chewing gum.

On the opposite bench Benjamin Snow sat with one arm resting on the blue and white Igloo cooler at his side. Occasionally he looked at Rachel as though he were trying to make her disappear, preferably by turning to dust or possibly evaporating into thin air. Benjamin Snow could do that with his eyes. On the island he was the law: constable, an old word for policeman, though sometimes Grapes called him the "town beadle," which caused her to think of Ben Snow as some kind of humongous bug.

The cooler was designed to hold a six-pack. You saw them all over the island as people went to and from their boats and the beach.

"How long will these tests take?" Snow asked.

"A day or so," Page said.

"You'll give me a full report?"

"Age, sex, health—"

"Cholesterol," McNeil added.

"I want a full report," Snow said.

"Mine's up over two-sixty," McNeil continued. "Got to get that mother down."

Across the harbor Rachel watched the schooner turn on her mooring. Her stern sported a mahogany escutcheon: *Northern Lady*. "Eight thirty-two," she said.

Page looked at his gold wristwatch. "Yes, the launch is late." He sounded tired.

"No, high tide," Rachel said.

"I'm going to conduct a search," Snow said.

Both detectives merely stared at him.

"There's got to be a body," he said.

"We don't know exactly what it is yet," Page said. "It might be wise to wait—"

"No," McNeil said. "Go ahead, pull on your waders and get out in the clam beds. Muck around and see what you dredge up."

"Will they bury it?" Rachel asked.

All three men looked at her, baffled.

"The heart. After they look at it under a microscope?"

Page took a long breath and was about to speak, but there came the blast of a horn and they all turned and watched the ferry enter the jetties.

McNeil got up and went over to Snow's bench. After a moment, Snow took his arm off the cooler and McNeil picked it up. "They're very thorough on the mainland," he said. "We'll be back in the morning."

Snow wouldn't look at him.

They all walked down to the end of the pier where other passengers waited. The ferry eased alongside with a final reverse thrust of the engine. It approached so slowly that it seemed that the pier was moving forward—though Rachel had known this sensation since she was a small child, it still fascinated her.

Page took two elastic bands from his coat pocket and put them around his wrists. Each had a small button which he carefully positioned on the inside of each wrist.

"Without them he gets wicked seasick," McNeil explained to Rachel as he handed her the rest of his pack of gum. "The man turns absolutely green."

Samuel's men crowded around the stretcher once it was on the table in the main hall. The long boats used to be kept here; now it was where the men ate. Self-sufficiency, that was the game plan. The members of the crew were men who had in one way or another fallen out of society. Some had been in mental institutions, others in jail. All had demonstrated renewed desire to take care of themselves. At the Rescue Station they cooked, cleaned, did laundry, performed all of the tasks necessary to live on their own again. Some stayed a month, others eight or ten weeks. Most of them returned to the mainland, to families, to jobs; but there were some who settled on the island so that it was not uncommon to see them in the village. The tourists, particularly the children, thought the crew odd at first; but when they saw how easily these men blended in with the other islanders they came to see them as another unique aspect of Angel's Head. They were part of the island's charm. Of course there were those tourists who were of the opinion that Angelians were a little cracked anyway. After one season they usually tried Nantucket, Martha's Vineyard, or Block Island.

But now, as they stared down at the army blanket which covered the body, Emerson knew that Samuel was faced with a difficult choice: whether or not to let the entire crew stay for the unveiling. He was a benevolent dictator, unabashedly so. In order to remain at the station the men had to be obedient. They had to share in the assigned duties—kitchen, laundry, whatever. But he was also understandably protective. Some of them were extremely fragile. They at times suffered setbacks. The four crewmen who had retrieved the body from the beach had, of course, already seen it; they were clearly distraught. There was alarm in their faces, a kind of retraction in their posture. Their heads, elbows, shoulders were oddly aligned and when they moved they looked like Cubism in motion.

For a long moment Samuel stared at Emerson; then he turned to Cyrus, who was standing near the head. As Cyrus pulled back the blanket, one crew member gasped, another took a step backward. None of them looked away. It was the body of a man in his mid-forties. Though the body was bloated, it was clear he had been lean and agile; and though the skin was now pale, it was still apparent that he had had a deep tan—not one of these New England tans that are sustained for a month or two during the summer, but a tan that seemed to go deep into the flesh. It took a moment for Emerson to realize he recognized this man. But somehow he wasn't sure, and he was distracted by the sudden, painful contraction of his scrotum.

"What did that?" one of the men asked.

The body had been gutted like a fish, expertly cut from abdomen to sternum, and his lower internal organs had been removed. Several ribs, however, were neatly sheared off, and he did not think that could be done with a boning knife.

"Cleaned," Samuel whispered, as he covered the body again with the wool blanket.

Emerson had not been able to see whether the body was still in possession of its heart.

"Don't sit on the fish!" Rachel yelled across the Boat House.

The boy who had just sat down on the bench along the far wall sprang up and grabbed the seat of his neon orange shorts. His parents, sunburned, dressed in pink and white alligator clothes, looked at him and laughed. At first the boy didn't get it, then he broke into an embarrassed smile. There was no fish.

"Not a bite," the husband said.

Rachel took their rented fishing rods off the counter and stood them in the corner with the other tangled messes. "Bluefish are unpredictable," she said. "They hit all of a sudden, eating everything in sight, and then boom they're gone."

"Well," the wife said, singsong, "let's all go up to the inn and have us a drink and some dinner. Maybe we'll find some fish on a plate!"

The parents moved toward the door, but the boy stayed put. "I'll be right up," he muttered, coming over to the counter. "I want to look at this stuff a minute."

His parents found that a wonderful idea and went out the door and trudged up the path toward the inn.

The boy stared down through the glass in the display case: jigs, poppers, lures, boning knives, boxes of sea worms, squid, and chubs. He was a year or so older than Rachel and his nose was coated with white cream. His eyes were pretty to look at and she watched them until he looked up at her.

"What's your name?"

"Eric Grier."

"I'm Rachel Flood."

"Some guests say the Floods are strange."

"You have no idea."

He smiled, revealing braces. "How often do you tell people not to sit on the fish?"

"About a dozen times a week." She took the key off the peg and placed it on the counter. "Want a Coke? It's on the house. Get two."

Eric took the key and went out to the old vending machine on the porch. He unlocked the lid and removed two bottles from the water. The Coca-Cola machine, dented, red with white letters, was an artifact—all summer long tourists coming in to buy bait or rent a catboat would pause to marvel at it. She thought the machine was a nuisance because she had to drain the water regularly and scour its metal compartment. Cyrus insisted upon it; he had a thing about rust.

Eric came in off the porch, a bottle in each hand, but she turned away and began pulling at the tangled nylon filament on one of the rods. He placed her Coke on the counter but she kept tugging on the line, only making it worse. She studied the reel by the fading light from the open window, knowing he was watching her. Picking up a boning knife from the counter, she cut away the snarled line. "There, all better."

They heard someone running down the path from the inn. She stuck her head out the window and, looking toward the cove, she saw Grapes bump the *Seraphim* up against the pier. The footsteps grew louder, and several cooks in white came jogging around the side of the Boat House, passing just beneath her. Looking up toward the inn, she saw her mother running down the hill.

Rachel led Eric out onto the porch. Doc Walter's blue car, old enough to have fins, pulled up at the pier. "Something's happened," she said.

35

They all went down to the end of the pier, where Grapes was tying off the launch. Something lay in the back under a blanket.

"It's big," Eric muttered, standing just behind Rachel. He sucked hard on his Coke bottle. "What is it, a fish?"

Her mother and Doc Walter got in the boat. There was only the sound of water lapping against the boat's wood hull. When the blanket was turned back, revealing the head, her mother took hold of the gunwale, but she couldn't keep her balance as her legs buckled beneath her.

Five

MARK HAD LEFT ALL HIS KEYS IN MICHIGAN EXCEPT THE ONE to the apartment above his aunt's garage. He had lived there in the seventies, and, like his Aunt Mae, whose house was at the head of the crushed seashell drive, it had hardly changed in the intervening years. Same mice-infested furniture, same chipped dishes in the cupboard. He hadn't lost his instinct for ducking the slanted ceilings, and there was the view from the bathroom: if he stood with his hip against the towel rack while pissing he could just see water beyond the spire of the Old Meeting House. For decades his aunt and uncle had run a wholesale fishing operation out of the garage and on particularly humid days or after a heavy summer rain the apartment still smelled faintly of decaying sealife.

He was on his second cup of instant coffee when he heard them coming up the outside stairs, two men, one with a heavy tread and the high squeak of rubber soles, the other the light tap of leather. He pulled on a sleeveless green and white Michigan State University sweatshirt and went to the screen door. The large man was black and he seemed to be enjoying himself, while the white man looked like he needed a vacation. Before they said anything Mark knew they were policemen. There was something about plainclothes police that was the same in New England, the Midwest, anywhere. A reporter Mark had worked with in Lansing once said, "They have badges for eyes."

They identified themselves as state police detectives and said their names were Page and McNeil. "We'd like to ask you a few questions," Page said. "About Eliot Bedrosian."

Mark stared at them.

"Any problem with that?"

"No," Mark said. "How'd you know I was here?"

After a moment McNeil smiled. "It's a small island, man."

"Uh-huh." Mark led them into the tiny living room and offered to make them instant coffee.

McNeil shook his head and took the only other chair, a rocker that had been unsuccessfully stripped of paint. Page looked about the place as though he were afraid he might catch something. Reluctantly he sat on the sofa. "You used to work for the island's newspaper, *The Current?*"

Mark squatted down on the hassock by the window. "Years ago," he said.

"You covered Plummer's Marsh, Blacke's Channel, and all that?" Page said.

"Yep."

"It developed into quite a story, for such a small island." Page was wearing a light gray sport coat, and he was careful not to put his elbow on the soiled armrest. "We've been doing some reading at the library."

"Mrs. Gains still work there?"

Page nodded. "When'd you return to Angel's Head?"

"I don't remember the exact date offhand."

"You've been in Michigan, I understand," Page said. "You fly or drive back?"

"Neither. I took the train."

McNeil burst out laughing. "Shit, from Michigan? You got some time on your hands, huh?"

"I always liked the idea of trains. I took the Lansing train into Chicago, then the Chicago train to Boston, and the bus down here."

Mark had seen two cops work people before; he decided to keep his attention focused on Page. "I sold some things before coming back, and stored the rest in a friend's barn. My car probably wouldn't have made it to Niagara Falls, and somebody offered me eight hundred for it. As you know, cars are rare on Angel's Head."

"So you plan on staying here permanently?" Page said.

"I'm at that point where I don't have any plans."

McNeil leaned forward, nodding his head. His deep voice was barely a whisper. "In my experience, you dump your notion of a plan, you end up with a life. I grew up in Detroit, and I came East some twenty years ago, thinking I'd get away from all the crime and murders. Now look what I been doing ever since—even on a pretty little piece of island there's somebody going to cut out somebody's heart."

He had a newspaper tucked in his back pocket, which he took out, unfolded, and handed to Mark. It was the week's edition of *The Current*—

the logo was still the same, a seagull flying above a row of very uniform waves. Mark read the headline and lead graph:

POSSIBLE MURDER VICTIM FOUND ON NAUSET

The body of former Angel's Head resident Eliot Bedrosian was found Wednesday morning on the bayside of Nauset Beach. Bedrosian, 46, a real estate developer now reportedly residing in Florida, was apparently cut open from the abdomen to the chest before being dumped in Pleasant Bay. Meanwhile, authorities are still trying to determine whether a human heart discovered at the Angel's Head Inn on Tuesday might have belonged to the victim.

"Aren't they jumping to conclusions," he asked, "connecting the body and this heart business in the lead? Isn't it still coffee shop speculation?"

"Good point," McNeil said, leaning back in the rocker.

"Important thing is they're reading it in the coffee shops," Mark said, "and Max loves that."

"Maxine Bulikoff," Page said. "You used to work on the paper with her."

"We were the paper," Mark said. "Now I believe she owns it." He handed the paper back to McNeil. "This story will sell a few extra copies no doubt, but she's also probably catching an earful because she had to bump a piece on the Ladies' Auxiliary Clambake to page two."

McNeil actually smiled, something which Page seemed to resent.

"So you and Maxine did all the stories on Eliot Bedrosian and the salt marsh," Page said.

"Fascinating, wasn't it?"

"Not really," Page said. "Only New Englanders can get really worked up about a salt 'maahsh.'"

"True. You mustn't be from the Cape."

Page didn't answer.

"I didn't detect an accent," Mark said.

Page commenced to review what they had read of Eliot Bedrosian and the salt marsh. He had the story straight, and Mark filled in where it seemed appropriate. In the fall of 1974 he had first learned of an "interest" in what was known locally as Plummer's Marsh, named for a hermit who decades earlier had lived in a cabin above the flats. Randall Flood, who worked for his father Emerson at the Boat House, mentioned it to Mark on one of the many afternoons when time on the island seemed to stand still. To some it was boredom; to them it was off-season. On such days nothing newsworthy ever happened anywhere between Buzzard's Bay and Provincetown. Sitting in the back room, amid outboard motor parts and an ice box full of beer and live bait, they did damage to a bottle of twenty-year-old Glenfiddich that had been a gift from a well-to-do Labor Day charter. Emerson was safely out of the picture, up in Wellfleet, repairing someone's leaky boat. A fine mist fell on the cove and nothing moved except the tide.

"Saw some government-looking vessel out to Plummah's last few days," was all that Randall said that afternoon. It was tucked in between speculation about Red Sox trades, the Bruins' chances of winning another Cup before Bobby Orr's knees gave out, and what the prospects were of finding carnal satisfaction through the coming winter months. Randall was a strapping, fair-haired Yankee and he had a boat, which meant that during the summer the college girls working at the inn sought him out. Winter was another story, and he wasn't above getting involved with some mean-looking women with babies and food stamps. Mark's prospects, in every season, were less promising.

The following morning, intrigued by the phrase "government-looking vessel," Mark drove his VW van out to Plummer's Marsh. Standing at a bend in South Point Road he scanned the whole marsh with his cheap binoculars. It wasn't duck season yet so things were peaceful. A half-sunk wooden skiff floated in one of the inlets. Then he saw two men in a gray pontoon boat in one of the tidal creeks. Though there was clearly nothing clandestine about what the men were doing, he just couldn't figure out why they were doing it.

Their boat was loaded with what appeared to be surveyors' equipment: delicate instruments carried in hardshell cases, folding tripods, a duffel bag full of accessories. They followed the meandering route of the channels well out into the marsh. The man in the bow studied a map and a compass, and directed his partner, who handled the outboard motor. At various points across the marsh they got out, wearing hipboots, and waded through the cordgrass. They set up their instruments, took readings, and before leaving each site drove a wooden stake with a tiny orange flag on it into the peat.

Toward noon, they were about halfway to Blacke's Channel, which ran between the southern tip of the island and the mainland. Mark drove down to the end of South Point Road. He took off his shoes and socks, rolled up his jeans, and walked out on the marsh. He frequently sank up to his shins and the muck was very cold. The nearest stake was about fifty yards out. The little orange flag had small black print on it: "Army Corps of Engineers." He headed back into town and got some lunch. It took a couple of hours for his toes to thaw out.

"You must have gotten someone at the Corps to talk," Page was saying.

"It took a while," Mark said. "At first nobody knew what we were talking about, or nobody was in his office. But Max knew somebody—a kid who had worked on Angel's Head as a summer rent-a-cop when he was in college, and now he was a corporal in the Corps."

"He snooped around," McNeil said, "and he was the one who mentioned 'environmental hazard,' right?"

Mark looked down at the newspaper rolled up in McNeil's hands. He always saw a daily for what went into it, the interviews, the phone calls, the dead ends, the fights with the editors. "After several phone calls with this Corporal Lewis," he said, "Max and I drove up to the Army Corps of Engineers offices on Trapelo Road in Waltham. We took Lewis out to lunch. He was a black kid from Worcester who was stuck at a desk filing paper for some colonel. He called the place 'de plantation.' All he knew was what he overheard; whatever was going on wasn't strictly classified, but something was"—here he smiled—"'fishy.' He could only give us two leads, but it got things moving: one was the word 'condominiums,' and the other was the name Eliot Bedrosian."

Page placed his elbow on the armrest. McNeil nodded ever so slightly.

"In the early seventies," Mark said, "we didn't even know what a condominium was. When we found out we got a little exercised over the possibilities. Max continued to work the Army Corps of Engineers, while I looked up Bedrosian because we knew each other slightly." He finished his cold instant coffee. "Bedrosian bumped his head once and believed I saved him from bleeding to death. The rest—well, you've read the clippings."

"It's history, as they say." McNeil glanced at the clock on the kitchen wall.

"No one keeps an eye on a clock like a reporter," Mark said, "or a cop."

"You still reporting?" Page stood up.

"Taking some time off."

"Laid off?" McNeil said. "Or fired?"

"It's called leave without pay."

"I thought good reporters only got fired."

"That's probably true at good papers."

"This Bedrosian thing have anything to do with your leaving the island fifteen years ago?"

"Maybe."

Page asked, "He have anything to do with your coming back?"

"I needed a vacation."

McNeil got up and with a large, gentle hand stilled the rocker before heading to the screen door. "Were you surprised that Bedrosian came back to Angel's Head—considering what happened here years ago?" he asked.

"Nothing Bedrosian did ever surprised me."

"And you're not surprised Bedrosian's been killed?" Page asked.

Mark looked at both men.

"Nothing ever surprises journalists," McNeil said.

"I suppose," Mark said.

"In that respect you're like cops."

Mark went out on the landing and watched them descend the stairs. Their shoes made a sharp, crisp sound as they walked up the seashell driveway. It wasn't a sound you ever heard in the Midwest.

His Aunt Mae came to her kitchen screen door, glanced out at the men, then called up to Mark: "That was that woman on the phone, Max! She'd like you for dinner at seven!" Aunt Mae might be the last of the generation to wear an apron about the house all day long. She was his mother's older sister and since his parents had died she was his only real remaining family besides his sister who lived in New Mexico. He loved her dearly but her timing had always been lousy.

He looked at the two detectives, who stood at the head of the driveway, watching him. He smiled at his aunt and waved, "Thanks, Mae!"

"That's okay, honey!"

Six

BENJAMIN SNOW STOOD AT THE END OF THE PIER, STARING across the cove at the *Northern Lady*. He looked like he was having second thoughts.

"You want I'll take you acrost, Ben," Emerson said, climbing down into the dinghy. He glanced at Rachel, and snapped: "No, you're not coming."

She looked crushed, like a dog told to stay.

Cyrus turned to Rachel and said quietly, "You've chores up to the Boat House."

The girl stared out toward the schooner with intense longing, then walked up the pier, her sneakers knocking angrily on the deck boards. Cyrus followed her, his stride long, slow, barely audible.

Once Snow positioned himself in the stern, Emerson untied from the cleat and began rowing. Pulling so much weight made the dinghy move haltingly across the cove.

"You sure this is all right?" Emerson asked.

"What do you mean, all right. This is my island, my jurisdiction."

"You said those detectives had some men coming out this afternoon to go through Bedrosian's boat. Wouldn't you rather wait?"

"I would not," Snow said.

"If you say so."

Snow was in his mid-forties and since he'd begun to put on weight he looked more and more like his father. He gazed off toward the jetties and the morning sun which was still low above the water. "I still can't believe Bedrosian came back here. The guy was a serious boat-recluse. I rarely saw him around the village, and usually then at night. I was up to Vera's Lunch for a piece of pie one night and he walked in. It was all year-rounders, you know, and the whole place fell silent. He just walked up to the newsstand, picked up a couple of papers, paid up, and walked out like nobody'd take notice. Every islander watched him, Emerson, it was the weirdest thing. He had that way about him, he always did."

"Ever speak to him?"

"Not me!" Snow said. "He never created a problem, so I got no reason to give him the time of day. I got better things to do. But I kept my eye out for him."

"No doubt."

"You ever speak to him, Emerson, I mean address him directly?"

"Address him? Sure, now and then. Always something to do with his boat. Mooring fees. Or when he'd come into the Boat House to purchase supplies." Emerson stopped rowing. "He never let on like there was this past to him and all. That he'd had anything to do with the Floods."

"How's Anne doing?" Snow asked.

"Hasn't come down from her room since fainting last night."

Snow gazed at the gunwale, where he was picking at the chafed wood.

"What you're really asking," Emerson said, "is whether Anne saw Bedrosian at all."

"Am I?"

Emerson began rowing again and pulled the dingy up alongside the *Northern Lady*. Bright sunlight glanced off her white hull, the reflections dancing on the water. Emerson shipped the oars as Snow stood up and took hold of the schooner's stern ladder. Emerson tied the line to the chrome rail, and they climbed aboard. She had a long, lean, neat deck: perfectly coiled lines, polished brass fittings, smooth teak.

"Must be thirty-six, maybe thirty-eight feet," Emerson said.

"Some stick," Snow said. "This guy win Megabucks?" He opened the hatch and led Emerson below. Ducking into the cabin they both stopped and stared. Everything was pink. Spattered pink: the curtains, the bench cushions, the tabletop. The air was close and smelled faintly rotten. There was a plastic bucket on the floor still half-full of water. "Christ," Snow muttered. He climbed back on top and Emerson heard him vomit over the side.

Bedrosian had been done here, and whoever did it made a hasty attempt to clean up. They had gathered up seawater in a bucket and poured it over everything, leaving a swirling pink film and no fingerprints, no footprints. Nothing but pink. Over next to the stainless steel sink lay a wad of soggy paper towels. It was a sloppy but apparently effective job.

Emerson could hold his breath no longer and went topside. Snow was sitting back near the wheel, a big chrome number, smoking a cigarette. His father, who had been constable on the island for almost thirty years, wouldn't have flinched at such a sight.

The deck was clean. There was no blood. "Must have brought him up," Emerson said, "and put him over the side in a boat. Probably wrapped him up in something. At night, I imagine. Or just tossed him overboard and let the tide take him out into the bay."

"Christ," Snow whispered, "gutted like a haddock." He made a fist, and a little wiggling motion. "Just run that blade up through the meat like our daddies taught us."

"Think it was done just with a knife?"

"A good sharp one. Why?"

"I was thinking of the ribs." Emerson looked up and down the length of the deck once. Neatly coiled line and anchor cable. Something was missing. "Fish don't have ribs like we do."

"No, they don't." Snow continued to stare toward the island. "You suppose he was alive long?"

"Maybe."

Rachel went down to gather chubs. At the end of the pier she pulled in the first line, raising the steel mesh basket up from the murky bottom. The long cylindrical basket had conical walls pointing in at each end, with a small hole to allow the tiny chubs inside after the bait. There were at least a couple dozen chubs wriggling in the bottom of the basket with a lump of salt pork. She wondered what the odds were of a chub getting in, then finding its way out again through one of the small holes. Once at school she had a teacher, Ms. Landis, who held up some cards—a tree, a horse, a snake, a bird—and asked the class to write a paragraph about the object they identified with the most. She assured them it wasn't a test to be graded, just a means of assessment. Rachel looked at each card, but never wrote anything on her paper. She handed it in blank, with her name printed neatly in the upper right-hand corner. Later, at the end of the week, Ms. Landis spoke to her after class; she didn't come right out and say it, but it was clear she wanted to know why Rachel hadn't identified with any of the objects on the cards. Their conversation was inconclusive, and finally Rachel was let go.

Rachel opened the basket and dumped the chubs into a pail of seawater.

"Whatcha doin'?"

She looked up toward the back of the Boat House. Eric stood next to an overturned dory. She said nothing. There were times when she could do or say nothing and almost will someone to do what she wanted. Especially boys. Bending over, she snapped the basket closed, peeled several starfish off the outside of the steel mesh, and dropped it back in the water. She heard Eric's feet on the decking, and when he was standing next to her she said, "Gathering chubs."

He took his hands from his pockets and squatted. His knees were smooth and his calves were covered with silky blond hair. He reached into the bucket and took out a chub. "Slimy," he said, laughing.

"Just try getting one on a hook when they wriggle like that."

The chub slid out of his palm, fell on the deck, where it flapped wildly. Eric tried to pick it up with his fingers, but the tiny fish squirmed free and disappeared between the deck boards. There was a tiny plop in the water under the pier.

"Sorry."

"You'll have to pay for it."

Rachel looked at him, her mouth set. He didn't believe her—it was in his eyes. They both smiled.

She put her finger on the wet spot on the decking. "I have always identified with chubs that get away."

He sat back on his heels.

She let him carry the pail for her as they walked up to the Boat House. Once inside she took the pail into the back room; placing it on the bench, she looked out the window at the cove. She could see Grapes and Constable Snow on the schooner. The tide was rising and the stern of the boat was toward the village, the same as the night, a few weeks earlier, when she had rowed out in a dinghy just after sunset. The western sky was streaked orange, and the white hull of the schooner seemed to almost glow from within. She rowed slowly, careful to dip her oars without splashing. When she neared the stern of the schooner she held her oars up and did not move, allowing the dinghy to drift alongside the hull. Its fading whiteness was frightening: she could feel her heart pounding, and she had to breathe through her mouth so as not to get winded. The cove was absolutely calm, though across the water came the faint sound of silverware from the inn's dining room. The hull had an almost sensual curve the way it rose out of the water. She thought of it as something alien, sleeping. Then, as she drifted near the bow, she heard the faintest thumping. It seemed to come from the depths of the schooner, possibly down in the keel. The noise became more distinct. Louder. Swifter. Until it gained a rhythm that seemed to intensify as it speeded up.

And there were voices. Not words. Sounds: groans and cries. A man's voice. A woman's voice. The voices rose together until there was some kind of release, and there followed gasps of anguish, sighs of relief. She expected to hear crying. She expected pain. But then, as the dinghy drifted under the schooner's bowsprit and entered water shimmering with the slightest breeze, she heard laughter, familiar laughter. Immediately she dropped the oars and began rowing furiously, pulling away from the schooner as quickly as possible.

Turning from the Boat House window, Rachel saw Eric now standing in the doorway. His eyes were raised toward a spot high on the wall to her left. He seemed possessed.

She glanced up at the wall: the spot. Above the shelves cluttered with cans of outboard motor oil, parts, and tackle boxes was a tide chart for 1957. Sticking out from its side at an angle was a sun-faded color photograph of a woman kneeling on a checked picnic blanket. She was holding a blue umbrella on one shoulder and she was naked. "Grapes calls her Sputnik. I don't know why. Nice tits, huh?"

Eric looked at her and after a moment he managed to close his mouth.

"They look like they're filled with air or something," she said. "I don't think mine'll ever get that way."

The boy flushed and stuffed his hands in his pockets. "It's the satellite."

"Cellulite," she said, grabbing the back of her thigh, "no, that gets you back here."

"The Russians were first."

"Uh-huh."

"They sent it up in fifty-seven."

"You're a strange boy," she said. "Want to help me count chubs?"

Emerson sat at the end of the bar and stared hard at Cyrus—sometimes it worked. Sitting next to Emerson, Snow finished his third sombrero. He was looking better. The color had returned to his face and his eyes seemed able to focus again. He had tossed his cookies again while Emerson rowed back to the pier.

"What you need is a good bowl of clam chowder to settle that stomach," Emerson said, watching Cy move down the bar toward them.

"What I need is a thorough blowjob."

"That wouldn't hurt you none either."

"You believe all that blood?"

Emerson nodded, but kept his eyes on Cy as he leaned on the bar. "Another, Ben?"

Snow nodded, absentmindedly staring toward the open back door of the bar.

"Life beyond the age of twenty-one," Emerson said, "is supposed to be like this: you sit at a bar and someone offers you another beer without your asking. As a courtesy. As the natural course of things." He finished his beer and pushed the empty bottle toward his son-in-law.

Cy straightened up and shook his head.

"Come on, Cy. We just witnessed a gruesome scene of a crime."

"You know your limit is one."

"The blood," Emerson whispered. "You should have seen it."

"Orders from the boss."

"She's been upstairs in her room since fainting yesterday."

"She'll know."

"How's she gonna know, Cy?"

"She just will."

"The woman is not omnipotent."

Cy appeared to wince, and Emerson saw an opening. He pulled a bill from his shirt pocket. It was a five and he slapped it on the bar. They stared at each other long and hard until finally Cy's fingers picked up the bill. He mixed another sombrero, got a second beer from the cooler, and brought them to the end of the bar.

Emerson drank down a good portion of the beer. Here it wasn't even twelve noon and he was on his second cold one. The day held rare prospects. Out the door he could see a cat sniffing around the dumpster. The island was loaded with cats. Many of them relied on fish scraps and anything they could catch—field mice, garter snakes, frogs. Rachel left out bowls of milk for them.

"It had to be his," Emerson said.

"The heart?" Snow said.

"Yep."

"But why was it hidden out to the shed?"

Emerson stared at Snow a moment, then he put his bottle down to watch the cat tear at some piece of fried fish. "It wasn't hidden," he said. "It was left out in plain view. To be found." He nodded toward the door, the cat. "You take in one of those cats, feed it, leave a window open for it to come and go, and what do they do?"

"Piss on the rugs. Claw up the furniture."

"They bring you a trophy." Emerson turned on the stool; Snow was gazing at him, and down the bar Cy looked on, his arms folded. "They catch something," he continued, "a field mouse, a garter snake, and they tear it apart and bring back part of it. They leave it out where you'll find it. The windowsill, the doormat. Then they stare at you with those proud yellow eyes."

Randall came up from the cellar, a case of beer on each shoulder. His massive arms eased them onto the bar and he began stocking the cooler. He paid them no attention. His blond curls were thinning now, and the top of his skull glistened with a sheen of sweat. Over the years the skin around his large blue eyes had darkened, and his broad face developed a perpetual look of bafflement. After his accident, after the years of trips to Boston for tests, the doctors finally said fourteen, maybe fifteen, and that's about as far as he would ever get. When his mother was still alive Emerson used to try to console her by saying that the boy was not unhappy.

He's a man, Sarah said.

Well, yes.

Of all the things, an outboard motor prop.

It happens. They're called freak accidents.

It was no freak accident.

I know. But there was no proof. No one saw it happen. Randall can't remember.

I wonder if he'd be better off if the blow had killed him.

Sarah.

Well I do.

I don't think it bothers him.

Just look at him!

He doesn't remember.

But I do.

Emerson watched his son close the beer cooler. He picked up the empty cartons, and without looking toward their end of the bar, he went back down to the cellar. He came and went; spent as much time with Samuel out at the Rescue Station as he did at the inn, particularly in off-season. Did chores about the inn. Worked on boats about the cove—repairs, cleanup, crewing. It was odd how some things remained intact, like his knowledge of boats and fishing. Probably because he had learned them so young, before he reached his teens. He loved the water and Emerson had taught him early. It was the only thing they had ever shared.

Cy shifted his weight against the beer cooler. Snow rubbed the back of his fingers along his cheek. He hadn't shaved this morning and his whiskers crackled. Randall's sudden appearances usually brought about an end to conversation.

"He's like a stray, living on the waterfront," Emerson said. He drank some beer. The other two men didn't respond. No one ever dared. "I wonder if his mother ever realized how little his life would be changed by it. Chances are he'd still be toting cases of beer up and down those stairs day after day."

Snow finished his sombrero.

"Again?" Cyrus asked.

"I must return to duty, to see if my rent-a-cops are vigilant in their protection of rights and property of the residents of this fair commonwealth."

"Tell me," Emerson said. "Does your eloquence always increase in proportion to your alcohol intake?"

"Fuckin'-A." Snow got off his stool and shuffled toward the door.

Cy busied himself straightening up behind the bar. Emerson stared hard at his son-in-law, but Cy just went about his business with his usual clear resolve.

Seven

RACHEL TOOK THE STAIRS TWO AT A TIME UP TO THE FAMILY quarters on the second floor. She walked down the hall past her room, Cyrus's room, Emerson's room, running one hand along the top of the wainscot, something she had been doing as long as she could remember—going back to when she was so small that she had to reach up to get her fingers on the rounded rail molding. The door at the end of the hall was open and her mother was sitting on her bed in her bathrobe. Beyond her, Cyrus stood in the balcony door, staring out at the bay. Neither of them noticed Rachel coming down the hall.

"One day," her mother said, "I take a rest for *one* day and everything comes unglued around here." Her voice was slightly hoarse. She must have just taken a shower—the room smelled of soap.

"It's just that it's July and we're booked solid," Cyrus said. "I can handle it."

"There's a short order of supplies off the ferry, a couple of waitresses are angry over station assignments—and Room 32 has dropped her ring down the bathroom sink—"

"I said I can handle it. I already got the ring out of the trap."

"No, I can't lie around here any longer. I want to get downstairs and see to—" She turned around and smiled at Rachel. "Well, hi there. Remember me?"

Rachel came to the bed and sat next to her mother. "How are you feeling?"

"Fine. I just needed to rest."

Rachel glanced toward the balcony door, where Cyrus continued to stare out at the bay. "This is really something," she said. "All of us here in this room—your room."

Cyrus turned around, but with the midday sunlight behind him it was

51

difficult to see his eyes. His tan shirt had smudges of what looked like grease or oil, and his jeans were encrusted with white sea salt. He was almost always active—working behind the bar, repairing something about the inn, taking care of the boats—so that to see him merely leaning in a doorway was peculiar. His gaze bothered her, and she realized there was something about his stillness that had always made her cautious.

"No, we don't get much time to sit and talk together during the summer," her mother said. She was pretending not to know what Rachel really meant—it was how she dealt with guests and staff: let them state the problem in their own terms. Rachel admired it as a tactic, but she resented the fact that she now had to spell out what she meant.

"I'm talking about Cyrus being here, in your room."

Her mother got up off the bed and went to the bureau. She sighed and said, "We've been through this, Rachel."

"I know. You and Cyrus have an 'arrangement.'"

Her mother had been in her room since collapsing on the pier yesterday; though she looked tired, her eyes were kind and patient. Rachel had missed her last night—all the activity about the inn seemed to lack cohesion without Anne Flood at its center. Still looking at Rachel, she said to Cyrus, "She's developed an interest in the heart."

"Uh-huh."

"But not just the one in the shed."

"There's another?"

"Hers—she has some interesting ideas about its conception."

Cyrus raised his eyebrows, and for a moment there was the faintest hint of a smile. "It's the books she reads," he said. "Some of the titles are, well, not for girls."

Rachel said, "I hate it when you do this, talk about me almost as though I weren't here."

Her mother opened the closet, sorted through the clothes, then pulled out her long orange and yellow skirt, a matching belt, and a lemon yellow cotton blouse. "You have an interesting theory: hearts might be synchronized at conception." Her mother went into the bathroom, and her voice echoed off the old tiles. "Sounds very romantic, doesn't it?"

"You want to know why your mother and I married," he said, "and why we now have separate rooms."

Rachel raised a hand to shield her eyes from the glare of the sun.

"Maybe it's none of your business," he said.

"She was pregnant when you married."

"Yes," her mother said from the bathroom. "We'd known each other a long time. When we were teenagers—not much older than you—Cyrus began working here at the inn. He helped out in the kitchen, he did repairs with your grandfather."

"Not much different from now."

Her mother didn't answer, but after a moment, Cyrus said quietly, "No, not much."

"Did you know my father?"

Cyrus turned and looked out at the bay.

"Did you love my mother?"

Her mother came out of the bathroom, working the belt around her waist. "There were some difficult years."

"The bridge," Rachel said.

"Yep, the bridge. And I was suddenly confronted with the burden of the inn."

"And you were pregnant."

"And she was pregnant," Cyrus said. "That was all right with me—"

Her mother came over to the bed. She was clearly perturbed that this conversation had gotten started, but now she seemed determined to finish it. "I wanted to have a baby, Rachel. I wanted to have you. Cyrus understood that." The light colors of her blouse and skirt caused her blue eyes to seem even brighter. "We have separate rooms now, Rachel, and it's a matter between *us*—"

"But why?"

Cyrus suddenly straightened up in the balcony doorway. "That is none of her business." He crossed the room to the door and, before stepping out into the hall, he said, "Check the bait traps today?"

"Already did," Rachel said.

She watched him go down the hall to the stairs.

When she turned around, her mother was sitting out on the balcony. Rachel joined her on the bench. When her mother placed an arm around her shoulders, Rachel could smell the sweet scent of perfume. On the bay white sails angled against the southeasterly breeze, and powerboats cleaved long wakes on the expanse of blue.

"Are you frightened by all this?" her mother asked softly.

Rachel shrugged.

"I am. I'm also exhausted. It's not just your heart that you can't stop, you know. It's all of you—your life goes on. When terrible things happen you must keep going. You've got to deal with the guests, the kitchen—check the bait traps. It's all you can do, Rachel." Her hand came up and stroked Rachel's hair, and she kissed the top of her head. "It's all anyone can do."

The Boat House was one of Emerson's refuges from the afternoon heat. He usually spelled Rachel there for an hour or so while she got lunch. A steady breeze came through the open windows; halyards clanged against aluminum masts, making the entire harbor tinkle like a Chinese ornament. He napped with *The Boston Globe* spread over his chest.

He was awakened by voices—Anne and Cyrus—out on the front porch of the Boat House. His chair was tipped back, the newspaper lying on the floor. He could look through the door, across the counter, and out the front windows; the lid of the old Coke machine was raised, and he could only see the top of Cyrus's hair, which bobbed up and down as he cleaned out the inside of the compartment. His labor was accompanied by the rasping sound of a bristle brush scrubbing metal. Emerson closed his eyes and began to drift off, soothed by the chiming halyards, the rhythmic scrubbing, the gentle sea breeze.

"I called Prichard up to Boston 'bout that order," Cyrus said.

"Straighten it out?" Anne said.

"The rest of the shipment will come out on tomorrow's ferry."

"And the cutlery?"

"Nope. Still on back-order."

Anne said, "This jockeying for stations between those two girls has to stop."

"Yep."

"I just told them the schedule's on the board in the kitchen. Read it."

"Straight. No questions."

"What about our guests without a reservation?"

"Page and that other fellow? They've been out and about. Haven't seen 'em since breakfast."

Emerson sat forward in his chair, lifted the newspaper off the floor, and dropped it on the workbench. He got up and walked out to the front door, looked through the screen at his daughter, who sat on the top porch step. She was wearing unusually bright colors. It seemed a wise, strategic choice. "Those two detectives," he said, "they were asking about you earlier."

Anne didn't turn around. "I figured they would."

"They've been dealing with Ben Snow since we came back from that schooner this morning. Going to bring some team of inspectors or some such out and go over that boat stem to stern."

Anne turned her head and stared up the hill toward the inn. "Well, I'm not going anywhere. They can find me."

Emerson pushed open the screen door and stepped out on the porch. The sun was hot on his bare head—it made him regret the beers he'd had with Ben earlier. He watched Cyrus scrub the inside of the Coke machine; sweat ran down his face, and the back of his shirt was soaked through. Dozens of bottles of Coke and other soft drinks cluttered the floor. "They're asking about Randall."

"Still no sign of him," Cyrus said.

"Think he's gone out to the Rescue Station?"

"Maybe."

"Might call out there on the shortwave, see if he's there."

Cyrus paused in his labor a moment and glanced up at Emerson. "Finding him's their job. I'm doing mine."

When Cyrus had first married, that's what Emerson saw in him: a young man who was willing to do his job. He seemed so rare in those days when all the other kids were interested in anything but honest work. Beach parties, drugs, booze, sex, and talking about the world as though being out here on this tiny island was a means of changing it all. Emerson found them tiresome. They were simply lazy. But Cyrus, he understood honest labor. Unlike most islanders, Emerson wasn't surprised that Cyrus and Anne married; nor was he surprised that their marriage turned out to be a life of chores, divvied up and done without much confabulation. For Cyrus, it was all he could expect—while for Anne it was confining and less than she had envisioned.

"How 'bout Rachel?" Emerson said. "She should have been back down here by two."

Anne got to her feet, the wind blowing her long skirt against her legs, and her hair fanning across her face. "I told her she could have the afternoon off," she said.

Emerson nodded. "She needs some time to sort this all out."

"She could sort out some of the tangled fishing line in there," Cyrus said, setting the bristle brush on the windowsill behind the Coke machine. "And I told her to do this at least a week ago."

Emerson said, "Kids her age come out here and get to go to the beach, go swimming, boating, fishing, whatever, all day long."

Cyrus poured his bucket of soapy water into the compartment, then reached down to pull the drain plug on the left side of the machine. He stood back with his hands on his hips and watched the stream of reddish

55

liquid squirt out, arch off the end of the porch, and pool in the sand. He stared at the dirty water as though it were the only thing that mattered.

Turning, Emerson looked at Anne, who was again staring up the hill toward the inn, where the two detectives stood on the bar patio.

Rachel heard them coming out of the inn. Their adult voices were soft, flat, careful. She closed her book and got up from the wicker rocking chair— she stopped its motion before going down the steps and around to the side of the porch, and crawled underneath. The shade was cool, finely striped by the midafternoon sun.

Page and McNeil sat in the wicker chairs, and her mother took the rocker. Rachel wondered if the seat was still noticeably warm. Her mother poured drinks over ice: tea with lemon. No one seemed eager to start. They drank, the wicker creaked, their feet shuffled on the boards directly above Rachel's head.

"I'm glad to see you're feeling better," Page said eventually.

"Thank you," her mother said.

"It must have been a great shock," McNeil said. His voice was not smooth like Page's. But it sounded friendly, almost brotherly. Rachel still had a stick of the black gum he'd given her.

"I'm better now," her mother said, though with little conviction. "It's hard to get rest at your own resort."

"This is quite an operation you run," McNeil said.

"Our summers are very busy."

In the distance seagulls cawed, and the sound of an outboard engine echoed faintly from the cove. Rachel watched a spider lower itself from the porch boards to the sand. She blew gently and the filament swayed languidly.

"You knew Eliot Bedrosian," Page said.

Her mother didn't answer immediately. "Yes, I knew him."

"Ben Snow says you've known him a long time," Page said.

"I knew him a long time ago."

"When did you meet?"

"Oh, early seventies. We met at a party, a beach party over on Nauset. That's how young people usually met each other on the Cape in the summer."

"They probably still do," McNeil offered.

"What was your relation to him, back then?" Page asked.

"Back then?"

"Yes. I understand he wasn't just a summer resident, but lived here year-round for several years. How well did you know him?"

"Year-rounders tend to know each other quite well," she said, "whether they want to or not."

"Didn't you date him?" Page asked.

"Is that what Ben Snow calls it, dating?"

"What would you call it, your relationship with—"

"Relationship," she said. "That was becoming a popular word then. We had a 'relationship.' But I don't think I've ever heard a really clear definition of what a 'relationship' is, have you?"

"Anne," McNeil said, as though they were old friends, "weren't you two a serious thing for some time? They used to be called an 'item'—two people who were very together. You could see it just by looking at them. My wife and I were an 'item' once. It was a lot of fun. But then of course we got married."

"I never thought of us as an 'item,'" Anne said. "And we were never married."

"You were intimate," Page said.

"I'll accept that. Yes, intimate."

Rachel looked down at the paperback lying beside her elbow in the sand. Somewhere in it she'd encountered the word intimate, and now she realized she hadn't fully understood what it meant. She knew that she and Eric weren't intimate. How far did you have to go to be intimate?

"Now," Page said, "Bedrosian left Angel's Head in the mid-seventies, after some bad land deals. He moved to Florida, where he got involved with real estate."

"I don't know what he did after he left the island."

"You never heard—"

"We had no contact."

"You looked after the inn."

"Yes. My mother was ailing then."

"You married Cyrus Martin."

"Yes."

"You had a daughter."

"Would you care for more iced tea?"

"Yes, thanks," McNeil said.

"No, thank you," Page said.

Rachel wanted to speak, to tell them what her mother was avoiding. But adults were so dense; they rarely asked the right questions. She looked up through the floorboards at their soles. Leather: Page. Rubber: McNeil. Her mother's bare left foot, slender and tanned; jiggling in the air because her legs were crossed and she always had this little jiggle when she sat that way. Rachel had tried it but it didn't work. Her leg just wouldn't jiggle like that, as though it had a mind, a life of its own.

When the iced tea was poured, Page said, "Bedrosian returned to Angel's Head this summer."

There was only the sound of ice cubes.

"He sailed up from Florida in the *Northern Lady*," McNeil said. "We understand he'd run into some trouble down there. Land deals again. Real estate's gone to hell everywhere, not just here in the commonwealth."

"You saw him this summer?" Page said.

Her mother put her glass on the floor directly over Rachel's head. A drop of cold water dripped between the boards and landed on her forearm. She moved back in the sand and her mother's leg stopped jiggling. Rachel looked up. Her mother was perfectly still. All three adults were perfectly still.

"Didn't you see him this summer?" Page insisted.

"It's a small island." Her mother leaned over, her hand came down to her glass, and for a moment Rachel could see her eyes, which appeared to be gazing not at the glass but at the gaps between the boards.

Page cleared his throat. "What was your relationship to Eliot Bedrosian this summer, Ms. Flood?"

Her mother sat back in the wicker rocker, without having picked up the glass. Her foot began jiggling in the air once again, the motion reminding Rachel of what some fishermen do with their bait to attract fish. Then the foot swung sideways and knocked over the glass, spilling iced tea on Rachel's head and T-shirt. There was creaking and shuffling above, until Rachel shouted, *"Christ, Mother!"*

She crawled out from beneath the porch, and getting to her feet she looked at the three adults who were now standing. Her mother looked angry; McNeil surprised, though pleased to see her. Page simply watched.

"Look at me!" Rachel screamed. "I'm *soaked!"*

"What are you doing under there?" her mother said.

The cold had given Rachel goosebumps, and she looked down at her enlarged nipples. She pulled the wet cotton T-shirt away from her skin, then let go.

"I talked to you about this eavesdropping—"

"It's not *true!"* Rachel screamed. "He's not my *father!"*

Page took a step forward. "Who's not?"

She threw down her book. "You're just a *dick!"* Turning, she ran along the side of the inn and into the backyard.

Eight

LATE AFTERNOON MARK WALKED THE BEACH TO WORK UP
an appetite. Another Chamber of Commerce day: blue sky, gentle sea breeze,
temperature in the mid 80s. It was on such a day when he had first seen the
island from the air, in a small plane from Boston. Mid-August, 1972, the
island was covered with the greens of maple, oak, and scrub pine, rimmed
by sand beaches; from several thousand feet, it didn't look like much headway had been made against the primeval forest. Previous to that flight he'd
always taken the ferry across the bay from Chatham. His mother, a native
Angelian, had married a GI after the war and they lived in Belmont, a
Boston suburb. Yet they returned for holidays and the summer months and
there they were taken in by his mother's family, the Boughs. But in 1972,
he was a Boston College graduate, and he had come not to visit, but to
work for an old man named Benjamin Cox who owned the *Angel's Head
Current,* the weekly that had "Served the Islands and Cape Cod for Three
Generations." From the air Mark thought he could actually see Angel's
Head more clearly: it was not the paradise of his childhood and his mother's
recollections; it was a fragile island amid the shoals of Pleasant Bay on the
elbow of Cape Cod.

The plane began its descent toward the small grass airstrip in the low-
lands on the west side of the island. From one of the back seats the crooner
began again, now singing "Old Cape Cod." Some of the passengers began
to sing along—it was an eighteen-seater filled to capacity. Then the crooner
was standing, moving up the aisle, his footsteps uncertain as he kept time
by tapping the lid of his beer can.

"Sir," the flight attendant with a trimmed Afro said quietly, yet with
the appropriate firmness, "we must ask you to take your seat and fasten
your safety belt as we are making our final approach."

"Fellow Pilgrims!" the crooner proclaimed. "My name is Eliot

Bedrosian and I'd like to welcome you to Angel's Head, the pearl of New England—"

The attendant politely took hold of his forearm. "Mr. Bedrosian. We must insist that at this time—"

"Hands off, *boy.*"

A few of the passengers drew in their breath audibly, and there followed a noticeable silence, save the perpetual noise produced by the prop engines.

Then Bedrosian's face went slack as he stared at the attendant. He placed his hand on the young man's crisp uniform jacket and shoved with all he had, and, just as he lurched forward, the plane banked even more steeply to the left, causing him to lose his balance—while the attendant merely stepped back with the thrust, never losing his footing. Mark tried to break Bedrosian's fall, but the man's skull cracked loudly against the overhead luggage compartment, and he fell heavily on the aisle carpet.

There was sudden confusion among the passengers. A remarkable amount of blood issued from Bedrosian's scalp. The attendant screamed for everyone to please remain seated and calm as he ran down the aisle toward the back of the plane, and over the PA system the captain announced their imminent arrival at Angel's Head, where the skies were clear and the temperature was 82 degrees Fahrenheit. The woman across the aisle rolled her eyes toward the nearest speaker and whispered, "Lord save us, he sounds just like Dean Martin."

Excusing himself profusely, the attendant made his way forward with his arms full of towels. Mark grabbed one, leaned over, and pressed it firmly against Bedrosian's skull. He could feel the man's pulse surging through the cloth, and within seconds there was on his palm the warmth and stickiness of blood. At that moment the plane touched down, and he was home.

It was because of that incident that Bedrosian always treated Mark as though they were kindred spirits. Sober, Bedrosian could be disarmingly engaging. He too was a recent graduate—from Harvard Law School—and he had come to Angel's Head with boundless aspirations. He took Mark into his confidence with ease, explaining that he wanted to build a practice on the Cape, dabble in real estate, and eventually go into politics. Mark had no doubt that Bedrosian could do almost anything he wanted; he had the finish, the look of a comer. He was at ease with the summer residents down from Boston, and he could throw a game of darts with local fishermen to while away a quiet winter evening. Whenever he encountered Mark they inevitably talked about the island, as if Angel's Head were their own secret find.

But there was something Gatsbyesque about Bedrosian. His darker side was revealed when he'd had a few drinks. A look or a sudden blunt comment would expose his nature. At times Mark admired Bedrosian for it. While many of their peers were in search of the ultimate high, Bedrosian seemed the consummate realist. He didn't wear trendy flannel, he didn't spout vacuous sentiments of peace and love, he didn't lose his head to the pervasive smoke of the early seventies. He had plans, long-range goals, and he seemed to see the horizon clearly. Mark was flattered when Bedrosian suggested that he himself was destined to considerable success as a journalist. Once when they were at a beach party they ended up staring into the driftwood fire together, sharing a bottle of tequila. The air smelled of salt water and dope. Someone with a guitar was doing a bad imitation of Bob Dylan. Bedrosian's eyes shone hard and black in the firelight. "It's not what they lack," he said as he passed the bottle to Mark, "it's what they're unwilling to acknowledge: ambition. I have it. You have it. They avoid it."

Mark looked at the bottle and said, "I have it?"

"You going to write for *The Current* your whole life?"

Mark shrugged.

"No. You'll eventually get on a daily up in Boston, maybe even go national, something like *Newsweek.*"

"Would I have to move off Angel's Head to do this?"

"We'll always have Angel's Head."

They both laughed. Perverted lines from *Casablanca* were in. They split the worm.

Bedrosian was right: though nothing else turned out as planned, as hoped, Mark would always have Angel's Head. The years in the Midwest he carried the island with him. His connection to that place—this place, where he was now, miraculously, walking the beach once again—became his source of survival. There were winter days when he would drive to an open field, crop stubble peeking through the snow, and he would walk, imagining himself on Angel's Head. It was as though he had ingested every brick, every clapboard, every village street, every stretch of beach. Over the years the perfection of the island increased in direct proportion to the imperfection of his life. Walking this stretch of beach now was like a prayer of thanksgiving. This was all the religion he had left.

When he came to the old abandoned clammer's shack, he sat in the shade, his back against its curled, weathered shingles. The bay was calm, the tide low. Seagulls and terns stood in the shallows. Mark closed his eyes and listened to the wind, to the birds.

He may have dozed. When he opened his eyes the light had deepened. Cape light was so rare, so unique. A few minutes in the late afternoon and the color of the water would go from blue to silver. Or gold. Or red. It all depended on the sun, on the angle of its descent. On the time of year. Angelians could tell whether it was the first week of August or the last week of August by the colors on the bay.

Mark looked to his left and saw him. He was standing about ten yards away. Getting to his feet slowly, Mark said, "Hi there."

"Hi there," Randall said. His voice was flat. It almost sounded like a question. He looked larger than Mark remembered. His eyes deeper, sadder. He appeared confused.

Mark took a step forward, but Randall turned his head toward the water, as though he were offended. His hair had grown out and the scars on the side of his head were barely visible.

"How have you been, Randall?"

"Tide's going out."

"Yes."

"Next high tide at nine forty-seven P.M."

Mark took a few more steps. Randall continued to stare out at the bay toward Strong Island.

"I haven't seen you in a long time," Mark said. He moved closer. "I used to write. To send stuff: a postcard of Wrigley Field, a Tigers pennant. But that was years ago."

"Bird Fidrich pitched for the Tigers."

"That's right."

"Sox should have got him. He's from Massachusetts."

Mark sat down in the sand and faced the bay. "Remember Pumpsie Green?"

Randall picked up a stone and scaled it out over the water. "Yeah, and his drinking buddy Gene Conley."

"Sammy White."

"Frank Malzone."

"Earl Wilson."

"Gary Geiger."

"Jackie Jensen."

"Pete Runnels."

"Bill Monbouquette."

"Dick Radatz, the Monster." Randall laughed. It was self-conscious, awkward, a laugh you'd hear from a boy who had recently entered puberty, his face sprouting pimples and whiskers, his voice dropping an octave. But it was Randall. A grown man with thinning hair, a round, hard belly, golden hair on his large, tanned forearms.

"You remember we used to drive up to Fenway?" Mark picked up a smooth stone. He waited. "We'd take your boat across to Chatham, to Ryder's Cove. That fisherman, Billy-something, used to drive us up in his truck. Afterwards we'd go for beers at the Newbury Steak House on Mass Ave, the bar with the big columns."

Mark waited, studying the stone in his hand; it was gray, streaked with black, flecked with silver, and he couldn't begin to imagine how long it had taken the ocean to make it so smooth. He wondered why we know this about stones, what part of our minds figures it out. Did such knowledge of stones make this stone in hand more beautiful? Could you still love the Red Sox without knowing their history?

"Billy Collins drowned," Randall said.

"I didn't know that." Mark threw the stone toward the water.

"His gill-netter broke up on the Monomoy shoals in a storm."

Randall started walking up the beach toward the dunes. Mark got to his feet and followed, moving up slowly until he was next to Randall.

"Eliot Bedrosian," Mark said.

They stopped walking.

"He's dead too," Mark said. "Why'd he come back?"

"Eliot Bedrosian—" Randall didn't continue.

"What did he want here, after the things he did?" Mark almost said the things he did to you.

"Eliot Bedrosian was a bad man."

"Who said so?"

Randall turned to Mark. He looked as though he were surprised to find someone standing next to him. It seemed to frighten him, and he took a step backward. This close Mark could see the slight depression on the right side of his skull, where the doctors had opened him up after the accident. It made his head seem lopsided. Deflated. When he started walking up the dune again, Mark let him go.

Nine

MAXINE BULIKOFF STILL LIVED IN THE SAME HOUSE OVER-
looking Crowell's Inlet. She still had dogs—now two yellow labs that
wiggled and sniffed around Mark's legs as though he were an incredible
find. She still had the bulging dark eyes enlarged by inordinately thick
glasses, and the hoarse, raspy voice, the result of over two packs of ciga-
rettes a day. But she no longer had the weight, not all of it. When she
hugged him in the doorway, setting the dogs into a dervish of jealousy, she
nearly yelled in his ear, "And you can almost get your arms *around* me!"

It was true. He stepped back to look at her. Her faded Yankees sweatshirt
and blue jeans hung from her shoulders, breasts, and hips. She was still a
large woman, but she had easily lost seventy-five pounds. The evidence
was in her face. Her cheeks, which used to be smooth and rounded, seemed
to have collapsed.

"And look at *you!*" she shouted. "Short hair. No beard. No 'stache. So
dahlink, you went Republican and bought stock in Gillette?"

"Looks can still deceive."

Laughing, she looped her arm through his and walked him into the
kitchen. It had been redone—the dark, bare pine boards, the enormous
Franklin stove which had once been the sole source of heat had all been
replaced by high tech built-in appliances with smooth black surfaces, white
ceramic tile counters, and fluorescent ceiling panels which seemed to flood
the room with shadowless light. Only the picture window overlooking the
inlet had not been changed.

Page sat on one of the stools at the counter. Mark was not surprised.

There was a bottle of peppered Stoly on the counter. Max went around
to the working side of the counter and poured three shots; they raised their
glasses in a toast and drank. Peppered Stoly. It made Mark smile; it made
his eyes water. Page appeared to have no trouble getting the liquor down in
one toss.

65

"So." Max poured another round, then leaned on the counter to stare at Mark, her eyes probing from behind the thick lenses. "You've come back, Mark. Everyone returns to Angel's Head. Everyone shows up in the village and makes a big production of it. How great it is to be back. How could they ever leave. They have law practices in Manhattan. They're doctors and professors in Boston. They throw their moola around, then in two weeks they're gone." She drank down her shot and waited as Mark and Page did the same. "But not you."

"No big bucks."

"No big production!" she said. "No entrance, no flourish whatsoever." She turned and stared at Page. "Not Emmons. He slips onto the island. Hovers on the fringes for God knows how long, and then—*then*—he decides to surface. When the coast is clear. He used to live in that little apartment above his aunt's garage, and let me tell you, we used to keep a body count, back when the phrase had real significance."

Mark shook his head. "Gross exaggeration. Max," he said, turning to Page, "used to refer to herself as the napalm of love."

Max slapped the counter and laughed hoarsely, alerting the dogs, who pranced on the slippery tile floor. Shaking her head and suddenly looking weary and distraught, Max went to the oven and pushed some buttons; there were lights, there were succinct beeps. "This is not like the old days, when we used to cook big pots of chili and spaghetti, drink cheap red, and smoke a joint sitting on the floor listening to The Band." She winked at Page. "How we got that paper out some weeks, fuck if I know."

"All-nighters," Mark said, pouring another round. "Pure adrenaline—and nips from Mother Russia."

"But now there's responsibility," Max said, returning to the counter. "And worse, accountability. This is what happens when you run things. When you own things. You know you're in a democracy when you lie awake at night fearing another lawsuit. It was more fun, more democratic when everybody was busy fucking everybody else." Suddenly Max had tears in her eyes, also enlarged by her glasses. "It was incestuous. It was called a sexual revolution. It hurt and it felt really good. Now they're all gone. Off-islanders making their fortunes in America." She sniffed and smiled. "Some are even dead."

"Bedrosian?" Page said quietly.

"Yes," Max said, "Eliot was one of us, in his own way." She looked like she'd break, and yet she appeared grateful. She threw back her shot and whispered, "We are defined by our enemies."

Mark drank his shot. He could feel it now. Its heat. Its illumination. Its clarity. He felt like he was back: the island.

The kitchen was humming. Cooks on the line worked full tilt. The ovens and grills combined to push the temperature well over a hundred. Waitresses and busboys burst through the swinging doors, balancing trays. Emerson sat on a stool by the back door, sipping a glass of Jim Beam he'd procured from a tray—the waitress said it was a mistake order. It was a godsend. The kitchen operated as usual, like an engine. But there was something different about it—the pace seemed more frantic, there was more bickering and swearing. The ship hath no captain.

He finished the drink, allowing the ice cubes to rest against his nose until it was numb, determined to catch the runoff coating the glass. With his head tilted back he was staring up at the wall phone, greasy from hands that had been prepping food. And above it, jutting out of the door jamb— at an angle often associated with a firm erection—was a sixteen-penny nail. It was coated with so many layers of white paint that a hardened drip hung from the nailhead. Emerson got up quickly and placed the glass on the stool; the loud knock was lost in the clamor behind him.

He left through the swinging doors, leaving the brightly lit kitchen and entering the candlelit dining room. Capacity crowd; civilized murmur. A man sitting at table eight wore blue slacks with little white anchors and he was telling his party about a golf accident where a guy got so upset over a missed give-me that he slammed his putter down, snapping it in two, and the flying broken shaft skewered his partner through the neck. Out in the front lobby Emerson grabbed some mints from the bowl by the register, went through the door marked PRIVATE, and climbed the stairs to the family quarters. Anne's bedroom door was closed. He stood in the hall a moment, stuffing the mints in his mouth, then knocked. She didn't answer, but he opened the door anyway. The room was illuminated only by the flickering light of the television. Some old black and white movie. The sound was barely audible. Anne lay on the bed in her white bathrobe. There was a bottle of Johnnie Walker on the nightstand.

"There's a grease fire in the kitchen," she said. "Heimlich maneuver at table five."

He went over and sat on the edge of the bed. She looked awful, the kind of awful only truly beautiful women can achieve after the age of thirty-five. His wife too had been beautiful, and what she did to herself appeared now in his daughter as a cruel form of reincarnation. "The staff

67

key to the shed's missing," he said. "It's not on the nail."

"Round up the usual suspects."

He glanced at the television. Claude Raines was wearing a military uniform and one of those French hats—flat top, short beak—at a jaunty angle. "Those mainland cops, Page and his friend McNeil, they were asking about keys to the shed."

There was eye movement: this was registering, but it seemed to render her more incapacitated, more liquid as she lay there bundled in terrycloth. He picked up the bottle, which was half empty, and ran his thumb over the label.

"Go ahead, Emerson. Take the night off. I am. Besides, it'll kill the smell of those fucking mints."

He took a fistful of ice from the bucket and let it fall in the glass. "They have the same beauty as stacked firewood."

"Attaboy."

"We've always understood each other."

"Absolutely."

Emerson took a drink, then handed her the glass. "The police have been going over that boat all day long."

"In the fall, when it starts to slow down? We could have a *Casablanca* night." On the television Bogart was sitting in shadows smoking. "You'd look good in one of those white dinner jackets."

Emerson took back the drink and finished it.

"I could be Ilsa Lund. Naw. She gets in the plane at the end and goes away."

"That's what it was about, going away?"

"Though I've always had a soft spot for the French girl at the bar who was dumped by Rick. She screws the Germans, and only the crazy Russian bartender really loves her. And she cries when they sing that French anthem there, whatever you call it."

"By plane? Or by boat?"

"We were going to go away and sail the Caribbean for the winter."

Emerson placed the empty glass on the nightstand and got up. "And then you'd come back to build a bridge."

Tears ran down Anne's cheeks and her head rolled back on the pillow.

She had a beautiful neck.

Her mother's neck.

They had haddock, brown rice, and a spinach salad. As evening came on the inlet disappeared and Mark could see the three of them, reflected in the picture window, eating by candlelight. There were a couple bottles of wine. Drinking always seemed central to life on the island. He reminded himself that he would have to watch it, and smiled at the thought as he poured from the bottle he had brought. Here drinking was connected with time, which seemed slower and more abundant than on the mainland. Drinking helped ease one through the long gray season; in summer it bolstered the illusion of escape, of perfection.

He and Max explained to Page how they had broken the story of Plummer's Marsh. Max had waded through the paper, the land deals, finally arriving at the realization that the various companies holding title to plots overlooking the marsh were, in fact, one big dummy company. Eliot Bedrosian was in some way connected to them, whether they were based in Boston, Providence, Hartford, or New York. One outfit even had a Dallas address, which they called the Texas Connection, but that paper trail went nowhere. What was clear was that some of the investors in these companies were major league. State senators from Massachusetts, Rhode Island, and Connecticut. A number of U.S. congressmen, one Nixon–Ford cabinet member, a former South Vietnamese general. And one of the five families of New York. Threads of the story came and went in the East Coast press. Before it was over *Sixty Minutes* sent out a film crew—though the story was never aired, leading to speculation about a CBS executive's connection to one of the companies through his son-in-law in Hartford. Much of it was based on weak substantiation, and the pervasive Watergate–Vietnam paranoia. "Our theme song," Mark explained, "was that Buffalo Springfield song 'For What It's Worth,' with its harmonic guitar notes that sounded like nerves snapping."

The island, like America, had become bitterly politicized, but in its own way: opponents of the bridge, known as islanders, would drop off homemade chowders and pies at the *Current* office when the staff was pulling all-nighters; yet on several occasions Mark's VW van was vandalized, presumably by Bridgers. Shouting matches in the coffee shops and bars were not uncommon. The joke was that things were so bad that even Jeanie's Salt Water Taffy Shop needed a bouncer. Through it all Plummer's Marsh and land overlooking it remained virtually untouched. "If there was a bottom line," Max said, "it was that nobody ever *proved* anything—and it sold a lot of newspapers." She was leaning on the table, staring intently at Page. She might have been dissecting the man.

Page's slow eyes sought Mark for confirmation. "I've often thought," Mark said, "that I—self-pitying fool that I am—had suffered most because I left. Because I felt driven out, driven off the island. So many people looked at you during and afterwards in a way that said 'You did this. You made it all up.' But I think now it was harder to stay." He looked at Max and she nodded. An acknowledgment, and appreciation.

She took Mark's hand. "I'm something of an institution now."

"You stayed." Mark looked at Page and said, "This woman kept the faith."

Rachel decided it was time to sit up. She untangled herself from Eric's arms and propped herself up on her elbows. "You're a good kisser," she said taking a long, deep breath, "especially for a kid with braces."

"Thanks." He brushed sand from his short hair.

"I meant it as a compliment, stupid."

"I know."

They were on the far side of the cove, and the lights from the village reflected off the still water. The schooner now had a broad ribbon wrapped around its deck rail. When they had first walked around here to the beach near the jetty rocks the sun was setting and the ribbon was bright yellow, making the schooner look like some absurd present; but now it was colorless, just a white stripe in the dark. The police boat that had been tied up to the schooner was gone.

"How'd you know about *Sputnik*?" she asked.

"I read about it in a book."

"In school?"

"No."

"On your own."

He looked away, toward the jetties and the bay.

"Well you *should* be embarrassed. Reading a book without being *told* to—they must think you're a real nerd at school, huh?" She put a big wet kiss on his neck. Leaning back, she laughed. He looked at her smiling— she could see his teeth by the lights off the water.

"After the *Challenger* blew up I began reading about the space program," he explained, almost apologetically. "There was another accident, in the sixties. The astronauts were killed in a fire while they were still on the launch pad. I feel worse for them. There's no liftoff, no film footage of the explosion that you've seen a thousand times. They just burned up in their capsule and nobody ever mentions it."

"Except in books."

"Right."

"You are a strange boy, but I'll tell you a little secret. Promise not to tell anyone." She placed her hand on his thigh and put her mouth close to his ear. "I like to read too," she whispered, then stuck her tongue in his ear, causing him to duck his head and laugh.

Standing up, she said, "Come on, I've got something to show you."

He got to his feet and she stepped into his arms again. His body was long, lean, and warm, and his mouth was tender and determined. "Nobody has ever kissed me like that," she gasped. "Not even Todd Giles, better known as The Tongue. Once in class our teacher was asking us what we thought we wanted to be, you know, when we grew up, and Todd announces that he wants to be a role model."

"Are you nervous?"

"Why? Am I talking too much?"

"And you're shaking."

"I don't know," she said, "this is something else."

"I know."

They held each other tightly a moment longer, then began walking, hand in hand, around the cove. The night air was warm, humid, and smelled of the bay. They had left their shoes back at the Boat House, and their bare feet squeaked on the wet smooth sand.

"What's your father do?" she asked.

"He's an engineer at Wang. Mom teaches."

"When do you go back?"

"After Labor Day." He didn't speak for a moment. "It gets quiet here then?"

"Yep."

"You like it."

"It's okay."

"What about school? I mean, there isn't one here on the island, is there?"

"I go to Orleans."

"Across water, every day?"

"There's a ferry every morning. And there's a school bus on the other side. It's not that far across. We're not, you know, totally cut off from civilization until next Memorial Day."

"Sounds neat—taking a boat to school."

"Sometimes the ferry won't come during a storm, but my grandfather usually insists on taking me across. He's something else, Grapes."

"What do you read?"

She looked up at him. They were near the village now, and she could see his face clearly in the lights. It was getting easier to look into his eyes, his beautiful eyes, and this frightened her. He looked back, and she could see his fear too. She squeezed his hand tightly. "Let's not talk about books—"

"Or school."

"Right. I've got something really neat to show you."

They reached the porch of the Boat House and put on their shoes.

"Thanks, but I've seen Sputnik's tits," he said.

She slapped him on the rear as he was bent over and tying his sneakers. He straightened up and grinned at her. "This is going to be better, right?"

"Absolutely. But we have to move carefully, and stay in the shadows."

"Great: a mission."

"Quiet, and follow me."

She led him up the hill, but not by the path; instead they walked through the tall grass which was often chest-high. They were engulfed by the sound of crickets, and dozens leaped ahead of them in the grass, catching the light from the inn. They paused by the bushes at the back of the kitchen—inside there was the usual clamor of dinner time. Lightning bugs streaked all about them. Rachel watched the barroom screen door which cast an oblong of light across the patio. She knew from years of nocturnal voyeurism that people inside the inn can look out a window or a door at the night, stare right at you, but not see you in the dark.

"Is there any one thing you identify with?"

Eric looked at her.

"You know, a bird or a fish or something."

"Well, I'd have to think. The dark," he said after a pause. "See this? Hear the crickets, see the dark? I have always identified with it. It makes you—" he smiled, his braces looking like polished pewter in the soft light from the bar door, "it makes us invisible."

"Exactly." She reached in the pocket of her jeans and pulled out a key ring. "Now: quickly, and very quiet."

She led him across the yard, through the oblong of light cast from the bar door. Looking inside she saw that the room was crowded. People lined the bar, and couples sat at the small round tables, their faces hovering over the glass candle bowls as if they were the souls of the dead.

When they reached the shed Rachel inserted the key and unlocked the door, something she'd done in the dark often enough, but now it seemed a long, intense moment filled with fear and anticipation. She could feel Eric's hands on her shoulders as she pulled open the door. They stepped inside, and when she closed the door they were in total darkness.

"*Wow.*" He kept his hands on her shoulders.

"I know." She threw the deadbolt lock. "Isn't it great?"

"Yeah." It was nearly a sigh. His voice was beautiful, surrounded by the dark. "Is this where they found it?"

"Yes. In back."

"Why here?"

"Good question. Whoever did this understands the Floods."

"It's just a shed."

"No it's not. My grandmother died in here."

"How?"

"By her own hand."

"You're making this up."

"I was very young when it happened."

"How did she die?"

"She hung herself."

Slowly, Rachel stretched her arms out into the dark, then she took a small step forward.

"Tell me about Randall Flood," Page said.

They were drinking brandy from snifters. Like adults, Max had said as she passed the bottle. Her face was now flushed, and she poured herself another two fingers. Her enlarged eyes were wary and alert.

Mark waited for Max to light another cigarette; waited to see if she wanted to field this one. She leaned back and exhaled, as though she were being coy at a poker table.

"Randall," Mark said finally. "He figured it out, really. Found the link, you might say."

Max rolled her eyes toward the ceiling.

"We were stuck," Mark continued. "We'd run a few pieces about these holding companies picking up land above Plummer's Marsh, and we'd offered a primer in the economics of a condominium."

"A very appealing idea," Max added. "Lots of islanders suddenly envisioned their old saltbox with a couple ells tacked on converted into apartment condos, lofts, you name it."

Page's eyes gave away nothing.

"Randall took me out on the marsh in his boat," Mark said. "Picked the worst day imaginable: one of those gray March afternoons when the air is raw and wet. We pulled into Partisan Creek as far as the low tide would allow us to go. I was wearing long johns, two sweaters, a hooded sweatshirt, gloves, and waders. It felt like a moonwalk. We squished around the marsh for hours, looking for the stakes the Army Corps of Engineers had set. Randall had a hundred-foot tape measure, and we charted the stakes on his map. After several hours we were exhausted and soaked—the drizzle had turned to freezing rain—by the time we made our way back to his boat. The tide was rising, the wind was really starting to come in, and we sat under his canvas canopy drinking peppermint schnapps. We were staring at a bunch of dots on the map, and none of it made any sense.

"I remember my hands then—I used to smoke, a lot, and my hands were so raw and wet it took forever to light a cigarette. And once I got one lit, it would go out because the paper got wet from the damn rain coming in under the canopy. I thought that this was the dumbest thing I'd ever done: move out to the island just so I could freeze my ass off out on a salt marsh. You might say I had developed misgivings. Then, after several pulls on the schnapps, Randall takes a pencil and starts to connect the dots. Erasing here and there; drawing new lines. Eventually, he's got two sweeping arches cutting across Blacke's Channel and the marsh to that big bend in South Point Road—there by the old mill? I looked at it and said, 'What, a channel?' Randall stared out across the marsh toward the island. 'Maybe they want to build a marina over here. People in these condominiums'll come complete with yachts, ya think?' Ecology was just beginning to be an issue in the early seventies, and I said something about them never being able to slice up and dredge the marsh like that. Randall nodded and, stumped, we finished the bottle of schnapps. We left the channel and rode back around to the village side of the island, cutting through Blacke's Channel, which was then only barely deep enough. Even though we were rounding the lee side of the island, the chop in the bay was something."

Mark finished his snifter of brandy and placed his hand over the top when Max offered to pour him another. "After we passed through the channel into deeper water, Randall suddenly cut the engine back to trolling speed. He turned around, raised his arm, and pointed—first at Grummond's Neck on the mainland, then sweeping his arm across Blacke's Channel, to Plummer's Marsh and the south side of Angel's Head. In virtually any other weather it was a spectacular view, a real Cape Cod postcard. But I was shivering with the cold and just wanted to get into a hot shower and another bottle of something. 'Can't ya *see* it!' he shouted. 'It's a *bridge!* They want to build a fuckin' *bridge* acrost to the *island!*'"

Max stood up and began gathering plates and glasses. "Soon as we managed to get the word bridge into one of our stories," she said, "all hell broke loose." She looked weary. She didn't want to go into the rest of it, the battle between Bedrosian and the islanders. And, of course, Randall.

Page seemed to understand and he pushed himself away from the table.

After saying goodnight, Mark and Page walked down through the village. The fog had rolled in.

"She didn't want to talk about Randall," Mark explained, "and ruin a good meal."

"I could see that. Everyone has a limit, how much they want to tell. You must come to recognize that, being a journalist. I often find it interesting what people avoid talking about."

Mark glanced at Page, who kept staring down at the brick sidewalk. "For instance?"

"She also avoided talking about the bridge—the bridge now."

"I see." They were walking beneath a row of maples whose roots had buckled the old sidewalk so much that it was necessary to step over and around broken and jutting bricks. "This," Mark said, "is one of the unique pleasures of Angel's Head."

"Particularly after a fine haddock dinner."

"Precisely."

"How do you think Max feels about the bridge being built now?"

"Personally, I don't know. My guess is that she's in favor of a bridge if it will boost the island's economy. As a journalist, I know how she'll act—" Though Mark was concentrating on the sidewalk, he was aware that now Page was looking at him. "Max will cover the story, follow it wherever it goes."

"Professional neutrality?" Page said.

"Precisely."

They entered the east end of the village, where the fog swirled about the street lamps. Mark was quite drunk. He could only assume Page was affected too—he'd had just as much to drink. But he walked with his hands clasped behind his back, the collar of his sport coat turned up, his straw hat low over his eyes, and he might have just stepped out of Sunday meeting.

"You think journalists and detectives are similar?"

"At times," Page said.

"That's probably why they make such good adversaries."

"Yes, I suppose. In our line of work it's usually us against the local authorities. Working for the state, you're always an intruder, always on someone else's turf. Except when the Feds come into our state. But every town has a Ben Snow. I understand there was a boating accident—though Ben Snow seems to not know much about it."

"His father was chief constable," Mark said.

"What happened?"

"One of those freak boating accidents you read about. Randall was scuba diving in the cove and someone ripped open the side of his head with the prop of an outboard motor."

"This happened when?"

"The spring after the bridge business was finally over."

"Bedrosian," Page said.

"It was dark. There were no witnesses, no evidence."

"But everyone presumed so."

"Yes, they did. Bedrosian left Angel's Head shortly after that. People were very angry. Too angry."

"Too angry?"

"You haven't read enough issues of *The Current,* evidently."

They came to the end of the street that led to Aunt Mae's house. Stopping for a moment, they stood and listened to the moisture drip in the maple overhead.

"You love it out here," Page said.

Mark nodded.

"Why'd you leave?"

"That's a good question."

Ten

RACHEL PRETENDED NOT TO NOTICE THEM WATCHING HER from the pier. She hated this job the most: cleaning seagull droppings off boat decks. Kneeling made her knees red and sore, and scrubbing the deck with the bristle brush made her shoulders ache. The white crud swirled and worked up into a smelly lather when it was mixed with the salt water in the brush. She was rinsing down when she looked ashore again. Only Page was standing on the pier now. The big one, McNeil, was rowing a dinghy across the cove.

"Looks like fun," he said when he was alongside.

She drew up another bucket of water by the short rope tied to the handle.

"How come this boat doesn't have a canvas cover or one of those things that twirl in the wind to keep the gulls off?"

"'Cause the guy who owns this boat's an asshole."

"That makes sense." He dipped an oar and wiggled the dinghy closer. "Mind if I come aboard?"

She got on her knees, dunked the brush in the fresh bucket of water, and began scrubbing a new section of deck. He climbed aboard the boat, moving easily for such a top-heavy man. He was wearing a New England Patriots cap spattered with white paint and he was chewing gum.

"Nope," he said, leaning against the chrome rail. "It don't look like fun."

"Afterwards my eyes are always puffy and my nose gets wicked stuffed up."

He squatted down next to her, pulling a handkerchief from the back pocket of his chino shorts; his calves reminded her of footballs. Holding two ends, he formed a triangle and held the handkerchief out toward her. "Here," he said, "let me tie this around you so you don't have to breathe that stuff. They should get you one of those fiberglass masks."

She turned around and let him tie the handkerchief around her head. She could smell licorice.

"There, you look like a bandit, a regular outlaw."

"You on duty?" she asked.

"All day."

"And they let you wear shorts?"

"My mother couldn't get me to dress right, and I've been hopeless ever since." He took a pack of gum from his shirt pocket, and offered a stick to her. "This'll help cut the smell."

It was that Black Jack gum. She unwrapped it and for the first few seconds she just closed her eyes and chewed, allowing the sweet licorice to spread through her mouth and sinuses.

He stood up, leaned against the rail, and peered out toward the jetties. "What a day. Lord, what a day. In February, I'll remember this very moment. You do that? Freeze a moment in your mind so you can have it later, like a snapshot?"

She paused in her scrubbing, but didn't look up at him. When she continued, she asked, "What're they going to do with the schooner?"

He craned around and stared at the *Northern Lady*. "That's a very good question, Rachel. And we're not sure yet. It's still unclear who owns that beautiful boat."

She stopped and looked up at him. "The dead man did."

"It's not that simple. He didn't own it outright. We got some papers faxed up from Florida that suggest that the boat was leased, and the lease had expired."

"It's stolen?"

"You might say."

"So it's just going to sit there with that yellow ribbon around it, collecting seagull shit?"

"For the time being. It's evidence."

"Well, I'm not cleaning it."

"Okay by me." He smiled down at Rachel. "You ever been on her?"

"No. Why?"

"I guess he was an old friend of your mother's, so I just thought you might have gone out there with her."

Rachel stood up and poured the bucket of water on the deck. "That's where he was killed, on the boat?"

"That's right."

"Was it messy?"

"It wasn't pretty, Rachel. Somebody tried to clean up, but they didn't do nearly as good a job as this."

"God."

"This is very unpleasant stuff, isn't it? People out here on the island don't seem as happy as they ought to, especially in this weather." He folded his arms and gazed up at the cloudless blue sky. "You ever been south, down nearer the equator?"

She hesitated. "Uh-uh."

"Well, this sky today could be down there. The deepest, richest blue dome imaginable. Places like Florida and the Caribbean, they have it most all the time."

"My mother used to go out to the boat," she said. "At night."

He continued to gaze up at the sky. "With him?"

"I guess so."

"You saw them?"

She lowered the bucket over the rail again. "I heard them."

"What did you hear?"

"Them."

"Doing what?"

"You know."

"Oh. That."

When she pulled up the bucket there was a small fish in it.

"That's neat," he said. "Without bait. You know he was from Florida. I mean, did your mother tell you—"

"We were going to go there."

"When?"

"I don't know. This fall."

"What about the inn?"

She shrugged.

"Were you going to come back?"

"She said we'd back in the spring."

"Are you sure?"

"Yes. They were going to build a bridge."

"They: your mother and Bedrosian."

"And other islanders. A whole group of them have been talking about it. They all held meetings over the winter. They used to be against the idea of a bridge, I guess, but times have changed."

"And Bedrosian was going to help."

"Yeah. After we went on this sailing trip."

"It's nice down there, especially in winter."

"I didn't want to go, I told them."

"Why?"

"We'd have to leave Grapes. Randall. The inn. The island."

"My." He shook his head. "Why would anybody want to do that?"

"That's what I said: it was just stupid."

"What about Cyrus?"

"What about him?"

"What was he going to do if you all went to Florida?"

"I don't know. We didn't talk about him."

He placed his hands on the rail and pushed his weight off until he was standing upright. Looking toward her dinghy, tied to the stern, he said, "If you're almost through, I'll race you back." He swung one leg, then the other over the rail and stepped down into his dinghy.

"Naw, I got to do the Gould's boat next."

"Okay. Another time," he said pushing off. He draped his wrists over the oar and drifted on the smooth water. "That business with your mom on the porch the other day—"

Rachel pulled the handkerchief down off her face. "What about it?"

"You work that out with her all right?"

She stared down at him. It was remarkable that a man his size wouldn't just send such a little fiberglass dinghy straight to the bottom.

After a moment he smiled up at her and began pulling easily on the oars. "I'll be seeing you, Rachel. Don't scrub too long now, hear?" Across the cove on the pier the other detective was talking to Randall, Eddie, and Emerson.

Rachel got to her knees and placed both hands in the bucket of seawater. When the little fish was between them, she closed her hands, but it swam free. Turning, she reached for the brush, and found a package of Black Jack on the wood handle.

Emerson wanted Page to know that Randall and Eddie, one of Samuel's crew, were to be treated kindly. Too often tourists did otherwise—in a look or a comment—and islanders took exception. Randall and Eddie often worked together. Currently they were replacing rotted decking on the pier. Randall took the measurements, Eddie cut the boards, and Randall laid them in place and nailed them. Page regarded them with disinterest, which concerned Emerson.

"You do all sorts of jobs around the cove, I understand," Page said.

"Yep." Randall stared down at his tape measure; beads of sweat trickled out of his curly blond hair. "Thirty-six and five-eighths," he read out.

"Thirty-six, five-eighths," Eddie repeated.

"Repairs, boat work, fishing," Page said. He was leaning against the bollard opposite Emerson. His arms were folded and he gazed out at the boats in the cove. He was wearing his straw hat and a light tan suit, and before leaning against the bollard, which was as big around as a telephone pole and coated with dried seagull droppings, he'd carefully covered its top with his handkerchief. "You work just for the inn?"

"Sometimes," Eddie said. "Sometimes for the marina. Sometimes for boat owners." He had been an ad executive in Connecticut until he had a nervous breakdown. When he first arrived at the Rescue Station over a year ago, he wouldn't speak. He was an overweight, balding man who had probably handled nothing heavier than twenty-pound paper. Samuel prescribed walking, and he insisted that Eddie leave the Rescue Station at dawn with a knapsack of food, walk the beach all day, and return exactly at sundown. The theory, Samuel once explained to Emerson, was that a man who seeks the isolation of silence, needs to confront it alone, aided by nothing more than the sound of waves and shore birds. After several weeks of the walking regimen, Eddie began to come out of his silence. He lost weight. His skin became ruddy. He took to wearing an assortment of old hats. Though he remained a quiet man, and there was still a damaged fragility to his gaze, he befriended Randall in a way no one else on the island had—it became clear that he wasn't going to leave the bay. Now Eddie turned on the power saw and cut the pine board that lay across the sawhorses. The whine of the blade momentarily transformed Page; he seemed almost in a trance, and he remained perfectly still until the blade was quiet. Eddie tossed the cut board to Randall. There was the fine smell of pine pitch in the air. "We work for anyone who pays us," Eddie said.

Page said, "So if I came into the cove here in my boat and needed some work done or, say, needed a crew, I could hire you."

Randall laid the board in place and secured it with half a dozen sixteen-penny galvanized nails. The report of his hammer was doubled, echoing off the back of the Boat House. "That's right. Long as you pay up." He walked on his knees down the pier to the next gap where rotted boards had already been taken out. "Forty-three and a quarter shy."

Page continued to gaze out at the cove. His partner was rowing a dinghy around the *Northern Lady;* at present he was leaning over and peering into the water. "You work on any of these boats out here lately?" Page asked.

Eddie cut the next board and carried it down to Randall—it was too long to throw. Randall nailed the board in place; when he was done he sat back on his haunches and wiped the sweat off his face.

Page still didn't look at them. "You worked on the *Northern Lady* for Eliot Bedrosian." His voice was soft, tired.

After a moment Randall said, "No." He put down his hammer and got to his feet. "I never went on his boat."

"I thought you had," Page said. "My forensics team said there had been some work done on the deck recently. Replaced planks, I think, so I thought maybe—"

"Teak," Eddie said. "I did that."

Page said, "When was the last time you saw him?"

Randall stared at Eddie in disbelief. Finally he said, "I told you you shouldn't work for Bedrosian."

"Was it the night he was killed?" Page said.

"Yeah," Eddie said. "Earlier. It was still daylight, not you know when—"

"He was on the boat?"

"Yeah."

"Was there anything unusual about him?"

Eddie shook his head slowly.

"For instance, was he drinking?" Page waited. "Tests found that there was quite a bit of alcohol in his blood."

"He was always drinking," Eddie said. "That wasn't unusual."

"I suppose not," Page said. "Randall, I understand you had an accident some years ago."

Randall nodded his head.

"Some people think Bedrosian was responsible," Page said, "that he might have been driving the boat that hit you out there in the cove. Do you believe that?"

Randall did not look up from the last board he'd nailed. "I don't know."

"Then why wouldn't you work for him?"

"Bedrosian was a bad man," Randall said.

"A bad man. How do you know that?"

Randall still would not look up from the new decking. "My mother said so. She said that Eliot Bedrosian was a bad man."

Page nodded as though he thought this remarkably profound news; then he stood up and peeled his handkerchief off the top of the bollard. He folded it up, making sure the side that had been in contact with the seagull droppings was on the inside, and tucked it in his coat pocket.

Eleven

THE INN'S WHITE PICKUP SAT IN FRONT OF LESARD'S PACKAGE Store. Mark leaned against its hood and folded his arms. Village businesses love cloudy summer days: the sidewalks were jammed with tourists.

When Anne came out of the store she narrowed her eyes at the sight of a man leaning against her truck, then recognized him. "Oh, Christ," she said.

"Hi there."

"Are you kidding?"

The tourists streamed by, making it difficult to get from the store to the curb. She held a paper bag in front of her as though for protection.

"How have you been?" she asked.

"I've been worse."

She took a hand off the package and laid it on his forearm. "God, Mark."

"I know."

"Got time for a drink?"

"What an idea."

They went to the Rip Tide because it didn't have a view, which kept the tourists to a minimum. Several times she stared at him hard, then looked away and shook her head. At first she ordered wine, but then changed it to a gin and tonic.

"When did you get here?" she asked.

"A while ago. What happened to Eliot?"

"I don't know. He showed up at the beginning of the season. Same old Eliot, full of it: the stories, the bravado, the bullshit."

"Was he back for good or just the summer?"

She finished her drink, stared at his, and ordered another round.

"What did he want?"

"What he's always wanted," she said.

"You don't want to talk about Eliot."

"Not particularly. You know what I want to talk about."

"I know," he said, "but not after all these years."

"You're still a coward."

"Yes. I was afraid of this then, and I'm afraid of it now."

"Fine. We won't talk about that."

Their drinks came and they looked out the window a while; below there was an alley lined with small shops and art galleries.

"I had forgotten how tourists tend to infest the village," he said.

"It's not enough," she said.

"It's not?"

"Memorial Day to Labor Day. It's no longer enough."

"Businesses are hurting everywhere. We're in a recession."

"They're dying here," she said. "You have no idea how many of these shops will close for good after this season." She drank as she always did, quickly, almost without pause; but she didn't seem to enjoy it like she used to. "I remember you got a job on a paper in Chicago—still there?"

"That paper folded. I've been in Michigan for years."

"The Midwest. I can't imagine you anywhere but—"

"Me neither."

"You're just visiting—"

"I don't know, Anne."

"Divorced?"

"I lived with someone for a long time."

"Past tense."

He nodded.

"What about your job?"

"I'm 'on leave' from the paper."

She drank half of her gin and tonic. "You'll stay."

"I don't know."

"An Angelian again."

"I don't know."

They decided to have dinner and she called the inn to say she'd be late.

"This used to be called The Scallop Shell," he said when their dinner arrived. "Remember the walls were decorated with giant shells and lobster claws with painted faces on them? It's completely different inside, but it still serves the same seafood."

"This place has changed names three, four times—at one point it was called Lotsa Lobsta. But always tacky island atmosphere, good seafood." As she drank her wine, he studied her hand. Short nails and strong, slender fingers. "For all the worry about bridges, condos, and outside developers," she said, "things still ran their course. It's like the tides. Can't stop them. This place is run by an outfit out of Atlanta. More and more of the restaurants and shops are owned by off-islanders."

"But not the inn."

"Not the inn." She seemed disappointed by the question. "When we were kids I thought that tourists were like our parents. I waited on them because they were adults, and we were raised to be polite and cordial. A funny thing occurred to me several seasons ago: I realized I was waiting on the kids we grew up with—and it changed everything. I don't know why. There aren't any real adults anymore."

"You've had offers to sell."

"We have had offers to sell."

"Did Eliot make an offer?"

She stared down at her plate of broiled scallops and inhaled slowly. "You know you used to do this."

"Do what?"

"*This.* Ask these questions."

"I'm sorry. Let's just eat."

"It pissed me off."

"It was my job."

"What is it *now?*"

She got up from the table, threw her napkin on the seat, and left the restaurant.

Everything was bobbing, crazed, and the green horizon of land rose and fell at the far edge of the gray chop. All hands grinned wildly, even those who had been vomiting over the side. Their movement was a four-limbed grope for hand- and footholds; running down, then climbing up the deck, slick with fish blood and ooze, for they were drifting over a large school of mackerel.

"Never cared for mackerel myself," Samuel Cross announced as he watched from the flying bridge.

"They can be a bit oily," Emerson said, turning the wheel to keep the bow into the southeast.

"A fresh tuna steak is fine. Or blue, just caught. But I prefer haddock and cod—firm white Atlantic fish."

"Aye. Know what I miss?"

"You going to start in about your sex life, Emerson?"

"No. Steamers. My system can't handle clams in abundance any more. My farts smell like the salt marsh at dead low. And they are fearsome powerful."

Samuel took another pull from his flask. "Now we talk of what we can't do, Em: can't eat it, can't fuck it, can't stand the smell of our own wind. Christ." In Samuel's younger drinking days he was notorious for outrageous behavior. Lately, since Bedrosian had been murdered, there seemed to be an undercurrent of agitation which gave a hard gleam to Samuel's eye, and a sharp edge to his pronouncements. He held out the flask, but Emerson shook his head—the only time he wouldn't consider a drink was when he was piloting a fishing party.

Down on the deck things had quieted. The two dozen tourists handled rods and reels as though they were lethal weapons. Randall and Eddie helped keep people from hooking each other or hopelessly tangling their lines. They'd lost the school of mackerel, so Emerson nudged the throttle forward and cruised southeast.

"They believe the heart belonged to Eliot Bedrosian," Emerson said, "based on the tests and the fact that his body had none."

Samuel gazed into the wind, his beard flattened against his chest. "Can't say I'm sorry."

"No."

"Should have happened to the bastard years ago. He got the whole Plummer's business started. The young buck thought he'd come out here and take over this island—when Crosses and Floods and a handful of other families have been caring for it for over three hundred years. Never trust a generation that didn't go to war! They don't develop a full appreciation!"

"What about Vietnam?"

"A war, Em, a world war. Besides, it's always the Eliot Bedrosians of a generation who get out of going, then find something here at home to muck up."

"True."

"The *gall!* A *bridge!* Angel's Head is an *island!*"

"He isn't alone," Emerson said.

"Aye." Samuel looked weary.

"There's plenty of merchants in the village who would now welcome a bridge."

"And I suspect they have been forming secret societies, holding meetings and such. Bedrosian's return has galvanized them. You know who they are Emerson—they talk of a hotel on the water, and a convention center to attract year-round business. For that, they need a bridge. I wouldn't be surprised if they contacted Bedrosian and invited him back up here. They're nothing but a bunch of Tories!"

Emerson turned and hollered down, "Bring the lines up—we're heading back to harbor!"

Randall and Eddie obediently helped tourists reel in their lines. One boy got his hook caught in his sister's windbreaker and she began to scream. Samuel sighed dramatically, and climbed down from the bridge. It was unclear whether the sight of him calmed or frightened the girl into silence, but within a minute he had her unhooked and pacified. He moved about the deck, growling commands which made children cringe, and parents smile. Samuel was local color, and knew that for many he would be the most memorable part of their day deep-sea fishing.

Samuel was incorrect, though; he'd forgotten that the island used to be connected to the mainland, and in the seventies that simple fact thwarted Eliot Bedrosian's plans for a bridge across Blacke's Channel.

"Sand," Emerson had told them that winter morning that he visited the tiny offices of *The Current*. "The channel, Blacke's Channel, it wasn't always so deep."

They both had that long hair; Mark's was straight, shoulder-length; hers was a black cloud of shapeless frizz. Emerson couldn't understand why kids did this to themselves, but they all did it, he assumed, out of some anger, or possibly fear. It had to do with Vietnam. They stared at him as though they'd just gotten the real scoop on the Tooth Fairy. Finally the girl, heavy, with thick glasses, and wearing denim overalls like she was some cranberry farmer, asked him if he'd care to sit down. Mark offered him a cup of coffee.

Emerson sat on the cold aluminum chair and looked about the tiny office while they searched feverishly for sugar—remarkably, under all those heaps of files and newspapers, Mark found a packet and offered it as though it were ransom. "This little shack," Emerson said, raising the finely cracked mug to his lips, "used to be my uncle's fish house. He'd be your mother's cousin, several times removed, I think. Lost his leg in the First World War so he went into the wholesale end of the business. Packed it in ice out back there and trucked it to Boston, Providence, New York."

Mark sat on a cleared edge of the oak desk, while the girl filled the chair behind it. They both nodded stupidly, never taking their eyes off him. Emerson was then a man in his late fifties whose work around the inn and around boats kept him lean and strong. These kids looked like a different species, scraggly, pale, and ill-fed.

"Blacke's Channel—when was this?" Mark asked finally, pulling on his beard.

"Hard to say." The coffee was bitter, but Emerson liked the warmth that came through the mug; it was a cold day outside, with low January sunlight and a steady north wind that made branches clatter. "Way the channels move about the bay you could probably find several occasions when the island was connected—if you care to go back far enough through history."

"But in your lifetime," Mark asked. He was taking the lead because he was a distant relative. The girl, Jewish, New York, seemed to understand that there was a family privilege at work here.

"When I was a boy I remember walking acrost."

"To the mainland?" the girl asked in alarm.

"Only during extreme tides," Emerson said.

"This would have been," Mark hesitated, "between the wars."

"Before the Depression."

"Oh, right." They said this together.

Emerson smiled. What did this boy, this girl, growing up in places like Belmont and New York, know about the Depression? "Once I walked acrost to Grummond's Neck with my grandfather. It was a summer day, and I was so young it seemed like a remarkably long journey. We passed others, mostly horse-drawn carts loaded with scallops, clams, and carts of shingles coming the other way. I remember the smell of cedar—you know how its scent comes out in the sun?"

Mark nodded, but the girl's eyes drifted impatiently toward the window.

"During that walk he told me about when he was a boy. There was a terrific storm. Fishing boats were smashed in the cove, and several islanders died. But what no one could get over was how much the channels had shifted as a result of that one storm."

"Your grandfather told you this," Mark said, "so we'd be talking about well back in the eighteen-hundreds."

Emerson nodded. The girl was watching him again, her eyes big as eggs behind those wire-rimmed glasses—the kids all wore them and called them granny glasses. "He said there was a dispute among the relatives after the storm over what to do with the deeds."

Neither Mark nor the girl dared speak.

"I was young and it wasn't real clear, but as we were crossing to the mainland at low tide my grandfather pointed out how things used to be, and the gist of it was there hadn't been a channel between Plummer's Marsh and the mainland—not until after that storm."

The girl sat back heavily in the chair as if pushed.

"Land," Mark said.

"Well sand, and more of the marsh of course."

"The deeds to the land," Mark said carefully, "were in the family."

Emerson nodded.

"What did they *do* with them?" the girl asked, leaning forward again. "Did they *sell?*"

"I don't know."

Mark stared at the floor, then shook his head. With a haircut and a couple months of honest labor outdoors he'd be a decent looking young man. "Who'd buy?" he said, almost to himself. "They were angry because the land was gone—under the new channel. The deeds were worthless."

"Couldn't even clam there anymore," Emerson offered, though this seemed beside the point to his distant cousin. Emerson's grandfather, however, said this was the greatest loss—the clam beds had been some of the most fertile in Pleasant Bay.

"Do you know where they are?" Mark asked. "Were the deeds, you know, handed down?"

Emerson shrugged. "We can check, can't we?"

Mark heard her footsteps on the outside stairs, climbing up to the apartment above his aunt's garage. He went to the door in his bathrobe, let her in, and she kissed him immediately. Her mouth was hard and she smelled of gin.

"Why did you come back?" she asked, pulling at his sash.

"Now who's asking questions."

"All right then, don't talk." The bathrobe dropped off his shoulders. "Not for now."

The room was only lit by the street lamp at the head of Aunt Mae's driveway—but he could see her eyes, bright and determined: gin had brought her to that level where there was pace, and a phenomenal ease of transition.

They used the couch. She sat on the arm, undoing her own clothes with one hand while she fondled him with the other. When she took him in her mouth it was not like before, but he wasn't sure how it was different. He kept his hands on her head, feeling the fine grain of her hair, running his thumb gently along the skin revealed in her part. When he was as drawn out as he could be, he stepped away and put his hands under her arms. She stood and he folded her arms on top of her head. She turned for him slowly and he kissed her sides, from the armpits down to her hips. It made her quiver, it always had. Finally, she knelt on the couch, resting her elbows on the back, and he knelt behind her, pushing his face into her. She was wet, warm, and she moved slightly, arching her spine, bringing herself out to his tongue. His hands slid up across her belly and took hold of her breasts. She began to hum. He had forgotten about it. Low, monotone, almost like an inaudible frequency. He could feel it as much as hear it, running down through her body. She pushed harder against his teeth as his tongue flickered over her, and the tone of her humming became rounder, fuller, yet without changing pitch. He could taste the spermicide, which was tart and distracted him from her own juices. He thought about her preparing for this somewhere else, in a bathroom at the inn or, more likely, one of the bars in the village. As she began to rock back and forth against him, the couch groaning beneath her, the humming broke up into short gasps for breath, until she came and she cried out. He pushed deeper as long as he could, now holding onto the front of her thighs with his hands. When she jerked forward out of his grasp, he stood up. She reached through her legs and guided him inside her. He went all the way in until he could feel her diaphragm. Her hand was grabbing his hip, the nails pinching the flesh, as she tried to drive him harder and deeper into her. It seemed there was nothing left but relentless thrust. His hands felt the sweat break out on her hips, and in the near dark he watched the jounce of her flesh, how it rippled up through her back and into her shoulders, until his release, when he simply closed his eyes and followed it to its end.

They lay naked on the couch in the dark. The ceiling overhead was slanted and they could hear the rain on the roof shingles. They shared a beer.

"Tell me her name."

"Leslie."

"Good."

"What else do you want to know about her?"

"Nothing."

"All right."

"One thing," she said. "It is over?"

"Yes. She's in Seattle—"

"Shh."

"Sorry."

"Tell me about Michigan, why you left the paper."

"Tight-ass editor," Mark said. "Office bullshit."

"What kind of stories did you write."

"The last one: an outbreak of the carcinogen PBB outside of Lansing. The cattle had to be put down. I found myself standing above the mass grave of dead cows, breathing through a mask that smelled faintly of ether. Then there was also a story I was doing on a campus protest over a course called Human Ecology. Eventually I found myself in a bar watching a Red Sox–Tigers game, eating a thick, Midwest version of clam chowder. Somewhere around the seventh inning I was talking to the clams. Then I remembered I had this envelope in my pocket with this clipping—"

"What clipping?"

He looked at her in the dark. "Someone sent me a clipping from *The Current.* It said that Eliot had returned to Angel's Head."

"So you came back."

"You want another beer?" he asked.

"No. I should go." She picked her clothes up off the floor.

"The island is in trouble, isn't it?" he asked. "You said a lot of those shops in the village will be gone after this season." He watched her dress against the pale light coming through the window. "Eliot knew this. Fifteen years ago Angel's Head fought 'progress' but now it's a matter of survival. Your independence has always been remarkable, Anne. When so many fucked up liberals were against the bridge fifteen years ago, you used to say that it didn't have to be such a bad thing. I always admired that about you."

"So have other islanders," she said sarcastically.

"If you were ambivalent then, what are you now?"

She buttoned up her blouse.

"My guess is you're for it."

"You're right," she said, "it is a question of survival now."

"You're for a bridge."

"It's a necessity."

"Enter Eliot Bedrosian."

"If it's going to be done, do it right."

"He was working with a group of you."

"Just your local merchants, ordinary tax-paying citizens."

"There's opposition."

"There'll always be opposition. But one more winter of stores closing, of people moving off-island, and we figured next spring they'd listen."

"But someone who was opposed to the bridge killed Bedrosian in the worst, the most *typical* islander's fashion," Mark said. "They gutted him like a fish. Then they put his heart in the shed. A message."

"A message."

"Nice quiet island, but just below the surface—"

"It's war, Mark. It *is* a matter of survival. We need the bridge and we need it done right. Easy year-round access, which doesn't mean we have to build a freeway across the bay. Christ, some people out here think we're living in the eighteen-nineties. They're blind romantics, and they'd rather starve out here than have their quaint little romantic image disturbed. They don't see the realities of commerce, of the future. Do you suppose my daughter will stay here? If the inn can't hold its own, I'll have to sell. To the Japanese? To some Texan? A corporation? What difference does it make? They're already buying places in the village—eventually they'll have a bridge, and if it's inevitable then why not have Angelians do it. Do it right." She was angry now: her voice was clipped, strident; her movements swift and abrupt.

"I admire your conviction," he said.

"You make it sound so old-fashioned."

"You don't see the genuine thing much anymore."

She took a deep breath and let it out slowly. "No, I suppose not. But maybe that's what makes us here on the island a little different."

"I'd like to think so. But convictions can be dangerous. You have to know how to control them, Anne. Someone killed Eliot Bedrosian because of conviction."

"I suppose. All convictions are not justifiable. Is murder ever justifiable, Mark?"

"Eliot stayed on his boat in the cove all the time?"

Anne nodded.

"He didn't sail up from Florida alone. A boat that size, he must have had a crew."

She was bent over and he watched the curve of her back. Straightening up, she said, "Yeah, a couple of college kids, but they're long gone."

"Who's in the house on Goode's Lane?"

"You're unbelievable." She stepped into her shoes, their heels knocking on the hardwood floor. "How'd you know that? You follow me?"

"'Fraid so."

"That's a bad habit, Mark, following people."

"Sorry. You're still irresistible. And I wasn't the only one."

"What?"

"One night, the last night I followed you, there was some kind of a disagreement. There were three of you in the house: you, Eliot, and someone else."

She nodded. "Yes, Rachel."

"As I was leaving I heard someone else out in the yard."

"Maybe they were following you. Serves you right." She came over to the couch. "Well, yes—Eliot rented that house. It was too difficult for me to get out to his boat in the cove without being seen, so he got the place above the village." She walked to the door and paused. "Satisfied?"

"Tough question," he said.

"They're all tough, Mark." She let herself out.

Twelve

IT WAS CLOSE TO MIDNIGHT AND THE RAIN HAD STOPPED. Mark couldn't sleep and he walked down through the village, around the cove, and out to the jetties. The stones were large and flat, and they extended several hundred yards into the calm bay. He went to the very end of the south jetty and stood with the water lapping all around him in the dark. It always gave him a perfect sense of isolation. Of islandness. It was almost as though he were walking on water. He considered getting off the island in the morning, leaving before he got drawn back into this place any further.

He didn't know how long he'd been standing on the last rock when he heard the footsteps behind him. Turning, he peered into the lights from the village, and he could only see someone's silhouette. A man. A woman. He couldn't tell. Someone who moved easily over the angled faces of granite.

"Hello?" Mark said.

The silhouette kept coming.

A man.

A man carrying something on or over his left shoulder, and something long in his right hand. He stopped when he reached the last stone. In the pitch dark of the bay, it was impossible to see his face.

"Low tide at two forty-three," Randall said.

Mark took a long, deep breath. "You follow me out here, Randall?"

"Anne's back at the inn now."

"Is she? Did you follow her?"

Randall didn't answer but squatted and allowed what he had been carrying on his shoulder to slide off onto the rock. Fish: the village lights glinted off their scales. "Want some flounder?"

"No thanks."

Randall put down his surf-casting rod, produced a flashlight from his

95

pocket, switched it on, and laid it on the rock so its beam struck across the fish, six or seven flounder, their bulging eyes stunned in the glare. He unsheathed a boning knife and began cleaning the fish. Mark sat on the rock, picked up the flashlight, and held it so Randall could see better.

"Flounder are my favorite fish," Randall said.

"Me too."

"Not just the way they taste. They way they are. See? Bottom side is smooth and white. The side they always bury in the sand. Top side is rough and looks just like sand. They become part of the ocean floor. Only their eyes stick up so they can see what's coming. The best part is the eye. When they're young there's an eye on each side of the flat head, rough and smooth. But as they grow the smooth-side eye moves, it travels around to the rough side so they both stick up from the ocean floor."

"Adaptation," Mark said.

"How do they do that? Isn't it neat?" Randall took the first fillet, leaned over and swished it in the water, then laid it on the stone. Gazing up at the sky, he said, "Milky Way's up there tonight. Millions of light-years away." He took the flashlight from Mark's hand, pointed it at the sky, and flicked it on and off. *"Hello!"* he yelled. Laughing, he gave the flashlight back to Mark and began cleaning another flounder. "Mainland police out snooping around," he said almost to himself. "Pretty exciting stuff, huh?"

"Do you remember Eliot Bedrosian?"

"He got cleaned."

"Yes, but years ago—"

"The bridge."

"You remember?"

"I've heard about the bridge. I took Bedrosian to court."

"It was pretty exciting, for a small island."

"People tell me, but I don't remember."

"Anything?"

"I had a mishap, you know."

"I know," Mark said.

"Emerson says to ignore what some people say. Anne cries. Bedrosian shouldn't have come back. He's a bad man—I could tell first time I saw him." Randall held a fillet in his hand. It might have been a pet, something small and vulnerable, the way he gently laid it out on the rock. "Is it hard to follow the Red Sox in Michigan?"

"I couldn't get NESN or channel 38," Mark said, "but there are the box scores in the paper." He squatted and waited for Randall to look at him.

"Who told you I lived in Michigan?"

"Maxine." He began filleting another fish. "She said we used to fish and surf together."

"And she told you I worked for a newspaper?"

Randall didn't answer.

"You sent the newspaper clipping to me?"

"We used to drink together. Watch the Red Sox. She said we were like crew mates."

"Yes."

"Drinking's not good for you."

"It's a lesson I still need to learn."

"We got Eddie to stop drinking. It took a year. Nobody on the crew drinks. Samuel does, but he says it's a captain's privilege, and he drinks for the entire crew. Alcohol affects your mind. Kills brain cells. You can't remember things." Looking up from the flounder, his eyes were playful. "You want to end up like Randall?"

"I'm glad you sent me the clipping."

The tide was coming in. Mark could feel the coolness rising up off the water, could see the small constellations of phosphorescence dancing around the edges of the jetty rocks.

Randall swished his knife in the water, disturbing the constellations. Wiping the blade on his jeans, he said, "Water stars."

Rachel couldn't sleep. Many summer nights such as this the inn hummed with activity until quite late. Voices came from open windows. Laughter rose up from the bar. A piano was being played in the lounge. The thought of Eric up in his parents' suite was disturbing. She thought of ways she might communicate with him. Call on the inn phone. Send something from room service. A plate of chocolate chip cookies. Or maybe chubs. Chub under glass. His parents would love that.

She got dressed and went downstairs to the front porch, where she sat in one of the rocking chairs. Suddenly there was a creak of one of the stairs, and she realized someone was sitting in the dark on the steps. It made her heart jump. She got up from the chair, trying to catch her breath.

It was a man sitting on the bottom step, hunched over, one hand holding a bottle. He turned and looked up at her, his white beard glowing softly in the dark.

"Samuel?"

"Aye."

"Why aren't you out at the Rescue Station?"

"I'll go out tomorrow. The crew's fine without me. I trained 'em, you know. All this business about that developer—it's all coming back. It's like the sea, it all comes back." His voice was deep, resigned, slurred with drink.

Rachel joined him on the steps. "You're really plowed, aren't you?"

"Where'd you learn to speak to your elders like that?" Then he laughed as he got to his feet.

"Where are you going?"

"To my house."

"I'll walk you."

"Aye, you do that, child."

As they walked through the village Samuel sang portions of songs Rachel had never heard—sea songs about whales and boats, storms and women—and when he finished his bottle he carefully placed it on top of a fence post. They turned up the street toward Samuel's house. He put an arm around her shoulders for support. They were in front of his house and he stopped walking. Without the forward motion he seemed about to fall. Rachel was unsure whether she should try to catch him or just get out of the way. He was breathing heavily.

"Told 'em," he said.

"Told who?"

"Told 'em they was seen."

"Seen where?"

"In the shed."

"When? When Bedrosian was killed?"

"Eddie—"

"What about Eddie?"

"He promised to say nothing. See, we have to trust in one's rectitude, in one's moral conviction." Samuel coughed harshly. "Besides, Bedrosian got what he deserved." He reached out and laid a hand on her arm. "You are the hope of Angel's Head," he said. "We all look upon you with, well, affection. And maybe some a little envy. A little more than envy."

"Why?"

"It will be yours one day. A responsibility not to be taken lightly."

"The inn."

"Yes, that too."

He started walking again. Down the left side of the house, which was dark, and into the backyard. Rachel knew his wife had died years earlier, and that a cousin Chastity had been living in the house ever since. Island children treated the Cross house as though it were haunted. They held their breath when passing by; on Halloween they tended to smash pumpkins and cause other sorts of disturbances in the front yard. Chastity, who was rarely seen outside the house, was perceived to be a witch, and his wife Dorothea was, of course, believed to be a ghost who still wandered through the empty house.

"Where are you going?" she asked finally.

"You don't think I'm going in that house, do you?" He laughed until he started coughing, bringing up phlegm in his throat.

They crossed the backyard to a small barn. Samuel opened the door, switched on a light. Gardening tools hung from the rough wood walls, but in one corner was a sagging cot. He lay down and said, "Just turn out the light, will you?"

Rachel put her hand on the light switch but didn't turn it off.

"Listen," he said. "The bridge. It's coming around again. Killing some developer won't make it go away. This is an island, right?"

She nodded.

"And we are islanders."

"Yes."

"Angelians." He looked up at her, his eyes bloodshot.

"What, Samuel?"

"There's a nature to islands, and someone always wants to tinker. Build a bridge and it'll be ruined forever. Build a bridge and you cut out the heart of Angel's Head. Remember that, Rachel—when it's your turn at the inn, remember that. Now go." He began snoring immediately.

She wanted to ask him about the shed, about the heart. But he was asleep and she was alone. She turned off the light and suddenly she was frightened. Not as she might have been a few years ago, by the stories of ghosts and witches and haunted houses, but by something large. Something real. An adult fear. She closed the door and ran across the yard, never looking back.

Thirteen

MARK AWOKE JUST AFTER FOUR. IT WAS STILL DARK OUT AND cool, rain-cleansed air came through the screens. He wasn't surprised to see lights on in Aunt Mae's kitchen—islanders are traditionally early risers. He dressed and walked up the drive to the house, drawn by the smell of coffee and the sound of the marine weather report blaring from the shortwave radio she kept on the windowsill.

She stood by the range, her hands on her hips, leaning back slightly, as if to compensate for the weight old age had brought out in her chest and belly. "Hello, dear," she said as he kissed her cheek. "You must be hungry."

He went to the radio and turned it down. "Yes, sure."

"Sit then!"

He slid into the booth in the alcove and watched millers beat against the back-door screens. There was always a cool dampness to the house during the summer. He rubbed his forearms; his skin felt good.

She was perspiring from cooking and she wiped her brow and mouth with the back of her wrist. There was a pot on all four stove burners. "Well, most of this isn't for today. I just thought I'd make some things up and keep them in the fridge—it's been too hot to cook every night."

She brought him a plate of poached eggs on English muffins. The black raspberry jam was homemade. She sat across from him with her coffee mug and watched him eat.

"You had a visitor last night."

He nodded.

"I saw her go up the stairs."

"I'll bet you did."

"I keep my eyes open. Especially in the summer."

"Why's that?"

"All kinds of people come over on the ferry now."

"Their pockets are filled with money, Mae."

"Since Memorial Day we've had several reports of prowlers in the village. Used to be no islander ever thought of locking a door. You want another English?"

He shook his head.

"You eat too fast, just like your father. This woman—she's an islander?"

He smiled at her.

"She's not one of these tourists?"

"I haven't been consorting with an off-islander." Mark placed his hand on top of hers for a moment—it was warm, the skin loose about the knuckles—then he slid out of the booth.

He took his plate to the sink. The shortwave radio on the windowsill was tuned to the marine weather band: two- to four-foot seas, westerly winds, Nauset high tide at 9:24 A.M., light afternoon sea breeze, visibility ten to twelve miles. Cape weather reports were a form of music.

"Two to four," he said. "Not bad for the Cape in July."

"They get in the cellar," she said.

"Who does?"

She looked up at him with alarm. "You don't listen to me!"

"Sorry, Mae—I was trying to catch the weather. Who gets in the cellar?"

"Animals!" Backlit by the light coming through the screen door he could see the outline of her scalp beneath the thin, white hair. "Raccoons, or maybe a groundhog. Sometimes at night I lie in bed and I hear scratching and gnawing. I knock a shoe on the bathroom tub: they stop, but moments later when I'm back in bed, they start in again."

The thought of this old woman banging a shoe on the bathtub in the middle of the night brought on a gushing sense of futility. His aunt lived alone and she feared that animals would eat the house from under her. How could he leave Angel's Head again? He slid out of the alcove booth. "I'll take care of it, Mae."

"Would you? That's a dear."

He went out to the backyard. It was a typical Cape Cod house, weathered shingles, with glossy white trim. He could smell the moist cedar. So much wood siding; in the Midwest most everything is covered with vinyl or aluminum siding, which made perfect sense from an economic standpoint, but these shingles could last the better part of a century, and at certain hours of the day they took on a luminous sheen under the sun, not unlike the scales of a fish.

Opening the steel bulkhead doors he descended the wood steps into the cellar. The smell Mae had referred to wasn't all that powerful. It had yet to overcome the natural cellar smell of damp concrete and forgotten things—beach chairs, old cans of paint, varnish, and shellac. One window was open, its latch broken; another was missing a pane of glass. The raccoons had gnawed the floor joists, and possibly rubber insulation on wiring. He wondered why they were desperate to get inside when the woods must offer so much food this time of year, but he admired their determination and stealth.

He measured the glass, found a notepad on the workbench and made a list:

> *glass 8 x 11*
> *points*
> *glazing*
> *latch*
> *pipe wrap*
> *poison*

He stared at the list a moment, then crossed out *poison*.

He walked toward the back of the cellar, to renew an old acquaintance. In the dim light from the windows he could see that it was still lying on the wall rack he'd built with two-by-fours, and was covered with a dropcloth. When he was younger he would simply have gone to the wall and gotten down to business. But he almost felt as though he had to wait for his younger self to get out of his way, to take the object of his affection back up the bulkhead stairs and out into the yard. Finally he removed the dropcloth, unveiling his surfboard. As he stared at it he felt a moment of wonder, appreciation, and embarrassment, as though he had just encountered the naked body of a beautiful woman.

He wrapped his hand around the board's curved edge. Rails: sleek, thin, low—for speed and control. From nose to tail it was eight-foot-nine, to his thinking the perfect length for Cape Cod surf. Under his fingers nothing about it was really flat; every inch had the slightest contour, falling away from the center stringer, rising patiently toward the pintail. Down through the old wax the fiberglass was a pale white. Underneath was a plastic blue translucent skeg, which he had filed down for sharper turns.

Stepping back, he took in the whole board. For several minutes he didn't move as he slowly shed everything he'd brought back to the island with him—every purpose, design, hope, and expectation. Every loss, every failure, every fear. What was left was one pure, simple desire: to catch the morning swell.

Rachel and Eric crossed the large jetty rocks in the first light of dawn. Along the arc of beach to the south they could see the lanterns of the fishermen who'd been up all night. She led him down to the little hollow she'd found. They climbed in underneath the rocks and spread their towels out on the cool sand. Crawling out again, she said, "I have learned that there's only one way to do this." She ran screaming, dove in, and swam hard underwater until she was over the shock of the cold. Coming up for air, she turned around and looked back toward the jetty through her wet hair. "It's great," she said.

Eric stood at the water's edge, staring at her distrustfully. Slowly he made his way into the water, stopping after every couple of steps. He stood still when the water was halfway up his thighs, and raised his arms as each swell rolled past him.

"That's good with the arms," she said, "you look like a symphony conductor."

"It's cold," he said.

"This is nothing."

"Are you touching?"

She floated on her back and kicked herself farther out. "Who cares," she said to the morning sky.

She heard the splash as he dove in, and he churned out toward her. When he reached her, she let her body drop into the water, and he slid into her arms. His skin was wet and silky. Her nipples felt so big and hard they might burst. Without the use of their arms, they couldn't keep their heads above the surface. They kissed as their bodies sank deeper into cold.

Emerson was at the Boat House preparing for the morning fishing charter that would leave with several dozen groggy tourists. He was leaning over the guts of a Penn reel spread out on the glass counter, convinced that the springs and screws they put in them nowadays were getting smaller. The news was on the radio and the sportscaster was just finishing up when a man stepped in off the porch. He wore green trunks, a white T-shirt, and even though it wasn't quite dawn, a pair of those reflecting sunglasses Emerson hated.

"Sox win?" he said quietly.

"Nope."

"I need a boat."

"Morning charter leaves the pier at six."

"I'm looking for a skiff."

Something about the man's voice sounded familiar. Emerson straightened up and stared closely at the man. Grinning now, the man slid off those glasses. *"Well!* If it ain't—" and he took Mark's hand as it crossed the counter.

"Been a long time," Mark said.

"Yep. You look almost grown up." Emerson continued to shake his hand vigorously. "What brings you back?"

"I heard there's a decent swell on Nauset."

Emerson withdrew his hand and leaned on the counter. "You're not serious about going over?"

Mark nodded.

"I always thought you boys were crazy. The way Randall'd get excited over a storm that lay hundreds of miles away, and watching the tide chart."

"I'd like to try for the last few hours going up to high tide. All those years in the Midwest, I was haunted by the thought of surfing in a Cape Cod sunrise. Today's the day."

Beyond him, through the door, Emerson could see Mae's old Rambler, with the surfboard angled in through the front passenger window. "So you're not grown up—well, let's see what we got." Emerson led him outside and down to the pier. "Lord," he said, his voice resonant above the water, "the sight of you jumps my innards back a few yards!" He paused and, looking up at Mark—he didn't remember the boy being so tall—he said, "Why is it that you came back now?"

"I know, it is strange, isn't it?" Mark had put his sunglasses back on and Emerson could only see a fine, rounded image of himself in each lens.

Mark took the skiff, a sixteen-foot aluminum hull with a twenty-horse Johnson, out past the jetties and northeast across the bay. It was the time of morning when the light seemed thrown up from the water into the sky. He ran past Fox Hill and Bassing Harbor to Allen Point, where he crossed the bay and beached on the backside of Nauset. At this point the barrier beach was no more than a couple hundred yards wide. He carried the board and his wetsuit over the dunes, and came to the outer beach. Not a soul in sight in either direction, though a half mile to the north the beach was covered with thousands of gulls. The swells were slow, but held up by a slight offshore breeze.

The ocean was bone-chilling around his ankles, but once he started paddling, the thin layer of water that got inside his wetsuit was heated up by his exertion. There wasn't any real difficult white water to work out through, but it had been years, and by the time he was seventy yards out he was exhausted. He sat astride the board and drifted for at least ten minutes, letting the ache in his shoulders subside. Looking east he saw a set of waves approaching, and tried for the second and fourth ones, but the swells simply lifted him up momentarily, then ran by, breaking a good twenty yards closer to the beach.

He paddled toward shore, and after another period of rest, he watched the next set forming, and this time tried for the third wave, which carried the board forward, then shot him down the steepening face. He pushed himself up and stood off-balance for one brief moment, gliding down, straight down, until the nose purled—stabbed below the surface—and stopped. He plunged forward, arms outstretched, and hit the water face first. Curling up into a fetal position, he covered his head as the wave broke over him with an enormous crack.

Though it was cool in the shade under the rocks, they were sweating now. She turned to let Eric untie the top, and when her breasts were free she leaned back on her hands. He kissed them, sucked the nipples, rolled them between his fingers. Placing one hand on the back of his sandy scalp, she pressed his head closer to her heart. It was becoming difficult to breathe. She couldn't keep her balance on one arm, and finally she fell back on the blanket. He slid on top of her, and their loins pushed into each other. She had to keep moving, her heels digging into the sand, and she angled her pelvis up to meet his thrusts. She felt she could take any amount of weight against her there, so much that the bathing suits between them no longer mattered. As he began to come down on her harder, he made hoarse, coughing sounds, and she completely lost her breath. She closed her eyes to the glare coming off the water. Holding tightly to his back, she wondered if she was about to pass out.

He caught one, finally. Thirty seconds, possibly less, of scooting diagonally to the right across the face of the breaking wave. There, in the small, tight curl, it was just as he remembered: remarkably still, poised, balanced above the spinning water—an endless sheet of water flowing under his board at an angle, then rising up into a wall beside him. For one moment, he reached his hand out and dragged it along the smooth, tubular wave. Then, just as the whole wave closed out, he cut back and rode its churning white water all the way to the beach.

With what seemed to be the last of his strength, he carried the board up to the first dune, then peeled off the wetsuit. He lay on his back in the sand and stared at the sky, the water, the morning sunlight. His skin was taut, numb. His mouth tasted of salt water. They used to ride dozens of waves, staying in the water for hours, and when they'd finally come out they would still be shouting, hooting, and screaming. He spread his arms out in the sand, filled his lungs with air, and let it out.

Rachel slept in Eric's arms, his body curled up against her back, and she dreamed that she was swimming naked between the jetties. Doing the backstroke, the sun was hot on her breasts, until a large seagull flew overhead, blocking the light. She heard a voice and she stopped swimming. A man's voice, no more than a murmur, though it seemed to come from a long way off. Treading water, she looked back into the cove. The water there was shimmering, and the moored boats appeared to be melting. The murmur came again. She turned around and looked out into the bay. Far off a man was walking on water. So far off that she could not tell whether he was walking toward her or away from her. She tried to call out, but couldn't gather her strength. The water around her was getting cold, and it seemed to be heavier. Squeezing her. Sucking on her skin. And no matter how she tried she could not get anything to come up out of her lungs. Not a whimper, not a cry, not a scream. The murmur continued, the water on her lips tasted of blood, and still she could not scream out across the bay.

Fourteen

EMERSON AWOKE SUDDENLY. HE HAD THE FEELING HE'D forgotten something. His head had been cocked back against the wall and his neck was stiff. Big band music was playing on the station out of Plymouth, and he reached up and turned off the radio. He looked up at the clock—it was almost ten—then left the Boat House with a sense of urgency. Stopping on the porch he saw nothing had changed except the angle of light—the sun was higher, and from up the hill he could hear the breakfast crowd at the inn.

And there was a voice.

Rachel's voice, calling his name. It was nearly lost in the sputter of an outboard engine.

He went down the porch steps, pain shooting through his right knee, and headed toward the pier. When he turned the back corner of the Boat House he could see the cove. Rachel and the boy she'd been hanging around with were jogging back along the shore from the jetties. Mark Emmons was steering the skiff between moored boats with the throttle wide open. Rachel yelled something which Emerson couldn't understand. She was pointing toward the cove.

Emerson felt stiff-jointed and slow—when it was clear that Rachel, the boy, and Mark were all reacting quickly to the same thing. He scanned the cove, but at first he saw nothing, just boats at their moorings, all with their sterns toward the jetties now that the tide was falling. Then he saw it, the blood smeared on the white hull of the *Northern Lady*. And he saw it in the water beneath the bowsprit: a body floating face down.

Rachel and the boy followed him out to the end of the pier.

"Who is it?" Rachel asked. "Grapes, who is it?"

Mark cut the outboard and let the skiff glide toward the *Northern Lady* and bump gently against the bow. His ears were ringing from the sound of the motor.

It was a man's body, tied about the waist with rope, which meandered across the oily water, then rose up to where it was lashed to the bowsprit of the schooner. He was rolled slightly on his side, as if weighted, and he stared into the water with a bewildered expression. It was Samuel Cross. His throat had been cut, the wound washed clean in the water.

Now Mark could hear voices, and looking toward the village he saw that people were walking down from the inn. They crowded out onto the pier, their combined voices at once festive and horrified. No, not horrified: taken aback. This was an imposition, an intrusion upon their breakfast. Only summer people could sound that way. Every islander recognized it.

Someone was rowing out in a dinghy, a large man who was having trouble keeping the oars in the oarlocks. It was Ben Snow. The dinghy banged into the stern of Mark's skiff.

"You didn't touch anything?" he said, winded.

"No."

Ben stared at Mark, squinted, then said, "Jesus, *you.*" Ben leaned around so he could get a look at the face in the water and almost lost his balance in the dinghy. *"Samuel?"*

"You going to just leave him there?"

"Guess not."

Mark stood up in the skiff and untied the line from the bowsprit of the *Northern Lady.* Ben made an awkward attempt to haul Samuel over the transom of the dinghy, but gave up—he was in clear danger of capsizing. He sat down heavily and gasped for air. "You'll have to tow me in," he said, looking at the crowd on the pier. He tossed Mark the dinghy's bowline, then gathered Samuel's body up close to the dinghy and held it fast by the rope. He looked embarrassed. "Slow," he said. "Not to the pier with all those people. Over to the dock at Vachon's Marina."

As the body was being towed across the cove to Vachon's Marina, Grapes said to Rachel, "Go up and lock the Boat House."

"What?"

He nodded toward the crowd that was rapidly gathering at the cove, and said, "With this kind of confusion you want somebody to clean us out of hundreds of dollars' worth of tackle?" He didn't wait for a reply. "Then go in the Boat House, lock it, and stay there." He hustled on his bum knees off the pier, and started around the cove for the marina.

Rachel didn't know whether she wanted to scream after him, or cry. She was frightened—Grapes never spoke to her like that, never ordered her to do something. She realized that he was trying to protect her because he too was frightened.

She led Eric up to the Boat House, locked the front door, then went to the back room, where they could look out on the cove from the open window. It was like a cocktail party; people chatted pleasantly as they stared across the cove toward the marina. She took the binoculars down from the pegboard above the workbench. Peering across the cove, adjusting the lenses, she brought the body into focus as it was being lifted out of the water by Ben Snow and the man in the skiff. She saw the khaki shirt, the white hair, the white beard, and lowered the binoculars.

"Who is it?"

"Samuel." She backed away from the window, trying to catch her breath.

Eric took the binoculars from her and looked out the window. "He's the guy that takes care of the crazies."

"You're sounding like a tourist."

"Sorry."

She came to the window. "He was really drunk. I walked him to his house. He was talking about the night of the other murder." Eric turned and looked at her. "It wasn't clear. He told someone they were seen going in the shed that night."

"Who?"

"I don't know."

They leaned out the window again. Across the cove a small group of men now stood on the dock at Vachon's Marina—Ben Snow, Grapes, the man in the skiff, Emil Vachon. The body lay on the dock, covered with a tarp.

Out on the cove Cyrus was preparing the *Angel Gabriel,* the inn's newest charter boat, to go across the bay. He had the Reverend Peele on board.

"Where are they going?" Eric asked.

"Probably across to the Rescue Station for Samuel's crew."

"Bring them back?"

"I don't know what they'll do."

"You should tell someone about what Samuel said—"

"No. I don't want to tell anyone about last night."

"Why?"

"Not now."

"You're shaking." He took her hand.

"No I'm not."

"I can feel it in your hand."

She tried to pull her hand free but he held tight. "I had this dream," she said, "and a man was walking on water."

"Only Jesus walks on water, men drown in it."

"This isn't a game, Eric."

"Okay."

"I just don't know what's going on."

"All right. We don't say anything to anyone right now."

She looked at him, then leaned out the window again, holding his hand tightly. Down on the pier her mother was trying to get her guests to return to the inn. She wore a white dress and her hair was up—Rachel thought she looked stunning against the water.

Fifteen

THERE WERE FEW LIGHTS ON THROUGHOUT THE INN WHEN Mark climbed the hill. After hours. Years ago he'd climb this hill after hours.

Expected.

Beckoned.

Now, drawn.

He went into the front lobby, and found Anne sitting alone at the dimly lit bar. She had a bottle of Scotch in front of her and she pushed it toward him. "I saved my first drink for you."

"You still do that, use those old movie lines."

"I stopped doing it a long time ago," she said, "but I started up again this summer. It used to be fun."

"I never liked it."

She reached over the bar and got him a glass.

Running his hand along the mahogany bar, he said, "Place never changes."

"No, it never does." She poured him a drink, and refilled her glass. "You come back every summer and the inn's about the same. Gives you that sense of continuity, of renewal. You come back after years and you feel like you've rediscovered your home, your youth, all those things you're supposed to lose for good. It's really what keeps us in business. Not what we are, but what we remind people of—that's what tourism's all about. But you stay here month after month, and the place hardly changes. The seasons change. The weather changes. *You* change—you age. But the inn just sails on across the placid waters of time." She studied him a moment and smiled. "This can't be your first drink."

"No, the boys had a few down at the marina after the police boat took Samuel's corpse back to the mainland. Jesus, *corpse*. That's what did it. It wasn't a body, it wasn't Samuel, it was a corpse."

"How's Emerson doing?" she asked.

"Lot of talk about sex, blizzards, and hurricanes."

"I try to keep that old fool alive, but not by setting an example."

"What about your brother?"

"He's upset. Doc Walter gave him something."

"Tell me about your brother, Anne. About Samuel. About Eliot."

"What do you want to know?"

"Everything."

She drank her Scotch.

"Last night after you left," he said, "I thought about leaving, getting off the island before I really get hooked. You're right—nothing ever really changes here. But now, I don't know. I think it's too late."

"I don't know everything, Mark."

"Well, tell me what you do know. Start with Eliot."

Anne finished her drink; took her time pouring another. "Since Eliot sailed up from Florida, the schooner has rarely left its mooring. He just sat there, waiting for me. Finally I rowed out one night."

"Old islanders must have loved that."

"We were discreet—Eliot insisted on it, and I must admit it was kind of fun." She smiled briefly. "Aside from the seasons, that's the only thing that changes when you get to be our age, don't you think? We become discreet. When we were kids fucking was something to display, throw in the face of the world, of the adults. Now that we're the adults, it's something to be done at night, in the dark, in private. It's hypocritical, but, shit, you've got to embrace your hypocrisies—they're all you've got, right?"

"After your brother's accident—"

"How could I even speak to Eliot?"

Mark nodded.

"When he showed up at the beginning of the season, I saw a different man. He wanted different things. He wanted safe harbor."

"He wanted a bridge. Still."

"He wasn't alone, Mark. I told you, a lot of us want a bridge. This time it wasn't going to be just his doing. A larger group of islanders was going to back the thing."

"And Eliot would help develop it."

"He is good at it. All he needs is cooperation. Next year, we'd have that, I'm sure. Things work slowly here, you know that. But more and more islanders have been coming around. They all know something has to be done."

"But, Anne, your brother—"

"Eliot had nothing to do with Randall's accident."

"You believe that."

"I do."

"You know who did it."

She shook her head, but Mark felt it was a gesture of affirmation. "All these years, all that shit. See what happens when you stay on a place like Angel's Head? Your sense of time, your sense of dimension, your sense of everything gets screwed up. The people who leave take on these enormous proportions. You're haunted by what you missed. What you're missing— present tense. You understand that, Mark?"

"You think it must be somewhere or someone else."

"Yes."

"I left Michigan for the same reason."

"There you go," she said. "And you know how Eliot was—he had that bigger than life quality. He could take you away from this. From your life. What it is. What it isn't. What it had become."

"What has it become?"

"Intolerable."

They drank for a moment, staring at each other in the mirror above the bar.

"You loved him then," Mark said. "I knew that. It hurt."

"Everything hurts. So what's the difference?"

"So you might as well get laid."

"I used to believe that, yes."

"You still do."

"I don't know what I believe now."

"Tell me about Cyrus."

"Guess."

"Working relationship."

"Half right."

"Just working."

"Cy knows his limitations, knows what he needs, and he gets it. The bar and maintenance of the inn are his domain. In return he provides good, cheap labor." She leaned her shoulder against his, now seeming weary. "He has his own room upstairs. What he does with the waitresses and the *touristas* is his business."

"Okay. Tell me about Randall."

"Randall—"

Mark turned his head so his face was in her hair. "I saw Randall on the beach the other day and last night. He doesn't remember me. I think he knows he should, but he doesn't. I still haven't met a better man than your brother. He was one with his element, as they say, and some of it used to rub off on me." He shook his head and started to pull away.

Anne put an arm around his neck. "No, tell me."

"At night we used to get loaded up good, you know, and we'd talk about all sorts of stuff. Your brother played the waterline hick but he was no dummy." She nodded and laid her forehead down on his shoulder. "We used to speculate about the future. He knew his life was this island, knew you and he would eventually take over here, and though he never said so directly—that wasn't his way—he let me know that he hoped I'd stay. That I'd—he just wanted me around as a life-long beach bum."

She raised her head up and he felt the warmth of her cheek against his. "That you'd win the sweepstakes," she said. "That's what he called it, The Sweepstakes: who gets to marry Anne and live forever with us here at the inn. It was important to him, and he was worried about it, but he could never speak seriously, and in some ways he was protective, jealous—all those things your brother's supposed to be. At times he'd get ugly, particularly there toward the end of the bridge business. He thought I was some kind of traitor because I thought a bridge to Angel's Head wasn't such a bad idea. He screwed I don't know how many waitresses and chambermaids around here, but he sometimes couldn't handle his sister sleeping with more than one boy at a time. But his heart was good."

"His heart was very good."

"'Was good': I do that a lot—talk about my brother in the past tense." She began to cry. "Do you have any idea how hard it's been running this place by myself? How many times I wished it had been both Randall and me? It seems all I've ever done is the inn. Everyone else comes, and then they go. And each of you takes a little piece of me."

She came off her stool, led him into the lobby, and found a key to a vacant room. Quietly they moved through the ells, along the carpeted halls and stairs, until they entered a freshly painted room with antique furniture and curtains billowing with a soft ocean breeze. It was like years ago: after work, after closing bars, after hours, they took a room at the inn.

She had managed them all with a sense of tranquillity that was unnerving. Possibly it was the drugs: usually her drinking was accompanied by something—a joint, a pill—anything that would push the night upwards into a higher clarity. Men were merely another enhancement, another drug.

She was a bridge. On the other side lay Eliot Bedrosian. Their connection through her had taken on greater weight as the months of litigation slid by. Once there were lawyers and deeds and lawsuits, with all the *Current* coverage and the intrusion of off-island media, the lines were clearly drawn. Mark and Eliot went to considerable pains to avoid each other, a difficult thing to do in so small a place. Anne remained their sole link.

Now Eliot was dead. But Mark could still feel his presence. It frightened him; it drew him in deeper.

Mark awoke in the morning to the sound of seagulls above the bay. Sunlight poured through the curtains. Anne was already gone. She had an inn to run.

It was early and the dining room wasn't open yet. He walked down to the cove. His aunt's car was still parked in front of the Boat House, and he had left his surfboard over at the marina. He stared across the cove toward the *Northern Lady*—a launch was tied alongside, and several men were moving about the deck. The *Angel Gabriel* was tied up to the pier; Cyrus had the engine hatch open and there was an assortment of tools laid out on the deck. He looked up and saw Mark, then went about his business.

Mark walked down to the pier. "Long time, Cyrus."

"Seems to be the summer for pigeons to come home." Cyrus fidgeted with the carburetor. He was as lean and wiry as when he started working at the inn. Only his dark eyes seemed pushed deeper into his sockets, and he'd shaved off his enormous sideburns. "Or maybe it'd be more accurate to say the alewives have returned to stream to spawn and die."

"You've cultivated a sense of humor over the years."

"Dry as a martini, salty as the air: bartender's fare." He took a wrench, lay flat on the deck, and hung his arm, shoulder, and head down into the engine compartment. There came the resonant clink of metal on metal.

"Who's that out on the *Northern Lady?*" Mark asked.

"Police."

"Heard you went out to get Samuel's crew."

"They didn't want to leave Nauset."

"I can understand that."

"Left the reverend with them, whatever good that'll do."

"Any ideas why this is happening?"

"Yep."

Mark waited, and finally he said, "Thanks for sharing that with me. Let me give you my view."

117

"An outsider's perspective."

"Sure. The economy's bad everywhere. Angel's Head feels it, for several seasons now, and there's an increasing and real fear that the island will be virtually taken over by outside concerns. Just look at the village: several restaurants are corporate owned, the pharmacy and hardware are chain affiliates. The movie theater's no more. Tourism's down and over the past few years some islanders have been reconsidering the idea of a bridge. In fact, they're certain it's an inevitability, and they decide that it would be better that they initiate it rather than some corporation."

"You used to write this stuff in the newspaper, didn't you?"

"Call it an editorial."

"They're the part that don't need any substantiation, right?"

"Sort of. Anyway, these islanders who are coming round to the idea of a bridge aren't like the people who first warmed to the notion fifteen years ago. Times have changed. These people are rational, pragmatic—in fact, some of them are even women."

"Imagine that."

"But the idea of a bridge still gets a strong and immediate reaction from certain quarters. Now, suddenly, they find themselves the 'reactionaries' and, I suspect, greatly outnumbered. They feel they should do anything to preserve the island. Its integrity. Its solitude."

"They have a mission," Cyrus said without raising his head out of the engine compartment. "Enter Eliot Bedrosian, Mr. Bridge himself."

"The developer," Mark said. "He's back and he's, ah, consorting with people in favor of the bridge."

"It's a marriage of convenience."

"Cyrus, you *have* developed a sense of humor."

"I try."

"The developer is not just killed, he's gutted—like some cod. And his heart, his least vulnerable organ, is left where? In the shed at the inn. Why? A message? A warning? Could it be an act of war, war over the bridge— the second bridge war? What's one sleazy developer compared to the future of Angel's Head?"

Cyrus continued to work on the engine, his shoulders straining against some ungiving bolt. "And Samuel Cross. What about him?"

"I don't know. I suspect he'd remain opposed to the bridge. What do you think? You knew him better than I did. You made regular trips out to the Rescue Station."

"Samuel was a strong believer in tradition," Cyrus said.

118

"But was he killed in retaliation? Has it gone that far?"

Cyrus paused in his work. The muscles in his shoulders and arms seemed to relax. "Something has gone too far."

"Which side are you on?"

Cyrus raised up out of the engine compartment and sorted through the tools on the deck until he found another wrench. Staring up at Mark, he said, "Why'd you come back? You think you can crawl into the past and disappear? Least Bedrosian sailed into harbor aboard a boat nobody could miss. You put on those shades and walked around for a while, thinking nobody'd notice?"

Mark remembered the night at Goode's Lane. The hand that drew back the curtain. The glimpse of someone stepping behind the garage. He took his sunglasses from his shirt pocket and, facing Cyrus, put them on slowly.

Cyrus lowered his head and shoulders back into the compartment and went at the engine with both arms. "You and Eliot back on the island the same season. There's a sense of order to it. It has set Anne in motion, that's for sure. I thought she'd finally begun to wind down."

"I'm under the impression you and she have an understanding."

"That we do." Cyrus got to his knees and put down the wrenches. He continued to stare down into the engine compartment. "And I'm not about to explain it to any of the guests."

"Understood."

"I doubt that very much."

"You always seemed to be following behind us, me and Eliot."

"I like the view."

"And you're still here."

"And I'm still here."

"You only have to say she's your wife. And I will understand."

"Would you?" He got to his feet and looked at Mark as though he were about to say something. Instead he went up to the wheelhouse and started the engine. The diesel rumbled deeply, and its vibration caused the water around the boat to shimmer, the lines fine and uniform as a topographical map.

Mark was getting in his aunt's car when a busboy came running down from the inn. He gave Mark a note:

I have a problem with Randall.

Anne

Mark returned to the inn and found Anne on the second floor in the family quarters, standing at an open window in the living room.

"It's Randall," she said. "He's in the bathroom. Locked himself in an hour ago. He's been asking for you."

Mark went over to the closed bathroom door. He knocked but there was no response. "Randall. Randall, it's Mark."

Nothing.

He looked at Anne. In the morning light she looked weary, exasperated. Life on the island had taken its toll.

From the bathroom there came loud groaning and pinging sounds—as though large springs were being stretched—then there were footsteps, climbing, moving overhead, crossing the attic floor; then more climbing, the sound of each footstep going higher, becoming more distant.

Anne pulled up the screen and leaned out the window. "Great. He's up on the roof."

Mark tried the doorknob; to his surprise it opened, but it bumped against the bottom of a ladder that had been folded down from a ceiling hatch. He climbed up into the hot, musty attic. Next to the chimney a broad shaft of sunlight, aswirl with dust motes, angled down through another hatch in the roof. Mark climbed the wood stairs and stepped out onto the slate shingles. It was a steep-pitched roof, and Mark worked slowly along the peak. Randall was leaning against the chimney, staring out toward the bay. He was wearing an old raincoat, buttoned to his throat, collar turned up.

"Nice view," Mark said when he reached the other side of the chimney. He squinted up at the sky—there wasn't a cloud anywhere—and held his hand out as if to check for rain.

"Samuel liked the rain," Randall said loudly. "Said he was in California after the war. Didn't like it: no rain." He squatted down and leaned his back against the brick chimney. "But for years he's been an Angels fan. He was one of those Red Sox–haters. Told me it started with Ted Williams. So when the California Angels joined the majors, he followed them. Because of their name." Randall eased himself down until he was sitting on the slate tiles. Mark sat next to him.

"He died an Angels fan!" Randall laughed as he reached in a pocket of the raincoat and pulled out a can of pitted black olives; from the other pocket he produced a can opener. He opened the can and scaled the lid down into the yard; then he stuffed his fingers into the black water and pulled out at least a half dozen olives, which he crammed in his mouth. He ate the olives rapidly, noisily, the dark juice running down his chin. When he was about halfway through them, he stopped and handed the can to Mark. Mark ate a few, then he ate a few more. It was hard to stop.

"Mom used to get so pissed at me in the kitchen," Randall whispered. "I would go through cans of olives and there wouldn't be any for the dinner guests."

Mark handed the can back to Randall. He ate the rest of the olives, then drank the juice.

"Out to the Rescue Station Samuel used to keep one shelf stocked up—just for olives." Randall turned and looked at Mark. "Is your mother still alive?"

Mark shook his head.

"Me neither."

Randall continued to stare at Mark. His chin was dark with olive juice. He seemed almost in a trance.

"What do you want to do?" Mark asked.

Randall put the empty can down on its side and let it roll, clattering and bouncing on the slate tiles, until it seemed to leap off the edge of the roof; after a moment of silence, they heard it hit the ground. He gazed up at the sky. "Nauset."

"The Rescue Station?"

Randall wiped olive juice from his chin and gazed out at the expanse of blue water.

Sixteen

Standing.

The mere thought of it made Emerson want to vomit his entire burning innards. But he heard them coming up the porch steps and he managed to get himself on his feet next to the bed. His arms were spread—one hand holding the bedpost and the other the windowsill—so that when they entered the cottage he must have resembled some high-wire performer, his body frozen in the taut, angular moment of imbalance and horror before plunging to the circus ring below. He sat back heavily on the bed, and his dizziness actually convinced him that the entire cottage was turning slowly to the left. "What time is it?"

"It's almost two o'clock in the afternoon," Rachel said as she entered the bedroom.

Mark Emmons stood behind her, leaning against the doorjamb, while Randall stood by the fireplace in the living room. Though sunlight poured through the windows, he was wearing a raincoat buttoned up to his neck.

Emerson suddenly felt memory—and panic—surge in as he recalled last night at Vachon's Marina. Waiting for the police boat to take Samuel's body back to the mainland. Shots of Johnnie Walker chased with beer. Tales of blizzards, hurricanes, bluefish runs. Stories from an era when red lipstick and nylons had the power of a drug. "So what is this," he nearly shouted, "some sort of committee?" Glancing down, he noticed his shorts were stained with dried yellow pee.

"We need to get across to Nauset," Mark said. "Randall wants to return to the station."

In the living room Randall was holding the conch shell to his ear.

"Get Cyrus to take you when he returns with the fishing party," Emerson said.

"No charter today, Grapes."

"What?"

"No one signed up, and he's off in the *Angel Gabriel*."

"It's July, there's always a fishing party."

Rachel shook her head.

Slowly Emerson got to his feet again. He felt weak, but at least the room remained stationary. Rachel handed him his pants, and as he stepped into them he put a hand on her shoulder.

"They're checking out," she said, "people are leaving early. They were boarding the ferry in droves this morning. And later in the day a new load arrived—cameramen."

She held out a tan shirt, but Emerson was stumped as to its purpose or function. "What cameramen?"

"Boston, Hartford, Providence—somebody said CNN was here." She turned the sleeves of the shirt right-side out for him. "There's reporters crawling all over the island."

Emerson pulled on his shirt and began fumbling with the buttons. Then he paused and looked up, first at Mark, then at his granddaughter. It was as though they had been speaking in a foreign tongue, and he finally understood what they were trying to tell him. "Here on the island. Media? Again?"

Mark stood on the stern deck of the inn's old charter boat, *Seraphim,* looking aft. As she crossed the bay the island seemed to rise up and spread out until its familiar double-wing shape lay distinctly against the sky. The last time he'd been on this old launch it was the middle seventies and he went fishing with Randall, Emerson, and Samuel. They had run down to Chatham Light and out the Nauset cut-through to the open Atlantic. They found a school of blues off the tip of Monomoy and took dozens until the tide changed; then they caught nothing but junkfish: skate, sand shark, and the horrendous-looking seadogs—which had spiny wings and hopped around on the deck, barking. They had been fishing in brilliant sunlight, but as usual a dense fog bank lay several miles off the Cape's elbow. When the wind shifted to onshore, they ran back toward Chatham, but the fog rolled in before they entered the cut-through. Emerson throttled back, while Randall stood lookout on the bow. The channel markers emerged out of the fog as if by magic. When they were safely in Pleasant Bay, Samuel opened another round of Narragansetts. The air was damp and chill. There had been something peculiar about this outing, something collusive about Samuel and Emerson: two old war veterans who thought this new genera-

tion of pot-smoking, flag-burning, draft-dodging war babies was the beginning of the end. Mark was surprised that they invited him at all.

Samuel took a long pull on his beer, set the can in the crook of his
arm, and began filling his corncob. "We wanted to have a word with you,"
he said. His beard was a thing of beauty, the way the hair lay against his
long cheek in graying eddies. "I understand Emerson spoke to you about
Blacke's Channel."

"The deeds," Mark said. "Last winter—" He stopped; it might be unwise to voice his frustration, for several times after Emerson had first mentioned the deeds Mark had made inquiries, only to turn up nothing. He
had pretty much let the thing drop—which was an integral part of life on
Angel's Head, the theory being that what's left after you let something
drop is what's really important.

"This bridge business, this Eliot Bedrosian," Emerson said, "t'ain't just
gonna go away."

"No it's not," Mark said. "Next issue of *The Current* will run a story
about the permits being issued. All the state and federal agencies and such-
and-such boards and commissions on the mainland. Bedrosian's people
have cleared all those hurdles." Emerson continued to gaze out at the fog,
but Samuel was now sucking hard on his pipe and watching Mark intently.
"They could start construction next spring."

"Next spring," Emerson repeated.

"If you had these deeds," Samuel asked, "what would you do with
them?"

"Read them. See exactly what they say."

"Then what," Emerson said, "feed them to your media?"

Media. Like condominium, the word was new. The media was keeping
the military from conducting the war in Vietnam; the media was causing
riots in cities and on campuses. To these men the media had the invisible
power of certain fish.

"The deeds exist," Samuel said, "and they've got to be used."

"Like a weapon," Emerson said.

"Maybe like bait," Randall said.

"Let's look at them," Mark said. "And get some legal advice."

They stared out the misted windshield, their silence couched in the
deep rumble of the diesel engine. Dead ahead, looming up in the fog, lay
Angel's Head. Mark sensed their love for the island, their fear of losing it.
Losing its islandness. He sensed it because he felt it too, and he didn't
know how to tell these men. It was something you didn't say outright. But

it was there, in the way you talked about the salt water, boats, tides, weather, and fish.

"Where are the deeds?" he asked as the launch entered the jetties.

Samuel leaned out the side of the wheelhouse and beat the corncob into his open palm, releasing ashes into the air. Then he took his can of beer from the crook of his arm and finished its contents. "They are in my wife's possession," he said, a wry grin developing within his great beard, "and we thought you and Randall might take it upon yourselves to obtain them."

"Couldn't you have told me sooner?" Mark asked.

Neither Emerson nor Samuel answered; they both continued to peer out the windshield at the fog. Mark glanced at Randall, who rolled his eyes and shrugged.

The Boat House was empty when she came in, flanked by two men toting video equipment. Rachel got up off the stool and involuntarily took a step back from the counter. "Regina Langley," she whispered.

Regina Langley's smile was just like on television at the end of the newscast, though here her makeup seemed much heavier—caked about the crow's feet and accentuating the sharp cheekbones, the beveled jawline—and her eyes didn't possess that studio-lights glitter, but were simply dead on. Rachel had seen those eyes in schoolteachers. "Well *hello,*"Regina Langley said, but her eyes were taking in the walls, the counter, the displayed fishing and boating gear. "Yes, this is perfect," she said.

The man to her left hoisted a video camcorder to his shoulder, and after adjusting a knob, he said, "Light's okay." Regina Langley opened a black briefcase and began uncoiling a microphone and its wire. The other man came to the counter holding a large plastic bag and, carefully keeping his hands out of the way, he let a dead fish slide out onto the cutting board. Regina Langley continued to smile at Rachel, though the fish between them seemed an impediment to any true pleasure in the exchange. Her hair was amazing: it was as though the woman had just been hit by a puff of wind that slammed the front of her hair up into a cresting wave—and it had been miraculously frozen that way. "What's your name?"

"Rachel Flood."

"Rachel, we were wondering if you'd like to help us."

"Okay."

"With a spot we're doing for tonight's broadcast."

"Okay."

126

"You know how to clean fish?"

"Yes." Rachel looked at the haddock lying on the cutting board.

"Would you mind showing us, demonstrating your, ah, technique for our viewing audience?"

"Okay."

The two men moved quickly in a kind of mechanical syncopation. Wires were connected, a small, intense light was held up, and something that resembled an umbrella was unfolded and opened, its soft gray material somehow concentrating the light in the Boat House. When the cameraman said "Go," Regina Langley was suddenly just like on television. Warm, personal, yet determined to get to the heart of the story. She held the microphone up to her moist red lips and spoke as though all of New England were sitting right there in the Boat House, eating dinner from folding trays. Finally she turned to Rachel and said, "And our young friend here, Rachel Flood, is going to show us how a fish is cleaned!"

Rachel looked at the woman, whose eyes were now lit with genuine inquiry. They seemed to be freezing something deep inside Rachel; she picked up a boning knife from the counter, but just stared at the fish lying on the cutting board.

"Cut," Regina Langley said finally, and dropped the black mesh dome of the mike against her green blouse. The intense light shut off, dropping the Boat House into what now seemed the near darkness of ordinary afternoon light. "Rachel, if this is *too* much, maybe we could get someone else from the inn? Maybe one of the chefs?"

"No, I can *do* it!"

"We're just looking for twenty seconds here, okay?"

"Okay."

The intense light came on again, and Regina Langley said, "So, Rachel, how's an expert do it?"

"It's easy," Rachel said, "you just—" She slit the fish open from anus to head, and peeled back the white flesh, revealing the organs.

Regina Langley whispered, "Absolutely yummy."

Walking.

By the time they reached Nauset Emerson's hangover had begun to recede. The hangover was, he believed, his natural state of being, and anything that helped push it back, whether it was drink or a snootful of salt air, was only temporary. Climbing the dunes forced his body to call up some reserve energy. He worked up a good sweat.

They found the Rescue Station empty. Randall instinctively looked toward the beach and spotted Samuel's crew with Reverend Peele. He led the way down to the water, where the men stood in a circle on the wet sand. They were silent, their hands joined, their eyes closed. Emerson was reminded of ancient peoples; the stillness, the unity of the circle caused him to stop, to keep his distance. Randall simply took his place within the circle: he would always belong. Mark was holding back as well, but when Randall beckoned he joined the circle—the men made room for him, and they all joined hands.

Emerson sat on the side of the dune. It should be so simple, to step forward, take an offered hand, and shut your eyes. Feel the sun's warmth on your lids. Allow the breeze to billow your clothes about you as the cold seawater engulfed your ankles. Samuel had been like a brother since childhood. Yet the bond had always been maintained against specific activities: drinking, fishing, fussing about boats. This other thing, this circle of men, Samuel had come to late. It signified a departure. A revised philosophy. Emerson admired Samuel for all of this: the Rescue Station, the crew, the circle on the beach. But he had never been a part of it—rather than join, he'd prefer to sit alone on his cottage porch, watching the evening light change on the bay. He preferred to observe. He sought isolation where Samuel developed community. Jokingly Samuel had once said, "You are an island, Emerson." The day they had found the heart in the shed Rachel had said that everything was an island—the comment stuck with Emerson, disturbed him in a way he could not explain. He was frightened by his granddaughter's sense of islandness. It seemed entirely too soon.

And it had to do with Randall. For the Rescue Station, and what Samuel had made of it, stemmed from Randall, from his accident. After several years of getting nowhere with doctors in Boston—they all said his recovery would be limited—Samuel brought Randall out here to the Rescue Station and somehow provided an environment which tended to stabilize the young man. His behavior had been so unpredictable after the accident. His relationship with Emerson had been difficult at best since he was a child, but the new Randall—that was how all the Floods saw him—would have little or nothing to do with Emerson for long periods of time. Most often he simply fled from his father; but occasionally he became violent and threatened him, once even hitting him on the shoulder with a boat oar. So when Samuel took him out to Nauset, Emerson felt relief where he thought he should be overcome with loss. He knew enough to leave well enough alone: Samuel was trying to help. Over the first few years at the

Rescue Station, there was a noticeable improvement in Randall. Slowly he began returning to Angel's Head and assuming simple chores around the inn. He'd still be difficult and unpredictable, but it was easier for everyone to allow his return to the Rescue Station. Whatever Samuel was doing with Randall seemed to work, and the Floods saw no point in interfering. Eventually Samuel gathered more men—damaged men, Emerson thought of them. They came to the Rescue Station, and whatever discipline or therapy or magic Samuel used it was clear that it worked, for most of the men eventually returned to their former lives, or built new ones, in a condition that allowed them to at least function, to cope. As a result, Samuel had gained a reputation; to some he was this wacko islander who took in hopeless cases, to others he was something of a mystical guru.

The men in the circle remained standing, absolutely still. It was a ceremony of sorts. They were saying goodbye to a member of the crew. It must be very difficult for these men, who seemed so innocent and fragile, to understand Samuel's death. The circle was intended to be a form of affirmation. Of continuation. Of renewal.

You believe in ends.

Sarah, since your death I no longer know what to believe in. But ends I can accept as a matter of course. Things do end. Samuel's end. Randall's life, as it was, ended. It was a kind of death. And look what it did to you.

It sent me away. Your rationality could no longer hold me. It was as though the earth lost its gravity.

So you killed yourself.

I sought a way out. I saw death behind everything in life. It was driving me mad, and finally I went to see what it was for myself.

My life has never been the same since.

I'm sorry. I thought you so self-sufficient.

I'm nothing of the sort. And what did you find?

Emerson opened his eyes. His tears blurred his view of the circle, the beach, the ocean. He looked into the wind, which swept his eyes clear.

The circle was broken, and Reverend Peele led the crew back toward the Rescue Station. Stretched out along the beach, they might have been children. Some paused to inspect a seashell or a piece of driftwood.

Stand.

Stand and walk.

Emerson got to his feet slowly, and walked over the dunes to the Rescue Station.

They called it the common room.

Long and dark, it had seen generations of men.

Men who resided here in the solitude by the sea.

Men who waited for a storm, a ship in distress.

Men who could act responsibly when there was disaster.

At the far end of the room, facing east, there were two sliding glass doors installed, the only sign of modernity. Emerson sat in a straight-backed chair at the long table and gazed out at the sand and sky. Mark stood by the glass, feeling the sun's warmth on his face. Between two dunes he could see the ocean.

"These murders," Mark said, "they must be connected."

"Aye. It's all connected," Emerson said. His aged skin was translucent in the sun. "Like the land, the sky, and the ocean, it's all connected. Bedrosian's heart. Sarah. Randall. Samuel. It—we—" he smiled as he gazed out at the Atlantic, "are as connected as water." He glanced up at Mark. "What brought you back to Angel's Head?"

"I returned because I have missed this deeply. And because I learned that Eliot Bedrosian had returned to Angel's Head."

"You were drawn back. Angel's Head does that. It always has." Emerson turned and looked at Mark now. "What do you believe in?"

"Did. 'What did I believe in?' would be more appropriate."

Emerson waited.

"I think I believe in the story. Telling the story."

"News."

"Well, yes."

"Seeking the truth," Emerson said.

"Investigating the facts. Putting them together. Reporting them."

"It's very powerful, this reporting."

"It can be," Mark said.

"Important."

"Sometimes," Mark said. "The bridge is important."

"In all my years on this island, the bridge—that whole time—is unique. It brought out things in Angelians that I'd never seen before—a fear of everything off-island. Deep in the heart of most islanders there's the need to stare across the bay. The water protects us, it makes us different. Once there's a bridge, it'll never be quite the same again."

"You're against the bridge, still?" Mark asked.

"I'm afraid of the bridge."

"I thought you believed everything was 'connected.'"

Emerson nodded. "So, there are the contradictions."

"Samuel was opposed to the bridge?"

"Yes."

"Actively opposed."

Emerson hesitated. "Yes."

"If Bedrosian was killed by someone against the bridge, was Samuel killed as a form of retaliation?"

Emerson took a deep breath and let it out slowly. He continued to squint out toward the ocean between the dunes. "Islanders in favor of the bridge now are people like my daughter. They consider themselves enlightened in their own way. They believe it's essential to have the bridge, and have it built the way the islanders want it. But are they willing to kill Samuel Cross to prove their determination? I don't know. This is a matter of possession, possession of the future. Some people will do anything for that."

Mark turned and looked into the common room, where the crew sat around another table with Reverend Peele. Randall was sitting alone at the foot of the stairs, gazing into the sunlight with eyes wide with an innocence and horror Mark had seldom seen before; he might have been in prayer.

"Yes," Emerson said quietly, "I've been wondering the same thing."

"You think he's capable of doing that to Bedrosian?"

"I don't know. I'm his father and I don't know what he's capable of at any given moment. But that's true of all of us, isn't it?"

Mark nodded. "The crew wants to stay here."

"I don't blame them," Emerson said. "Reverend Peele is goin' to stay too, for a while."

"Think they'll be all right?"

"I hope so. Samuel taught them well."

Seventeen

IN SEASON RACHEL USUALLY ATE HER MEALS WITH THE STAFF in the kitchen, but tonight the inn was almost empty—remarkable, for July. Many of the guests had checked out during the day and ferried back to the mainland. At her mother's suggestion Rachel ate in the dining room. Some of the other tables were occupied by staff, dressed like tourists; they winked at Rachel, and talked stupidly about boating and the beach, like tourists. The detectives Page and McNeil, who had that afternoon checked into the inn, were seated by a window with some other men, who the kitchen staff said were the Feds. Rachel's mother sailed through the room once, looking delighted.

What was more eerie was that some of the real guests were familiar faces: Dexter Connelly from *Channel 8 Eyewitness News,* Paula and Bob Logan from *Channel 24 News Day,* and the Boston columnist who's always photographed with a cigar. Regina Langley was not in the dining room, but Rachel heard her name mentioned at several tables. Dexter Connelly, his rich baritone carrying easily from the far side of the salad bar, questioned the woman's professional integrity, but had to admit she had great visibility. There was speculation that she was about to go national.

At 7:30, as if on cue, most of the guests left the dining room and drifted into the bar. Rachel finished her scallop plate quickly and followed; she sat in the back corner with Grapes, who was drinking coffee and not looking too pleased about it. Mark Emmons was at the end of the bar, reading the newspaper, seemingly unaware of the TV personalities sitting near him. The group asked Cyrus to turn on the TV: and there was Regina Langley, standing with the Angel's Head Inn in the background. The group of TV people applauded and whistled as though they were a bunch of college kids on a Memorial Day drunk.

Regina Langley strolled along the edge of the cove as she described the recent events on Angel's Head. There was a photograph of Eliot Bedrosian. There was footage of his schooner, the *Northern Lady*. Back to Regina, who was now wearing a different outfit, including the green blouse she'd had on in the Boat House. She sat on the pier, looking both alluring and a little spooked, as she talked about someone named Lizzie Borden. This brought hoots and whistles from the TV people, and Grapes swore under his breath. Regina Langley was saying something about famous murders in New England—but Rachel couldn't hear her over the chatter at the bar. Then there was a rapid progression of photographs: two young people—Eliot Bedrosian and Rachel's mother—arm in arm walking the beach; Cyrus splitting logs with his ax raised above his head; Randall wearing a wetsuit, diver's goggles, and an oxygen tank; Grapes at the wheel of the *Seraphim*, looking menacingly over his shoulder; Samuel Cross and a woman Rachel didn't recognize, who seemed to be trying to cover her face with her hands; and finally the Rescue Station on Nauset.

The group at the bar was going wild. Cyrus leaned against the beer cooler with his arms folded. Mark Emmons drank his shot, chased it with beer, and scowled at the newspaper spread beneath his elbows. At a corner table McNeil chuckled, but Page seemed on the verge of nodding off. The Feds had disappeared. Rachel didn't dare look at Grapes, and her mother was nowhere in sight.

On television Regina Langley was walking up the pier—the *Northern Lady* in the background—and as she approached the camera her jiggling breasts made the silk blouse appear to flash electric in the sunlight. Fade out.

Fade in: Regina Langley was now in the Boat House, standing across the counter from Rachel. Looking at herself on the TV screen, Rachel thought she appeared odd, small, fidgety, and her hair was too flat against the sides of her head, as if she hadn't washed it in a week. The group at the bar suddenly became quiet as the camera zoomed in on Rachel's hands, her boning knife—and as she deftly slit open the fish Regina Langley's voice-over asked "And we all wonder: where will it all end?" Pause. "From Angel's Head, this is Regina Langley for *Eyewitness New England*."

Mark watched Emerson hustle his granddaughter out of the bar. One of the TV dolls turned and called after her, "We know you didn't do it, honey!" which brought out more laughter. Fresh drinks were ordered and Cyrus went to work. His movements were swift, efficient, professional; he was cordial, all business. The man was a bartender. He came down the bar, poured Mark another shot of Scotch, and opened another beer.

Mark raised his eyes from the newspaper he had spread out on the bar—the new issue of *The Current,* which he'd been trying to read throughout the broadcast. "Regina Langleys," he said quietly. "There's hundreds of 'em now. Every city, every state has one. I think they grow them in a field somewhere."

"All you fucking media people are the same: bottom feeders." Cyrus turned and walked back up the bar.

Mark did his shot. He watched the group down the bar. They had the clothes, the hair, the chiseled features of all broadcast people. They looked as though they always expected to be recognized, but sitting in a group like this there was something silly, even adolescent, about their preening.

He gazed down again at the *Current* spread on the bar. Max's sentences were clear and taut. They had a substance and sinew that was a ways acrost the water from the broadcasters' face lifts and hair transplants. *A ways acrost the water,* a phrase old islanders used, often in reference to opposite ends of a spectrum. The mainland was a ways acrost the water from the island, and they wanted to keep it that way. The newspaper story said that in 1975 the deeds had been obtained by a *Current* reporter, which had led to prolonged litigation. Eventually the plans for a bridge across Blacke's Channel were defeated. Not a clear-cut court decision, but by attrition: the seemingly endless court dates, hearings, appeals, and petitions which finally caused Bedrosian's backers to pull out. Invest their money elsewhere. Thwarted at Angel's Head, Eliot Bedrosian went south and worked real estate development plans using money that had been traced back to a drug lord named Robert Marshall. Alleged drug lord Robert Marshall, who lived somewhere in the Caribbean to avoid the IRS, the DEA, and probably half a dozen other federal agencies. Throughout the eighties Bedrosian built an empire of condominiums and malls on Florida wetlands, only to have it collapse around him in the nineties. Losses estimated at over two hundred million dollars. A familiar American scenario. So he sailed north and returned to Angel's Head this summer. For what? Max's newspaper copy could not say for certain.

Mark looked up at the television, which had now been switched to the Red Sox–Indians game. Even on the small set he found the green of Fenway Park soothing. One thing that truly impressed him about Regina Langley's broadcast was the photograph of Samuel Cross and his wife. That she had obtained a photo of Dorothea Cross was the reason Regina Langley would go national, while the idiots down the bar would probably remain local

135

throughout their careers—and none of them even expressed appreciation for that one photograph, how difficult a feat it was: how Regina Langley even knew such a photograph existed was miraculous.

He got off his stool, took some change from the bar, and went to the pay phone back by the dart board. He looked up Max's number and dialed.

"Hello?" she said.

"You still write a neat sentence."

"Thanks. I had good competition as a kid."

"You see this spot on TV?"

"Everybody on the island did, I imagine," Max said. "Where are you?"

"The inn. Place is almost empty, except for us media types."

"I was thinking of heading down there."

"Bring your trench coat, and a can of hair spray."

"You going to be there a while?" she asked.

He thought about checking in at the inn for the night—taking Anne up on her standing offer. He thought about going back to his apartment before he did himself too much damage.

"All the broadcast plastic in here," he said, "I'd love to buy a real journalist a drink."

When Rachel and Grapes got upstairs her mother rushed down the hall. "I can't *believe* you *did* that!"

"Anne," Grapes said.

"She told you to cut open that fish in front of the camera—"

"Rachel didn't know how the film would be used."

"*All* of New England watches that stupid program!"

"Anne, she's just—"

"*Shut up!*" She leaned forward as though she were about to take a bite out of him. Her face was extremely red—it always was when she'd been drinking. She pulled strands of hair off her face.

"Mom, she was very nice, I didn't think—I clean fish every day. They come in with their catch—it's too slimy for them to handle—"

"They're all leaving—the place'll be empty for Labor Day! We're all a bunch of *looneys!* Axes! Knives!"

"*I didn't do anything!*" Rachel yelled. She felt herself filling up, and rather than cry in her mother's presence, she turned and went back down the stairs. Her mother was screaming after her, and when she opened the door to the lobby her mother's voice seemed to pass her and expand, swell out into the lobby. Only a few guests sat in the clusters of antique furniture. They turned and looked at Rachel, at the open door and stairway to the private quarters, and their eyes registered guarded curiosity. Some of the children showed genuine fear, and cuddled closer to their parents. Then, after a moment, they acted as if they had not heard. A man refolded his newspaper and began to read. A mother continued to inspect her child's blond hair for ticks. Rachel closed the door carefully, and she crossed the lobby as though nothing had happened.

She went out on the front porch, placed both hands on the railing, and took long deep breaths. After several minutes her breathing returned to normal. All the while she stared out at the bay.

She returned to the lobby. Louise was at the registration desk, her jewelry chiming about her wrists and neck. Rachel wrote a note on a piece of stationery: *The jetties at 9*. She folded the paper, placed it in an envelope, which she labeled *Suite 304A*. Louise gazed at the envelope as though it might leap off the counter. She had been with the inn every summer since Rachel could remember; she was the closest thing to glamour the place had, and with her makeup her eyes seemed in a perpetual state of astonishment. "Might this be urgent?" she asked, picking up the envelope.

Rachel shrugged.

"Well, we'll have it sent right on up."

"Thank you, Louise."

Eighteen

"WHAT I DON'T UNDERSTAND," MAX SAID—AND MARK NODDED, knowing what she was thinking—"is where this Regina Langley digs up a photo of Dorothea Cross."

"Most likely," he said, "she paid someone for it."

Max sipped her vodka gimlet, and again she gazed toward the bar, where Page and McNeil had been drinking and watching the Red Sox game on television. "We don't have one photo of her on file. Plenty of Samuel, but none of her. It was part of her reputation: the recluse who fought the bridge. Rarely seen, let alone photographed." She glanced toward the bar again. "We have company."

Page and McNeil came to their table. Mark and Max invited them to sit, and it might have been a séance the way the four of them leaned over the candle bowl.

"We've been reading more of the old issues of *The Current,*" Page said, "and it occurred to me that I remember you two. I was fresh out of police academy and working up in Brockton when the Angel's Head bridge thing was in the news. I remember seeing you being interviewed on TV by Paula Simmons."

"I don't remember anything about that interview," Mark said, "except that she had great perfume."

McNeil laughed. Both he and Page looked weary, done in; they were cops drinking off-duty in a strange place, a scene journalists knew well. Page looked toward the bar and raised his hand. They were the only customers left, the waitress was gone, and Cy was cleaning up. When he came over with their drinks, Page gave him a twenty and waved off the change, then leaned forward again. "They are all a little strange out here, aren't they."

"In winter they eat their young," Max said.

"Your stories in the paper, they're very good," Page said, "but there are things unsaid, left out. Tell me about the deeds, Dorothea Cross, and the bridge war."

Mark had had so many boilermakers that by now he'd come through the other side of drunkenness to a clear, remarkably lucid place. An island, of sorts, and he had the attention of two men who were interested in things that he'd done years earlier. "Emerson Flood told us about the deeds, and Samuel Cross told me his wife had them. It seemed the only way to fight Bedrosian's bridge. Samuel asked Randall and me to talk to Dorothea—"

"Samuel asked you to talk to his wife?"

"Yes. He hadn't seen her for over twenty years—since a few years after the war. Things do get a little strange out here, but there's always some hidden logic to it. Something—I don't know what—happened in their marriage and Dorothea became a recluse. Yet they remained married, and they continued to live in the Cross house. They divided it so that she primarily lived on the second floor, and he kept to a few first-floor rooms in the back. All this time an old cousin, Chastity, if you can believe it, lived with Dorothea. She did the cooking, cleaning, she did everything, and she was the only one who ever saw the woman.

"Anyway, Dorothea Cross was known as the Emily Dickinson of Angel's Head—without the poetry—and one summer afternoon Randall and I knocked on her door. Chastity admitted us to the parlor. She weighed all of ninety pounds but she had one of these hoarse voices that carried, and she announced that Dorothea was not receiving visitors. So Randall scribbled a note, something to the effect that the deeds she held might be valuable in thwarting Eliot Bedrosian. Chastity took the note upstairs and we sat in the parlor a long time, hearing only creaking floorboards overhead. Finally she returned with a note from Dorothea which asked 'How do you know I don't want the bridge?'

"We didn't of course. We only assumed. By that time the whole island was severely divided. There were those who were for the bridge—they were practical, Rotarian, usually Republican, and they thought it was time for Angel's Head to get with it, to join in on the progress that was America. In truth there were more of them—the Bridgers—and if this were a true democracy it would have been put to a simple vote and the bridge would have been built. You have to realize that twenty years ago this island was much more 'backward' than it is now. Things like phones were rare, and those that existed seldom worked, particularly if you tried to call the mainland, which reporters tended to do. Many of the houses still didn't have plumbing, and not a few were without electricity. To watch a Sox game you really had to come down here to the inn. But everybody had radios. AM/FM, shortwave, CBs. In houses, on board boats, radios were the perpetual link with the outside world.

"Then there were those who were opposed to the bridge—the 'islanders.' Vehemently opposed. Things were so clearly split everywhere then— the war, abortion, civil rights, the legalization of pot. The opponents of the bridge were usually either young or from the old families. They were associated with all that was going haywire on the mainland. They were elitists, and of course some of them had to be commies. A bridge, on the other hand, was American. Making money was American. If you opposed the bridge, you opposed the capitalist system—so it followed that you supported the alternative.

"In reply to Dorothea we wrote that we didn't know whether or not she was for or against the bridge. Then I added a phrase that was popular at the time—you always saw it written on the walls in public bathrooms: 'If you're not part of the solution, you're part of the problem.' Don't smile— in the mid-seventies it seemed profound. I sometimes wonder if it still isn't. We gave the note to Chastity and left.

"A week or so passed. One, maybe two issues of *The Current* came and went—then I heard from Chastity. She put a note in her subscription envelope."

Page looked at Max, confused.

She said, "We didn't just write *The Current*. We delivered the damn thing as well. One of us would go door to door here on the island, while the other took bundles of the paper across the bay to be distributed up and down the Cape."

McNeil smiled. "You visited Dorothea again."

Mark nodded. "And this time Randall and I were admitted to the second floor. Two straight-back chairs had been placed in the hall, and once we were seated Chastity withdrew back downstairs. After a few minutes the door to our left was opened slightly. I couldn't see anything but a corner of a bureau. Then, from behind the door, Dorothea said, 'Randall, if I gave you the deeds, if I had Tom Shaw put the deeds in your name, what would you do with them?' Tom Shaw was a lawyer living over in Harwich. Randall told her he'd use the deeds however he could to fight the bridge. She agreed to that—she said there would be a long, drawn-out legal battle, and she didn't have the energy for that. She said she knew she wouldn't survive it.

"Then we saw something slide out the doorway. It was a leather envelope, quite large and fat, and tied together with a piece of faded blue satin ribbon. Randall picked it up; it looked like it had been handed down through generations. The door closed, and Chastity returned to show us the way out."

Rachel found Eric sitting on the jetty rocks, staring out at the darkness of the bay. The moon wasn't up yet and the Milky Way was spread across the night sky like a haze.

"Will you be leaving?" she asked.

"The morning ferry."

She sat next to him. The rock was cool beneath her, but his bare thigh was warm against her kneecap. She could feel the hairs. They were fine, soft, and they made her think of little animals. Gerbils and chipmunks.

"I'm sorry your vacation's cut short, Sputnik." She felt light-headed all of a sudden and she lay back on the rock. The Milky Way appeared to move, thousands of flecks of light playing tricks on her. Slowly she pushed herself up again and leaned forward and kissed him. "The island's not safe. That stuff on TV, those people from Boston—it's getting crazy."

"I don't want to go back to Hartford," he said.

"Why not run away?"

"Right."

"If you ran away, where'd you go?"

"West, obviously."

"Well, I wouldn't take the ferry—you can't get away on the mainland. They always find people on the mainland."

"Well, I can't walk on water," Eric said.

"No, you can't." Suddenly she was reminded of the dream she had the day Samuel was found dead in the cove, and she remembered walking Samuel home the night before; he'd been alive, now he was dead. It seemed so simple.

"What?" Eric asked. "What is it?"

"I just remembered something Samuel told me the night he was killed. I don't remember exactly, but it had to do with Eddie."

"Eddie? One of those guys living on the beach?"

Rachel got to her feet. She stared across the bay toward Nauset. "My mother's driving me crazy—I'm thinking of running away."

Eric got up. "You are?"

"But crossing to the mainland's a mistake, Eric. They'll always find you."

ॐ

Chastity let Emerson into the parlor, her frail hands worrying the buttons of her green cotton blouse. "Those people from the television program, they offered me so much money," she said. "I need it and—"

"I know. It's all right."

"What difference does it make? Dorothea's been dead so long."

"It's only a photograph, Chastity, don't worry about it."

"They've all been here. Ben Snow. All sorts of police from the mainland." She sat down wearily and glanced toward the window. "He was sleeping in the barn."

At the window, Emerson looked out at the yard. Again that ribbon, same as the police had strung around the deck of the *Northern Lady*, encircled the barn.

"They've taken samples of everything," Chastity said, "in plastic bags like they were Sunday leftovers."

"He never came in the house last night?"

"Emerson, he hasn't set foot in this house since she died. He always slept out there."

"Did you hear anything?"

She didn't answer, and he looked around. Chastity's face, her skin reminded him of wood pilings in the cove. The years of seasons, of tides, of salt water cracked and withered the wood, leaving it hard and pale, sometimes gray, sometimes a bleached white. It was wood that could no longer absorb moisture. But it was a face, so weathered, so taken down to its essentials, that it was not without its beauty. "I'm not sure," she said. Her hands lay curled in her lap like seashells. "I dreamed, and in the dream there were voices. I awoke briefly, and I thought I heard footsteps, feet moving through the grass." Her eyes were moist, and it seemed the only moisture left in her body. "They wouldn't tell me anything—was he killed out there?"

"No, no," Emerson said. "I saw Ben Snow and he said that whoever it was came here and walked Samuel down to the cove. He was cut—on the cheek—to convince him to go with them. The police found a little blood on the cot. At the cove they got in one of the dinghies and rowed out to the *Northern Lady*." He thought of the blood smeared on the hull of the schooner. He didn't mention that—as it was Chastity seemed to be losing her breath.

Emerson sat on the sofa. He put his arm around her, and the blade of her shoulder nudged against his breastbone. Her hair in his chin was coarse, brittle. "I can't bear it," she whispered. "Samuel was like a ghost around here. He came and went from Nauset. I always knew when he was here—not entering the house was a form of respect for Dorothea. Now that they're both gone, this house feels—" She wiped her eyes with the back of her hand. "Do you think Samuel's death had anything to do with that other man's, that developer's?"

"Yes," Emerson said.

"Samuel was still against the bridge."

"I know."

"So many people are for it now. We used to just live by the bay," she said with effort. "We fished and clammed, and we didn't need much. We didn't have a lot of want. Now people never seem satisfied. Do you think this bridge is a good idea?"

"It's a matter of what's good or what's necessary," he said. "I just don't know anymore."

Emerson held Chastity while she regained her breath. The only other sound in the parlor came from the banjo clock, its tick soothing, hypnotic, yet its precision seemed to mock the old woman's labored breathing.

When Mark was drunk he often used to walk it off on the beach. If that failed, he simply slept in the hollow of a dune. When he left the inn he went down to the beach and found that the practice still had its pleasures on a summer night. A three-quarter moon was rising over the bay, and the salt air seemed to open his pores. He walked about a mile barefoot down to the lighthouse, then headed back. As he approached the inn, where now only a few rooms were lit, the long white building made him think of an angular oceanliner riding in waves of sand.

A woman came down the front porch steps. She was wearing a night-gown, pale blue in the moonlight. It was Anne—she had been walking in sand since her childhood and it did something to her stride. Graceful yet determined. Her hips had exceptional English and she was bent forward more than if she were merely strolling a sidewalk. Mark followed her around to the back of the inn, where she stopped at the shed. Turning, she watched him approach. Her eyes were enormous.

"They're all going," she said. "All our guests."

"They're afraid."

"You might as well leave too."

"I have considered it."

She continued to stare, her eyes hard, angry.

"But I'm staying," he said.

She said nothing.

"Disappointed?"

"Yes—because you'll never learn." She folded her arms and leaned against the shed door. "The rest'll check out tomorrow."

"Then I'll have the place to myself."

"What're you doing out here, Mark?"

"Walking the beach, wondering what it's like to lose part of my brain."

"Randall's memory, it's all disconnected," she said. "It comes in glancing blows."

"Glancing blows?"

She sighed, but he could not tell if her exasperation was with him or herself. "Suddenly he'll mention something or someone from years ago, and I'll ask him what about them and he'll tell me some detail, something that was said or done. Five minutes later I'll ask him to elaborate and he won't remember any of it."

"In a way I envy him—there's plenty I'd like to forget. Booze isn't thorough enough. Nor, I assume, are drugs."

"No, but they make it all more tolerable." She moved closer to him. Her face was white, her eyes and mouth black.

"What I don't get is you and Eliot—again."

She looked away.

"Years ago, that was one thing. We were all young—"

"And half out of our minds usually."

"But *now*—how could you fall in love with Eliot now? Particularly after what happened to Randall."

"Because—because he didn't do it."

Mark placed one hand against the shed wall. He felt he was close to something, something that Anne had been carrying all these years. "Everyone on Angel's Head thinks it was Eliot." With his other arm, Mark pointed down toward the cove. "Your brother was scuba diving there, hooking mooring lines to the concrete slabs on the bottom. He did it every spring. And in the evening someone ripped open the side of his head with an outboard motor prop. Part of his brain was pulverized. If the mouthpiece to the oxygen tank weren't still in his mouth, he would have drowned long before Ray Snow rowed out and found him. He bit down so hard on that thing he broke teeth! Everyone believed it was Eliot. Everyone. But there was no evidence, no fucking way to prove it."

"You don't understand," she said in disgust.

"What, Anne? What don't I understand?"

Anne walked out across the moonlit sand and disappeared into the shadow of the inn.

Nineteen

Walking.

Without the hangover, Emerson's remorse seemed more manageable. His gaze sought the blue horizon without the usual fire searing the back of his eyeballs. It was a bright summer morning and he had to admit that his joints felt well-greased and his stride long. His feet sank in the sand, his pant legs were brushed by dune grass, seashells crackled beneath his deckshoes. *Samuel.* He wondered if it was possible to live for these small pleasures they had shared since they were boys. Pleasures of the island. *Yes, Samuel. They will take your body to the mainland to be cremated; then I will spread your ashes on the bay waters you loved—as you wished.*

He entered the inn and found the lobby empty—it wasn't quite seven o'clock—except for one man, who rushed toward him pulling a wallet from his pocket.

"Flood," he said urgently, "I've got to get my family back to the mainland as soon as possible."

"The first ferry arrives at seven-thirty."

"Damn the ferry! My kids and wife were up half the night, scared out of their wits. I don't know what kind of operation you think you're running here, but last night that Regina Langley got them—"

Emerson attempted to tack to his port side, skirting the man and angling for the door marked PRIVATE. "First ferry leaves at eight-thirty."

But the man stayed with him, keeping his girth between them. He had a deep, smooth double chin that wiggled as he moved down the lobby alongside Emerson. "Here," he took several bills from his wallet, "sixty dollars to take us across in that launch of yours."

"Your money's good in the dining room, which opens in just a few minutes." Emerson went through the door to the private quarters, closing it firmly behind him; to his astonishment he took the stairs two at a time.

He knocked on Rachel's door and, after waiting only a few moments, let himself in—the curtains weren't drawn, the sunlight poured in on the made bed.

He went down to the kitchen and talked to the help. No one had seen Rachel. He sent a busboy to wake up Anne, but she wasn't in her room either. The cooks, the waitresses and waiters—no one had seen Anne or Rachel.

He did the once-through of the inn, occasionally asking a maid. The few rooms that had been occupied overnight were being vacated by tourists toting duffel bags and suitcases, rushing to get to the dining room in time to eat before the first ferry departed. He went down to the Boat House, but it was still locked. Just to be sure Rachel hadn't taken her anger at her mother and spent the night there, he let himself in and looked in the back room. It was empty.

Out the window he could see a long line of tourists on the pier. The ferry had just arrived; Ben Snow and one of his summer rent-a-cops were trying to herd the crowd aboard. Emerson left the Boat House and went out on the pier.

"It's like a bad allergy attack," Ben said. His tan shirt was already soaked with sweat. "Tourist count is way up there."

"Once they all leave you'll be fine."

"Sure," Ben said, "and then we all starve."

"'Fraid so."

"Thank you, Regina Langley." Ben looked like a man assigned a menial, undignified task. "Listen Em, I gotta ask ya. A couple of these news people staying up to the inn, they called my office first thing this morning demanding private transportation back to the mainland."

"What?"

"They seem to be allergic to the public, too."

"Didn't they come over on the ferry?"

"Ya, sure." Ben was on the verge of whining.

"They can take it back then."

"Well, that's what I said, Emerson."

"Fine—"

"But they claim it's different now that this story's been on TV. They'd get no peace on the ferry. It's wide open and the cattle would be sniffing all around them."

"They might even step in something."

"Look. The island's gotten enough bad publicity—"

"Now you're handling PR for Angel's Head, too?"

"I just don't think there's any point in aggravating these TV people." Ben now had the guilty, hangdog look of an adolescent boy. "So I said I'd arrange it with the inn."

"Arrange what?"

"Transportation, in the launch."

"You did, did you?"

"It's only six people, Emerson."

"Did you also offer to pay for my gas, oil, and time?"

Ben shook his head.

A man and a woman came around the side of the Boat House. They were tourists, right down to the Angel's Head ball caps, but they looked truly anguished.

Ben pointed back along the pier. "You'd better get in line."

"No," the man said, removing his sunglasses.

This was Ben Snow's job and Emerson began to walk away.

"Our boy," the woman said. "We're not getting on any ferry until we've found him."

Emerson stopped and looked at her. "He's missing?" he asked.

She turned to him and nodded.

"Since when?"

"Last night," the husband said.

Emerson saw the man's genuine concern, and it had the effect of amplifying his own, which had, until now, been a small, buried seed. This man was past parental anger. When he spoke, his voice was constricted yet blunt, as though he were admonishing himself. "We had dinner, then watched that, that program. Everyone was getting excited." He glanced at his wife for support. "I told him, Ginny—"

"We had too much to drink, Hal, period. We're staying in a suite, and when I got up this morning and looked in Eric's room—"

"Eric." Looking at Ginny, Emerson began nodding his head. "Eric Grier."

"He hadn't even *slept* in his bed." Tears rolled down from beneath her sunglasses. "I told him no later than ten-thirty, and ordinarily we would have stayed up until he came in but—" She turned and stared out at the cove.

"He's been hanging around the Boat House," Emerson said, "with my granddaughter."

"Yes, we've met Rachel," the man said.

For years Emerson had studied the people who vacationed on Angel's

Head; with anthropological detachment he watched the way they moved, the way they dressed, the way they spoke to each other, and he had concluded, unlike certain other islanders, that tourists were not really a separate species, but simply an extreme Darwinian mutation. Despite physical similarities, they had developed feeding habits and mating rituals that were distinctly different from the Angelians'. But now he looked at this man, dumbfounded; suddenly Emerson felt connected to this man and woman by one common, genuine emotion: fear. It was a form of communion. "I believe that Rachel and Eric might have disappeared. Together."

Hal nodded, while without looking away from the cove Ginny placed both hands over her mouth.

"Lost children are my specialty," Ben told them. "In most cases they're found in the shops where toys, ice cream, or comic books are sold." He started walking toward the village with a sense of purpose.

"Ben missed his calling," Emerson said. "He should be teaching third grade."

Hal Grier nodded in appreciation at the attempt at humor.

Ginny lowered her hands. "But they've been gone all night."

"Ben spreads the word and the kids always turn up."

Across the cove a small cluster of people had gathered on the marina dock where the *Seraphim* was tied up. They were dressed as though they'd just stepped out of a catalogue. Television people from Boston.

"We're going back up to the inn and wait." Hal had put his sunglasses back on and seemed to have regained his composure.

Mark sat on the top landing of stairs running down the side of his aunt's garage. A frayed Red Sox cap which he'd found stored in her cellar with some of his old clothes was pulled down over his face to shade him from the midmorning sun.

He heard footsteps coming up the crushed seashell drive. Through the cap's eyelets he could see that it was Anne. She wore sunglasses and carried four cans of beer dangling by a six-pack plastic ring.

"I thought you might be able to use one of these," she said when she reached the landing.

"Your timing's perfect." He pulled two cans off the ring.

Anne went into the apartment, where she kicked the two empty beer cans he'd already tossed into the kitchen. She stumbled and swore, then put the beer in the refrigerator. When she came out to the landing, he handed one of the beers to her, then took some aspirin from his shirt pocket. Holding his palm skyward, he felt her sort out two pills and take them. He popped what remained and washed them down with beer. They drank in silence for quite a while. There was the sound of birds from the woods behind the garage, and the sound of some talk show from Aunt Mae's radio up at the house.

"Mark, I don't remember hangovers hurting like this when we were twenty-five."

"They didn't."

"This island—it does this to you. The only Angelians that don't drink themselves to death are the ones that walk that Puritan walk with the straight back and the family Bible clutched to their proud bosom."

"Believe me, you can drink like this anywhere," he said. "Only the scenery's not as nice. I always prefer my beer with a view." He got up slowly and took her empty can into the kitchen.

She followed him inside. When he was at the refrigerator her arms came around his waist. "There are lots of good remedies for a hangover," she said as she undid his belt buckle. "See if this helps."

Floor sex, with a hangover. Cool linoleum. Filthy baseboards. Hardened pasta and a dried-up lemon wedge in the small space between the refrigerator and the counter. They sucked, licked, pulled, tugged at each other within inches of large black ants preoccupied with the transportation of food crumbs. It alleviated the headache, but was hard on the knees and elbows. Anne, astride, spread her arms out for purchase, one hand holding a stool leg, the other the refrigerator handle. Sweat ran down her breastbone, which he gently thumbed across her nipples.

For a long time afterward he lay motionless on his back, her head on his chest. The frosted glass bowl covering the ceiling light was littered with black spots: dead flies.

Finally she lifted her head up off his chest. "I always admired you for leaving, going out into the great big unknown."

"It's just a mall out there now."

"I was going to leave. Finally, after all these years." Looking at her he realized he'd been carrying the image of her profile in his mind all these years, and he was shot through with amazement that it was now right here with him. He had forgotten, though, how her gaze often suggested that she was conjuring up some horrid invisible abyss. "I guess that's why I fell for Eliot again. He offered an out: one fucking winter off this island."

"I thought he came up from Florida pretty broke."

"When you lose money like that, you're never really broke. He'd been salting some away—a winter sailing the Caribbean was his idea of a rainy day."

"This is my idea of a rainy day," Mark said, "returning to Angel's Head—broke, no job."

"When he showed up here I thought—I swear to God—I thought he'd changed. He was humbled. He was injured. The kindness and generosity appeared real. They should have been a tip-off. Then I started to see the cracks in the veneer. He hadn't really changed. He was a man who had to destroy what he couldn't have."

"What do you mean?" He took her hand.

Anne looked at him, her eyes suddenly fierce. "There's a deep connection between anger and fear—and regret. At first when Eliot came back, I thought—" She looked away and shook her head.

"He was going to help build a bridge," Mark said. "This time you were unified, you and all the islanders who saw that the bridge was now essential."

"I thought so too, at first." She was squeezing his hand, as though afraid to let go. "We were going to head south in the boat for the winter, then come back next spring and get to work." Her grip was becoming painfully tight. "Christ, that boat! He shows up in a fucking *schooner!* But that was always the thing about Eliot: he could offer that life—all those things that seem out of reach. I mean, all these years I've been cooking for tourists, taking their orders, listening to their complaints, and *smiling* through it all. Eliot could take me away from all *that*, but I had to *pay*." She turned back to him, angry now. "He asked too much, Mark. And I—" She paused, took a deep breath. "There were too many contradictions: he kept talking about the past."

"The lure of the past—it's powerful bait. I know."

"You and Eliot, both drawn by what might have been. I wanted to leave for what might be. The lure of the future."

"Who would gut him like a fish?"

She let go of his hand. "It could be any islander," she said, getting up off the floor. "Don't you see the perfection of it?"

"Yes, but the heart—in the shed."

"Someone with a sense of history—Flood history."

"It was an offering?"

"Maybe." Anne stood above him, naked, strong, still angry. She turned and walked into the bedroom and lay down on the bed.

"A warning?" Mark said, standing up. "Perhaps it was a means of protection?" He went in and sat on the bed. Anne placed her hand on his chest and twirled his hair in her fingers. "Or it was meant to look that way."

"Who'll protect me, Mark?"

He lay down beside her, and drew her to him.

She kissed him gently. "You may love me. We may love each other." She looked at him with steady, blue eyes. "But I will always protect myself."

Twenty

THE GROUP FROM BOSTON WAS PUTTING LUGGAGE IN THE
Seraphim, and when Emerson arrived at the dock they stared at him as
though he were some hired man in deep shit. None of them appeared
comfortable being outdoors. A slight breeze now came across the bay and
the women kept touching their hair with their hands. One of the men—an
anchorman for a Boston station—stood in the stern of the boat, holding a
bright red valise against his chest. His hair was absolutely silver. Emerson
put his hands on his hips: someone was speaking to him, but he didn't pay
attention. He kept staring toward the end of the dock. Usually they kept a
skiff tied up, a small aluminum hull with a Johnson engine. Rachel used it,
to ferry people out to their moored boats. He scanned the boats in the
cove, but the skiff was nowhere in sight.

"That was the understanding we had with the constable," one of the
men was saying.

Emerson stepped down into the *Seraphim,* took the valise from the
anchorman, and placed it on the dock.

"Didn't you hear what we just said?" the anchorman intoned.

Emerson picked up two pieces of luggage at a time and set them up on
the dock until they were all lined up in a row. "Get out," he said quietly, as
he untied the stern line from the dock cleat. He walked around the anchorman, took his keys from his pocket, and started the inboard engine, which
sent a blue cloud of marine oil up from the stern. He made his way forward
and untied the bow line. Still holding on to the dock, he looked at the
anchorman and said loudly, "Get off my boat." They all began talking, but
one of them lent a hand as the anchorman climbed out. Emerson returned
to the wheel, put the engine in gear, and slowly pulled away from the
dock.

Mark awoke first and he watched Anne sleeping beside him, remembering how in the midst of all the litigation over the bridge she had quite suddenly taken him up. One night in the bar at the inn she simply said to him "Wait for me after last call." That night he stayed with her at the inn.

In the morning they learned that Dorothea Cross had died. For a woman who had not been seen in public in years, her passing came as a remarkable shock to the island. Her absence in life had been a kind of presence; there was the feeling that she was somehow watching over Angel's Head. Providing the deeds to Blacke's Channel was proof that though she had withdrawn from island life, she had not abandoned it.

That Dorothea Cross bequeathed the deeds to Blacke's Channel to Randall Flood came as no real surprise. Dorothea and Samuel had led their separate lives for years. They had no children. Randall, the eldest male cousin, represented the next generation. There appeared to be a kind of justice to it. A blood logic. With Dorothea gone, Randall was elevated to something of a champion to the islanders. However, it resulted in vehement arguments among the Floods: Randall likened Anne to a traitor, while she maintained that no one had any right to tell her what she could do, and with whom she could do it. The issue, she maintained, wasn't the bridge, wasn't Eliot Bedrosian; it was her freedom to do as she wished.

Bedrosian's lawyers countered the deeds with the possibility of the state taking over Plummer's Marsh and Blacke's Channel by eminent domain. The pitch of the islanders' response was remarkable, for in a time when the United States was watching its troops being airlifted out of Saigon, residents of Angel's Head were promising to go to war if the government dared take over the privately owned Blacke's Channel. There was talk of sabotage, of bombings of state and federal institutions, of calling to arms the militia—which some local historians went to great pains to prove was still an official entity on Angel's Head, dating back to before the Revolution. Men marched on the village green in buckskin, tricorn hats, with shouldered muskets. An independence society was formed, proposing that Angel's Head secede from Massachusetts—and overtures were promptly received from Maine, New Hampshire, and Vermont. A more extreme group argued for nothing short of secession from the United States. An Angel's Head national flag was created, the original stitched by Aunt Mae. A national anthem was written. The national fish was the dogfish; the national bird the greenhead fly. Despite the hyperbole, or perhaps because of it, tourism was good. Strange times: the islanders' anger increased in direct proportion to sales. Now, in the early nineties, many of these same islanders' anger had turned to desperation and fear; it had become a question of what they were willing to do to obtain a bridge.

Anne rolled onto her back, with her arms over her head. Her breathing was deep, even; her face had lost its tension. He wanted to stay absolutely still and watch her sleep. There was little else he could imagine needing. The notion of going on from here distressed him. That was the difference between watching her sleep back then and now. He used to look forward; now he simply wanted time to stop.

Her eyelids fluttered, and though she didn't open them he knew she was awake. She said, "I'm still amazed that you came back this summer."

"I had no choice but to come back," he said. "There was nothing left out there. I wasn't lost, I was in exile."

"I know," she said. She opened her eyes and looked at him. "You start to believe that somehow you're living the wrong life, that there's a place where you belong, with the people you belong to."

"While you were sleeping I was thinking that I'm afraid in a way I've never been before. It's not just that I have no money, no job, and all that; it's that I don't know how to move forward. I feel suspended between the past and the future. We were such a generation of now fanatics. Do it now. For the first time in my life I've arrived at now, and it scares the shit out of me."

"When we were younger I didn't think of you as having much fear."

"I must have been better at hiding it."

"The trick isn't hiding it," she said. "No, the real trick is understanding the source of your fear."

Emerson had circled the island slowly but he saw nothing. When he returned to the jetties, he debated going into the cove and contacting the Coast Guard—the *Seraphim's* radio was down and he was waiting for a shipment of parts. He felt panic running cold beneath his skin. There had been two murders on the island and his granddaughter was missing. But she often took the skiff out on the bay. He was jumping to conclusions—she was fifteen and she had discovered boys. They probably just went fishing.

He saw the *Angel Gabriel* coming back from Chatham; Cyrus was up on the bridge. He pulled alongside and put the engine in neutral.

"You take those TV people back to the mainland?"

"Yep," Cy said.

"You haven't seen Rachel?"

"No. Why?"

"I think she's out with a boy in a skiff."

The two boats bobbed up and down near each other. From his elevated perch up on the flying bridge, Cy gazed across the bay toward The Narrows and Simpson Island. "You hear about the storm?" Their boats were drifting farther apart and he needed to shout. "Weather bureau's upgraded it. She's going to really blow tonight." Cyrus said something else but the boats were too far apart now for Emerson to hear.

It was a big bay. Coves, tidal creeks, islands, the kids could be anywhere. The wind was out of the southeast and the tide was nearly full. Emerson headed north.

The Johnson on the skiff wouldn't start. During the night they had gotten halfway across Pleasant Bay when it conked out. The wind and tide had pushed them far into the northern reaches of the bay, until they landed on the backside of Nauset. They'd slept in the dunes until midmorning, untroubled by their predicament; but now it had begun to rain, and Eric sat on the stern bench, rubbing his right shoulder. He must have pulled the cord dozens of times, but the Johnson gave nothing more than a weak cough.

"This one's always trouble," Rachel said. "Even Grapes can't quite figure it out." She had been standing waist-deep in the water, holding on to the gunwale so the skiff wouldn't drift into the nearby cordgrass. It was *Spartina alterna flora*, Eric had told her, the grass of the lower marsh which is usually covered by salt water at high tide—as opposed to *Spartina patens*, which covers the higher salt meadows and is only submerged during the abnormally high tide often brought on by storms. She had appreciated his knowledge, but now it seemed pretty useless, and she let go of the skiff and began walking back toward shore, careful not to step on shells or crabs.

"We could row down to the Rescue Station," Eric said.

"Be my guest."

"Well, it might be wise to wait for the tide to turn."

When she reached dry sand she sat down heavily, resting her arms on her knees. Eric threw out the anchor again, tugged the line till it took hold; then he jumped over the side and began wading in to the beach.

"You look like you're having second thoughts," he said.

"About running away, maybe."

"Last night you suddenly thought it was so important that we get to this Eddie guy. And now look."

"I know." She sighed and got to her feet. "It's just that I'm hungry."

"Me too. How far is it down to the Rescue Station?"

"Three, maybe four miles." She squinted up at the rain coming in off the ocean, then began walking south.

Twenty-one

MARK SAT OUT IN THE LIVING ROOM WHILE ANNE CONTINUED to sleep. The air had become tropical, and a heavy rain pelted the roof. He wore only a pair of cutoff sweat pants and sipped bottled water. Occasionally he poured some in his hair and let it run down his back.

The floor quivered as two sets of footsteps climbed to the apartment. He went to the door and saw Page and McNeil through the screen. Water ran off their hat rims. Mark opened the screen door and they came inside, removing their raingear. As with their first visit, Page sat on the sofa, while McNeil leaned back in the old rocking chair. Mark rested a haunch on the windowsill, where he could feel cool rain coming through the screen. Folding his arms, he glanced at the bedroom door.

"You told us you returned recently from Michigan," Page said.

"That's right."

"But you don't remember the exact date you got here."

"Your real question is, 'Did I return to Angel's Head before Eliot Bedrosian was killed?' Right?"

McNeil grinned and nodded his head. "Right."

Page's expression didn't change, until they all heard a sound—the creaking of floorboards—coming from the bedroom. He turned around and McNeil stood up as Anne came out into the living room, wearing Mark's green terrycloth bathrobe. She was still half asleep, her eyes puffy and red, and she stared at the policemen in anger.

"Isn't this something," McNeil said, "we were just looking for you at the inn."

"I'll bet." She went into the bathroom and closed the door.

McNeil sat down again, took a pack of gum from his shirt pocket and offered it to Mark, who shook his head. McNeil unwrapped a piece of gum for himself, and as he started to chew the room smelled of licorice.

"Black Jack?" Mark said.

"Mm-hm."

"I thought they stopped making that stuff years ago."

"They did," McNeil said. "Now they only make a small batch every few years—you know, sort of a novelty or nostalgia thing. Lemme tell you, it's made in Mexico, and it's harder to get than some of your choicest imported substances." He leaned forward and whispered. "But I got a stash— go on, take a piece."

"Thanks." Mark took the stick of gum, feeling he'd somehow entered into a vague and unwise commitment, and placing it on the windowsill beside him, he said, "Maybe later."

Glancing toward Page, Mark could tell he was upset. This was a man who required attention, who needed to be in control during an interrogation, and, Mark suspected, his loose, jovial partner delighted in causing diversions.

In the bathroom the toilet flushed, water ran in the sink, and then Anne came out, looking considerably more alert than a few minutes earlier. She stared at the three of them with open disdain, then went into the kitchenette. "Would you like something to drink?" she asked as she opened the refrigerator. "There's instant coffee, orange juice, ice water, and beer." McNeil shook his head, but Page merely stared at her. "Fine," she said. "This inn's closed." She took out a bottle of beer and twisted off the cap.

"There was quite an exodus from your inn this morning," McNeil said.

"It's amazing what a little bad publicity will do to tourism." She drank some beer and leaned against the refrigerator door. "I'll probably have to lay off some of the help."

"Is that what these two deaths are," Page asked, "bad publicity?"

"The way it's affecting the livelihood of the islanders, you can hardly suspect one of us, can you?" she said. "I mean, don't you have to establish a motive? If we don't book every room at the inn between now and the middle of October, we're going to have a very hard time getting through the winter. And I don't know if I can squeeze another loan out of the bank."

"Would you ever consider selling the inn?" Page asked.

"Are you making me an offer?" Anne drank some beer. She seemed to be getting brighter by the moment, and Mark wondered what she'd taken. "I have turned down all offers so far."

"So far," Page repeated. He paused, as if to indicate that it was time to change the subject. "You told us several days ago that you had a close relationship with Bedrosian when he lived here some years ago. We've since learned that you also had a close relationship with Mr. Emmons here—which still seems to be, shall we say, viable?"

"I suspect—" Anne left the kitchenette, came out into the living room, sat on the sofa and crossed her legs. "I suspect, Mr. Page, that you missed the seventies. Probably the sixties as well. You were at some police academy, learning how to dust for fingerprints." Suddenly she turned toward McNeil. "But you were in the thick of it. You worked undercover and busted kids dealing a lid of dope."

"Amen," McNeil said. "Sweetest job I ever had."

"I'm sure," she added. "We used to have these narcs come down here and work on the island for the summer. They'd have beards and long hair. They'd smoke grass with the kids. They'd ball the girls out in the sand dunes, and then toward the end of the season, they'd disappear without giving notice. A few days later Ray Snow and some Feds would go around the island arresting kids. It used to make people what we called paranoid."

"Your point?" Page asked.

"My point. My point is that to ask me if I had a 'close relationship' with Eliot Bedrosian and 'Mr. Emmons here' years ago misses the point. One, we didn't call them 'relationships' yet. And, two, whatever it was that we did to each other—we were often doing it with more than one person at a time. In short, we fucked around. A *lot*. We *all* did it. It used to be *fun*."

McNeil was grinning broadly, nodding his head as though to music. Page carefully placed his elbow on the armrest at his end of the sofa, and turned his head a few degrees in Anne's direction.

Mark took the stick of Black Jack off the windowsill, removed the wrappers, and began working the gum hard. When the taste of licorice burst in his mouth, he was reminded of DeFazio's, the corner store at the end of his street in Belmont, where he and his friends spent summer afternoons trading baseball cards. He wondered how such a childhood could lead to these present circumstances. Something was lacking, something he failed to understand at an early age allowed him to end up here at this very uncomfortable moment in a small, hot living room. He suspected that it was The Trade: he had given up his Roger Maris for a Pumpsie Green and a Frank Malzone, and later that season Maris broke Babe Ruth's home run record.

Anne was watching him as though she were sharing his vision, and her eyes were wide with awe. Whatever pills she'd taken had kicked in, giving her pupils a marvelous innocent light.

"Might I ask to confirm," Page said and cleared his throat, "if your present familiarity with Mr. Emmons is connected to some past association?"

"Yes."

"And did they know about each other?" Page asked. "Emmons and Bedrosian?"

She nodded her head.

"Of course we did," Mark said angrily.

"I see," Page said.

"I doubt it," Mark said. "I seriously doubt it."

Page leaned forward. "And you were good friends with Randall?"

This was like coming about; the wind forced you to move to the other side of the boat and everything leaned the other way. But there was always some warning—whoever was handling the tiller would say *Prepare to come about.* Here there was no warning and Mark felt himself caught off balance. He'd done it to people he'd interviewed, asked the question that suddenly made them sweat. Page was building toward something. "We are still good friends," Mark said.

"Yes," Page said, "you have a lot in common."

"We're both fools: we love the Red Sox."

"And you both hated Eliot Bedrosian."

"My feelings about Eliot are a little more complicated than that."

Page looked at Anne now. "We've been gathering evidence, and some of it belongs to your brother."

"For instance?" Anne asked.

"The murder weapons."

"Weapons?" Mark said.

McNeil said, "He was opened up with a fishing knife and a pair of cable cutters."

"Cable cutters?" Mark said.

"The ribs," McNeil said. He chewed his gum slowly for a moment. "Our divers found cable cutters in the cove, under *Northern Lady.* They probably were on the boat—that's not an unusual tool to have aboard a seagoing vessel. The lab found traces of blood in the wood-grained handle of the knife—"

"Whose knife?" Anne asked.

"Your brother's."

"And the blood?"

"It matched Bedrosian's."

164

"You sure it wasn't fish blood?" Mark asked.

McNeil smiled. "We're sure."

"So," Mark said, "that doesn't prove it was Randall."

Neither detective spoke for a moment. Then Page said, "No, it doesn't."

Anne got up from the sofa, knocking the empty beer bottle over with her foot, and went back into the bedroom, closing the door behind her. None of the men moved except McNeil, who continued to rock slightly in his chair.

"As to my original question," Page said finally. "About whether you were here on the island when Eliot Bedrosian was murdered."

"Like I said, I don't remember the date I arrived—" Mark took the black wad of gum out of his mouth; he carefully enfolded it in the wrapper, which he then flicked toward the trash barrel in the kitchenette. He missed. "But yes, I'd been back on the island about two weeks before Bedrosian was killed."

Twenty-two

FOR OVER AN HOUR EMERSON HAD SLOWLY CRUISED THE shallows of the northern reaches of Pleasant Bay. He had seen no one except two fishermen, who said they had seen nothing. He continued to run north along the back side of Nauset, scanning the dunes beneath an overcast sky. He was soaked to the skin by the rain, and the wind was now gusting to at least forty knots.

Finally, he spotted the skiff anchored in close to the marsh. He took the *Seraphim* in as far as he could and dropped anchor. Climbing over the side he waded about a hundred yards to the skiff; she was standing in less than a foot of water. There was no sign of Rachel or Eric. Emerson took the bow line and began to pull the skiff toward deeper water. The aluminum hull dragged and scraped across the bottom and his progress was slow, compounded by the fact that pulling such weight made him sink up to his ankles in the muck. His legs weren't what they used to be. It took a long time to reach water deep enough for the skiff to float. He climbed in, lowered the Johnson's prop, and tried to start the engine. He got nothing after maybe a dozen pulls, and he was not surprised—this engine had been giving him fits all summer. Using the oars, he rowed the rest of the way, and tied the skiff to the stern cleat on the launch.

Back at the helm of the *Seraphim,* he scanned Nauset again. The thought of wading in once more, coupled with the recalcitrant Johnson, made him angry, something he rarely felt toward his granddaughter. She'd been gone overnight—apparently with a boy. Emerson wondered if he was missing something, if there was a reason that she should be so angry herself that the only way to communicate it was through such behavior. He could accept the fact that she was becoming a young woman, and he knew from raising two children himself that at her age her actions would often be baffling to say the least—both to herself and to him. But this was something intentional. Conscious. She was doing this not just to herself—she was doing it to someone. To him? To her mother? He just didn't know, and he stared out at the water he didn't want to cross again.

"And what if I find them?" he said aloud. "What if I wade in there and find them in the dunes, naked and doing you know *what*? I am *not* your mother!" he shouted. "I am *not* your father!"

Emerson reached under the steering console and unclipped the air horn. He held it high over his head, pulled the trigger, releasing an ear-piercing bleat into the air. The sound of the horn seemed to disintegrate in the vastness of the bay.

The rain was coming in hard off the Atlantic. At the top of one dune Eric shouted something, but his voice was snatched away by the wind. Rachel gazed at the rubber bands connected to his braces, then she looked in the direction he was pointing. One gabled end of the Rescue Station was now visible above a distant dune. They continued on, leaning into the wind and rain, until they had reached the top of a dune that gave them enough elevation to see the entire Rescue Station. A large plane of water lay between the oceanside dunes and the Rescue Station.

"Oh my God!" Rachel shouted.

"What's happened?"

"It's broken through! The sea has broken through!" The waves rolled through the break in the first line of dunes above the beach and had formed a lake several hundred yards wide. The Rescue Station was almost perfectly centered in the plane of water. "The storm'll cut Nauset in half!" She screamed, but she could hardly hear herself.

They walked toward the Rescue Station. Rachel was shivering and the wind tore at her hair. When they reached the water, though, she waded in without breaking stride. The water was very cold, and they went deeper than their waists in some places. Occasionally a wave forced them to swim until their feet touched again. At one point Eric grabbed her arm and pointed that they should go back to the nearest dune, but Rachel continued on. The current was very strong, and she had to keep walking to the left, toward the open ocean, in order to make any headway down to the Rescue Station.

Emerson cruised south slowly, keeping close to Nauset, where there was some protection from the wind. He blew his air horn about every minute. From the flying bridge he could see out over the dunes, but the wind made it difficult to keep his eyes open, and his mouth tasted of salt. Though he tried to think of other things, he only seemed to recall other storms. There had been so many—hurricanes, blizzards, nor'easters. Sarah always anticipated storms by giving everyone orders. She'd cook up enormous amounts of extra food to be stored in jars and pots. She'd get out the kerosene lanterns and set someone to cleaning them thoroughly. Assigned to outdoor chores—securing the boats, bringing in extra firewood, closing shutters, sandbagging—Emerson was always soaked by the time the storm reached the island. Liquor was his reward. Sarah liked storms; she liked the fury of the elements, the immediacy, the heightened sense of survival. Anne was conceived during a January blizzard.

He saw so much of Sarah in Anne, it was frightening. Particularly in the way she dealt with Rachel. For long spells she was hard, aloof. She'd become so accustomed to giving orders around the inn that it seemed the only way she knew how to respond to the child. No wonder Rachel ran away. Anne, in her day, tried to do the same thing. She was always with some boy, and though she never really left the island, the drugs and alcohol created a distance he and Sarah could not cross. Rather than going out into the world, Anne went in, and as a result she became more lost. Rachel was lost and sought to be found. She was not searching for escape, but for discovery. She was looking for her father.

Anne would never say who Rachel's father was—no direct or indirect probing had worked. Emerson had often tried to calculate; there was Eliot Bedrosian, there was Mark Emmons, and there were God knows how many other boys. Boys she met in bars. Boys she went down to the beach with at night—more than once Emerson had seen her returning from the dunes at sunrise, wrapped in a blanket or sleeping bag. It was, he believed, something she was doing to them, himself and Sarah. After Randall's accident, however, after Eliot Bedrosian finally quit Angel's Head, Anne began to change, to settle in. She married Cyrus, and after Sarah's death, she took on the inn, she assumed the burden. After some years, she still occasionally saw other men, Emerson knew, but it wasn't something out in the open— it wasn't on public display. There was a sadness and resignation to these affairs, as there was in everything that Anne did. To dwell on it broke Emerson's heart.

Sarah, Rachel eyes every man as though he might be the one. Being raised without a father has left a blind side, which makes Rachel vulnerable. Which led her to this: running off in a skiff with a boy.

You can only watch over the child, you can't save her.

*My biggest fear is that I won't live long enough to see her acrost to the other side,
to the safety of adulthood.*

You fear that more than your own death?

Yes. I do not worry what it will be like, Sarah.

No, you shouldn't worry.

I will find you there.

I'm here, yes.

I do worry that I'll never complete my life—

This is one thing that is assured.

I mean its work; its worth, before it is finished.

Emerson, it all has worth. It is life.

When they reached the Rescue Station Rachel and Eric found the first
floor was flooded. The water in the long common room was knee-deep. It
was quite dark at first, but once Rachel's eyes adjusted she saw the crewmen, sitting on the stairs going up to the balcony. They stared at her,
looking cold, wet, and haunted. She didn't see Eddie among them.

"Where's Eddie?" she asked.

The men turned to each other, baffled—she might have spoken in a
foreign language—then, finally, one of them pointed upstairs.

"Maybe I'll wait here," Eric said.

"Why? You're afraid?"

Eric shook his head.

"There's *always* stories about Samuel's crew," she said. "Some islanders
love to tell them around the tourists. Make them think we're all a little
cracked."

Eric gazed up the stairs uncertainly.

"For a kid who knows so much about *Spartina flora,* you're pretty gull-
ible."

Rachel began wading toward the stairs, and after a moment she heard
Eric behind her. The crewmen parted for them as they climbed the stairs. A
couple of the men smiled now, one patted her on the back. But others
seemed confused, even distrustful. Without Samuel or Randall around, she
realized that she didn't feel absolutely secure herself.

"How did you get out here?" one of them asked when she reached the
top of the stairs. He was very overweight, bald, and he wore a faded Boston College sweatshirt with the hood up.

She smiled. "We swam."

He looked at her wet clothes but wouldn't smile back. He glanced at

Eric, then downstairs. "Just you two? You came alone?"

"'Fraid so," she said. "Disappointed, huh?"

Overhead the exposed roof timbers groaned and creaked. The sound of the wind and rain was deafening up here. "This place isn't going to make it. Have you called the Coast Guard or anything?"

"The radio's dead—it's hooked to an antenna on the roof that blew over. That was this morning, I think. Why do you want to see Eddie?"

"I came to talk to him."

"You're Randall's niece."

"Yes."

"You crossed the bay in this to talk to him?"

"Yes. What's your name?"

"Louis." He stuffed his hands under his armpits as though in an effort to contain them. He seemed to be thinking very hard; his brow wrinkled, forming a knot of flesh between his eyebrows. "All right," he said, "you can try." He led them across the quivering balcony and down a narrow hall, past several closed doors.

They entered the door at the end of the hall. Eddie was sitting by a window in a straight-back chair, staring out at the rain. He didn't seem to notice their presence. The room was bare except for a bed and an old bureau. He was unshaven and his eyes had a soft glow from the candlelight. He was an adult, a grown man, and Rachel wondered what it was about being a grown-up that allowed such total withdrawal. Her mother had once suggested that it had to do with the future, with losing any sense of having one. Rachel realized that she often thought about what was to come—tomorrow, next week, years from now. Without anything to look forward to, perhaps it was possible to reach this place where Eddie now sat. Louis pulled the hood back off his head. "He's been like this for a couple of days now—this is how he was when he first came out here. Wouldn't say or do anything. We were all upset after Samuel was killed. But Eddie, he was very bad."

"Why haven't you gotten help?" Eric asked.

Now Louis's eyes bulged fearfully. He took a deep breath and exhaled. "Some of us wanted to get him to the mainland, but others are afraid that if they see Eddie like this they'll take all of us off Nauset. We had been arguing more and more—then this storm hit."

Rachel stepped closer to Eddie. He was remarkably still, his hands folded in his lap. His eyes were pale blue; he blinked but he never looked away from the window.

"Eddie," she said. "I saw Samuel the night he was killed. He mentioned you. Why?"

Eddie blinked once.

"Before he was like this," Louis said, "he'd scream and cry—for hours. He often said something about it should have been him, not Samuel."

A wave crashed against the side of the Rescue Station, breaking the sliding glass door. The entire building shook, and they could hear furniture slamming into walls downstairs.

"We have to get out of here," Eric said.

Rachel nodded. Through the open door she could see down the hall: the other crewmen had moved up the steps, and were bunched together on the balcony. Several men shouted as another wave struck the station.

Twenty-three

AFTER THE TWO POLICEMEN LEFT, MARK WENT INTO THE BED-
room. Anne was standing in front of the bureau, rummaging through her
large leather handbag. There were already several plastic vials on the bureau; she took two more out of her bag, read the labels and put them
down. Her hands moved fast, as though she were clumsily performing a
magic trick.

"Can't find the right complement?"

She ignored him as she continued to search through her bag.

"In need of a downer, I presume." He picked up one of the vials and
read the label. "Christ, I can't even pronounce this."

"Mark."

"These cops walk in here and you pull *this?*" He slammed the vial
down on the bureau. "You don't think they could *see* what was happening
to you?"

"Fuck them."

"Right, Anne. *Fuck* everybody."

She found the vial she wanted, opened the lid and tapped out two
white pills. She popped them in her mouth and swallowed hard.

Mark picked up a handful of vials and threw them against the wall
above the bed. The caps flew off and red, blue, and white pills rained down
on the unmade sheets. "Those cops think your brother might have used a
pair of cable cutters on Bedrosian's ribs! They think that maybe I somehow
convinced or coerced him into doing it—and all you can do is *this!*"

Anne slapped him hard on the left cheek.

The pain rose up through his skin, spreading until the entire left side
of his face ached. He felt hot—and for a moment he felt the temptation to
raise his hand and slap her. But he realized that the pills insulated her from
such physical pain, and to hit back might only provide justification for

173

taking them. He said, "Last night at the shed—you remember *that?*"

"Yes, I remember that!"

"You were trying to tell me about your brother, about his injury."

"I thought you'd understand."

"You told me that Bedrosian didn't do it."

Anne took a step backward.

"You didn't finish," he said.

She went to the bed and began collecting pills; she might have been a child who has thrown a tantrum, only to find her favorite toys broken as a result.

"How, Anne? How do you know?"

"I just do!"

"You took his word for it?"

"What if I did?"

"No. You didn't need his word—you knew he didn't rip open Randall's head with an outboard prop—"

She threw the pills in her fist at him. They bounced and rolled on the hardwood floor. "You're going to tell me about the *past!*"she shouted. *"You?"* She smiled a moment, holding both hands on top of her head; then she raised her hands to the ceiling and let them fall to her sides. "You've spent all these years avoiding your life! You said so yourself! You don't *have* a past! You don't *want* a past! Pasts can be messy, they can be full of mistakes—errors in judgment. You just want today's news. Fresh copy—throw out the old papers!" She came around the bed, looking like she wanted to hit him again. "You come back here after all these years and the first thing, the first thing I want to get out in the open is the abortion. I didn't tell you until after it was done because it was *my* decision—*my* body. Have you heard of that? I thought I was sparing you, but instead when I tell you it's like 'how could you do this to me?' I didn't *do* it to *you!* And that was it, it was over between us after that, we both knew it. We tried but there wasn't a chance. You left, what, three, four months later?" She took a step closer to him. "You know *why* I have a daughter? Because having that abortion was the hardest decision I ever had to make. After Eliot, after you, I was all alone here on this island, and I got to the point where I needed to prove to myself that I could have a child. And you know who the father is?" She waited, staring into Mark's eyes. "It's no one. Her father's *nameless.* He was only a necessity—he was just a *tourist!* She's my *child!"*

"I understand why you had the abortion," Mark said quietly. "It's true I didn't understand fifteen years ago, Anne, and I'm sorry about that—

leaving you has been something I've been living with all these years. But what I don't understand is why did you almost kill your brother with a boat prop?"

She leaned back from him, as though she had been struck. "It wasn't on purpose—I didn't plan to do it. He provoked me and I got mad—"

"He provoked you?"

"To you Randall was a good drinking buddy, but he was always giving me a hard time. About the *bridge*. About *Eliot*. Don't you remember how we used to fight? That night he was diving in the cove I went out there in a skiff, to help him because it was getting dark. He started yelling at me, giving me orders—" Her eyes were large and moist, but they still held her anger and resentment. "I wanted to scare him. I wanted that prop to pass within *inches* of his face. I wanted him to *know* how much he was hurting me. But I didn't know I'd *hit* him. All I felt was the lurch forward as I turned the throttle on full. I took the skiff out of the cove and down the island to that house Eliot was renting overlooking Plummer's Marsh." Exhausted, she sat down on the bed. Gazing at her hands in her lap, she said, "About an hour later Emerson called—he was furious, accusing Eliot. I could hear him shouting through the phone. Eliot just listened. He didn't deny anything. He knew how much he was despised already—by so many islanders. All he wanted, all he really wanted at that point was to get off the island, and he wanted me to go along. Do you understand that about Eliot? He didn't say anything—there was nothing he could say—to convince my father, to convince Angel's Head." Tears fell on her hands as they worried the knot of the bathrobe. Still she wouldn't look up. "I couldn't leave then. I couldn't bear to tell the truth, but I couldn't leave, which I was desperate to do. So I stayed. I stayed and took care of all of them. The inn, Randall, my mother, who was never the same—I took care of all of it. That's really what my parents always wanted, but for me it became a form of penance."

There was nothing but the sound of the rain. Anne raised her head, stared up at Mark—then she looked toward the window and gasped. Mark turned around. Randall was standing outside the window screen. His hair was matted and rain streamed down his face. A small wet leaf clung to his cheek. He was watching his sister.

Mark went to the window and began to raise the screen. Randall backed up on the sloped roof.

"Wait," Mark said.

Randall climbed into the maple tree behind the garage and quickly descended to the ground. He ran across the yard, slipping on the wet grass.

"I've got to find him," Mark said.

Anne had lain down on the bed and pulled the sheet, dotted with pills, up to her chin—it made her body seem skeletal, mummified.

An enormous wave struck the side of the Rescue Station, and even Eddie responded to the tremors coming up through the floor. He looked at Louis, who was staring at Rachel.

"He'll walk?" she said to Louis.

"Eddie," Louis said loudly, "we've got to leave." He took Eddie by the arm and helped him out of his chair.

Rachel led them out to the balcony, where the rest of the crew stood with both hands on the banister as each new wave sent a shiver up through the floor joists. Overhead, the timbers appeared to sway. Pegged mortise and tenon joints groaned when a gust of wind hit the east wall. The wood crackled, like fireworks, and the balcony floor jounced freely beneath them.

Finally Rachel took Eric's hand, and they led the others down the stairs and into the water. They waded across the main room, down the corridor, toward the rear door. Inexplicably, Louis stopped and opened a closet door. Inside, lined up on hangers, were yellow rain slickers, and Eric and Rachel began pulling them out and throwing them to the others. Standing waist-deep in water made a rain slicker seem pointless. As Rachel pulled on the slicker she couldn't resist smiling at Eric. Dressed in brilliant yellow, the crew suddenly seemed festive. They gazed at her expectantly—she had gotten them this far.

She went to the rear door. The water was almost up to the old latch. The door was swollen in its jambs, and she had to pull hard to get it open. Outside there was nothing but water, wind-swept gray water from here to the nearest sand dune, about a hundred yards away.

They left the Rescue Station, walking single file. Eric was right behind Rachel and one hand held the bottom of her slicker. She thought of elephants in a circus. She thought of how her feet sank in the sand, how with the next step she might sink and sink, and continue to sink until she was below the cold water, below the sand, swallowed up in its darkness, squeezed to death by the unforgiving heaviness of sand.

Her slicker had a hood. She pulled it up over her head and tied the drawstring under her chin. With her ears covered, the roar of the wind seemed reduced, distant. Only her face was exposed—her hands were pulled up inside the long sleeves—and she turned her head away from the blast of the wind. Men behind her were shouting to one another, but she didn't look around. She kept her eyes on the sand dune ahead of them.

The water got deeper, and once she was over her head and had to kick and paddle. Eric was beside her now, doing a side-stroke. He grinned at her, and raised his face to the sky as though he were basking in the sun. To her right, Louis and Eddie bobbed up and down in water that was up to their shoulders. With one bob they'd move well ahead of her, and with the next they'd fall back even. Her arms grew tired—the long sleeves were stiff and made paddling difficult—and she began to swallow seawater, until hands were upon her, hoisting her up, and Louis carried her piggy-back. She coughed, and the seawater came up again, burning her throat and sinuses. Finally, resting her chin on Louis's shoulder, she closed her eyes.

Until she suddenly felt heavier. They were rising out of the water and she was becoming less buoyant. She opened her eyes and saw Eric walking in knee-deep water. Beyond him rose the steep slope of the sand dune. Rachel dropped her legs and began walking, but she held on to the back of Louis's slicker with both hands.

They came up out of the water and continued to climb the side of the sand dune. Walking was difficult, and frequently Rachel was crawling on her hands and knees. The sand was wet on top, but beneath it was dry and tended to give way, causing her to slide back down the slope. As they neared the top of the dune, the wind became even more fierce, pressing the slicker against her back and clutching her sides. It was difficult to move, and when she reached the top of the dune she was on all fours and out of breath.

Down the other side was easier. They were protected from the full force of the wind, though the rain still pelted their slickers. When they were all at the bottom of the dune, they stared at each other and out at the whitecaps. The rapid storm clouds seemed to be a product of the bay, as though the water had given angry birth to the clouds, and was unwilling or unable to let go, and thus remained connected by dramatic, sweeping black arcs of rain. *"I've never seen this!"* she shouted. *"I've never seen this!"*

Everyone was shivering; their lips trembled, their faces were rubbed raw. There was shouting. One of them pointed and they all looked toward Eric, who had fallen to his knees and begun digging frantically in the sand with his hands. The others followed suit—they all began digging holes in the side of the dune. Eric got down to dry sand, and continued until his hole was about three feet deep. He waved to Rachel, and indicated that he wanted her to sit down in the hole. She shook her head and continued with her digging. He shouted something she couldn't understand, but she went over and stepped down into the hole. When her legs were stretched out before her, he began to push the sand in over her. Louis helped. The sand was heavy on her legs. It was warm. She leaned back, spread her arms out and swept more sand over her, piling it up over her legs, her waist, her stomach, her chest. As her body disappeared, she got warmer.

Mark left his apartment and jogged toward the village. The wind was really up; trees and bushes were thrashing about wildly, and the streets looked barren—shopkeepers had pulled in outdoor displays, tables and chairs, awnings. Heavy gray clouds hung low over the village. A storm always made Angel's Head seem even smaller, more vulnerable.

He didn't see Randall.

Randall who had followed Anne to Mark's apartment. Who could disappear into the fabric of Angel's Head, like a flounder burrowed in the sand, only its eyes protruding. Who the police suspected of using a boning knife and cable cutters on Eliot Bedrosian.

They—Mark and Randall—were both murder suspects. It was an odd sensation: every moment of Mark's past could have been directed toward that sole criminal act. It could all add up. Once there was a motive, your actions could be interpreted differently. Page and McNeil had established a motive—jealousy. Probably the most common motive, new hot-blooded jealousy, old long-harbored jealousy, raging jealousy, a silent and cold jealousy. Everyone understands it; everyone is capable of it. Jealousy of person, property, reputation, fortune. What another has, what another has done. What you are not; what you might have been. The detectives had placed him at the scene, if you considered an island as small as Angel's Head a scene, and they thought that he and Randall shared something in common—a hatred of Eliot Bedrosian.

It had been years since Mark cleaned a fish, but it was something you never forgot—the way a sharp blade will part the flesh with remarkable ease, the softness of the organs in your hand. Cutting open a human being couldn't be much different. Everything would be larger, more substantial, warmer. And Samuel—he too was killed with a knife. Neither Page nor McNeil mentioned that.

Mark couldn't remember the last time he'd felt so alert, so clear—Randall used to call it a storm rush. A surge through your system, like a wave. Senses wide open, mind quick. It was another thing he only associated with life on the island. Everything was sharper. But not artificial, not drug induced, not even alcohol induced. Nature and the elements. Nor'easters, blizzards, hurricanes—they all created a natural rush. Years ago there had been another storm, a blizzard, which he always associated with the bridge business, with the end of the island as he knew it as a young man. The winter of '76 a blizzard was expected, and the bar at the inn was full. Many fishermen had come in to see this 43 pound halibut Lonnie Bradshaw had just caught; it lay out on display on a tub of ice, a pure white halibut, top to bottom. No one had ever seen one before, and the inn had bought it, with the intention of having it stuffed and mounted so it could be hung above the bar. Between the albino halibut and the coming blizzard, the room was in rare form. Mark had been sitting with Randall, Maxine, and Tom Shaw, the lawyer who was handling the litigation concerning the deeds to Blacke's Channel.

"Sand," Shaw said quietly.

"Sand?"

"Legal sand: this could go on forever." Shaw glanced across the crowded bar; islanders had things battened down tight by February, and they could pretty much have a drink, stare out the window, and watch the storm come in. "He understands it now." Shaw was facing Eliot Bedrosian's table in the corner, but Mark didn't turn around. They were all there in the bar— Emerson, who tended the bar then, Anne who waited on tables, while Cyrus was a dishwasher who periodically came into the bar in his soiled apron to replenish the stock. The bar that night was crowded but very quiet—a unique island trait: silence as the ultimate form of communion. "I could see it in Bedrosian's face in court today when the judge read his decision on Bedrosian's latest motion, not to consider eminent domain," Shaw continued. "A weariness, a glaze that sets in—it means a client is asking himself how long can this shit go on. He suddenly understands what the legal process really is—not the social construct that will promote justice, capital J, that will move inevitably toward the obvious conclusion that the client is right and deserves fair compensation, exoneration, acquittal, whatever—but some creaky mechanism that takes place in stale chambers, run by judges and bailiffs and clerks who are prone to narcolepsy." Tom Shaw studied his glass of bourbon a moment, as he rubbed the red spots on the side of his nose left by his glasses. "Today Eliot Bedrosian sat in that Barnstable courtroom and saw the sand. It was covering my legal pads, it was filling our coat pockets, it was drifting in the corners of the room, piling high against the wainscot there. When he got up during recess his feet sank in sand, and when he stood before the urinal his piss hit sand."

Mark was drinking boilermakers and snow struck the plate glass at an angle. The combination gave him a sense of abiding love that verged on the sloppy. He loved ice, he loved snow, he loved blizzards, and he was getting thoroughly lit. Hours passed in the bar. Darkness came on, the wind buffeted the inn, more people arrived—Randall and Max joined them. Villagers came by the table to chat, to buy rounds. Logs roared in the fireplace. There was a quiet sense of revelry, and every now and then Cyrus dumped another bucket of ice on this huge white fish in the middle of the room. Bedrosian remained through it all, sitting with a few supporters, a real estate agent, a pharmacist, the manager of the village five-and-dime—the island's commercial establishment, the Elect. Clearly, Angelians didn't know what was good for them.

Anne simply tended to business, waiting on tables—she had the uncanny ability to treat her lovers like ordinary customers. As the room got drunker—and became a cocoon of warmth and inebriation surrounded by the cold, howling blizzard—she seemed to conduct herself in a manner that was increasingly sober, methodical, efficient. Such normal behavior seemed remote, even surreal, in a tavern gone midwinter drunk.

It was quite late when Bedrosian came to Mark's table. Mark wondered if there was going to be some show of good sportsmanship, of reconciliation. He was hopeful, because unlike most islanders Mark still believed there was in Eliot Bedrosian a core of honor and fair play. That American fiber. Bedrosian stood above him without speaking; his silence wasn't the same as the islanders'; it provided neither comfort, nor companionship. Mark felt somehow responsible for this, Bedrosian's isolation: throughout the months of court hearings he'd avoided talking to Bedrosian except on an "official" basis; although he knew it was proper journalistic procedure, he always felt guilty about it, as though he were passing judgment before a verdict had been handed down by any court of law. You may be my friend until proven guilty. But they were never really friends. Acquaintances, yes—all year-round islanders were acquaintances. More than that: Mark had once stanched Eliot's blood. And they both loved the same woman. Women and blood—a strong, silent bond.

"You know the bridge would have been a good thing," Bedrosian said finally.

"No. I don't know that," Mark said.

"Well, you at least are smart enough to know it's inevitable."

"Is it?"

"It is—some day." He was purposely directing his attention toward Mark, excluding Shaw, Randall, and Max. "Just not in our lifetimes, maybe. But the *effects* of the bridge, *that's* inevitable. And you should know better."

"Why's that?"

"You're not an islander."

"True," Mark said. "That sounds like an accusation."

"A statement of fact. You're from the mainland, just like me. And you can see what anyone from the mainland can see: this island *needs* to be connected—it would improve their lot."

"You sound like some feudal lord who speaks lovingly of the welfare of his peasants."

Bedrosian's fist came down on the table, spilling Scotch and beer foam, and bringing a deeper silence to the room. "*Bullshit!* I see the need for the development—access to the mainland that would improve the quality of life!"

"What else do you see? Condominiums? Yachts in a snug harbor? Inflated land values? No," Mark said, "they seem to appreciate the 'quality of life' as it is."

"Who made *you* spokesman?" Bedrosian nearly shouted, pounding his fist on the table again. The room had become absolutely silent.

Randall pushed back his chair and slowly got to his feet. "We don't need a spokesman."

"You know what you're doing, don't you?"

Randall merely stared at him.

Bedrosian turned around and looked at Bradshaw's albino halibut. He picked up a steak knife from the nearest table and went to the tub. He swiftly jabbed the knife into the belly of the fish and worked the blade forward until its guts spilled out over the ice. "You know what you're doing?" he shouted. "You're making yourselves *extinct!* The way you live, isolated out here. It won't survive much longer! Unless it's *gutted*—" he picked up the fish organs and held them out—"*stuffed* and *mounted!*"

They all started to stand up. There was the scraping of chairs on the floor, the shuffle of winter boots. Practically everyone in the bar stood up, watching him in silence. Bedrosian stared around the room, his arm outstretched, then he slowly squeezed the fish guts, causing blood to run from between his fingers. The islanders didn't move; no one spoke. Bedrosian flung the organs down on the ice, went to the nearest door, and disappeared into the storm.

For minutes after he was gone, the islanders remained standing. As Mark looked about at their faces, he saw neither defiance nor victory. Their eyes told him that they knew Bedrosian was right.

Now Mark reached the cove, which was in turmoil. A long line of

181

tourists waited in the wind and rain to board the ferry—a sign said it would be the last ferry of the day. Boats were being hauled out of the water at the marina and the public landing. Larger vessels were heading out the jetties for more protected harbors. The Boat House was closed.

Mark started up the hill toward the inn. The dining room picture windows had been reinforced with masking tape—giant X's, as though marked for some pagan ritual.

Twenty-four

EMERSON SAW THEM—RACHEL, THE BOY, AND SAMUEL'S crew—growing out of the side of the dune like some yellow crop. Most of them were buried up to their armpits, but upon spotting the *Seraphim* they began to dig their way out of the sand.

Emerson began to maneuver the launch closer to the mouth of the inlet. With the most extreme high tides this creek was no more than twelve yards wide and always tricky to navigate, but now the mouth was three, maybe four times its most extreme width, and he was able to pull the *Seraphim* well up the channel. The water was so high he could bring the boat about without fear of grounding her keel.

The crew and the children came down to the water's edge, shouting and waving. Emerson dropped anchor, then got in the skiff and began bailing. It took some time—in tow, the aluminum hull was nearly swamped. When he rowed ashore, they all waded out to greet him.

"What happened?"

"The sea's broken through the outer beach!" Rachel shouted. "It was waist-deep in the station!"

"Inside?" Emerson looked toward the Rescue Station—he could only see a gabled end jutting above the dunes. "Not in my lifetime!"

It took three trips to get everyone on board the *Seraphim*. Emerson told the crew to go below and find clothing, anything that was dry. He and Rachel and Eric stood in the wheelhouse, staring out at the bay.

"Think it's too late to cross?" Rachel asked.

"I don't know. It was pretty rough, and I hugged the shoreline."

"This must be Samuel's doing." Rachel smiled at her grandfather.

"Yes, I thought of that," Emerson said. Since she was very young Rachel had always displayed an acute sense of the bay—its currents, tides, shoals, ledges, and marshes. She understood its spirit. "How bad do you think it'll get?" he asked her.

"You walk over that first dune, you're in seawater. And it's wide, Grapes, at least a quarter mile. It'll drive through to the bay somewhere overnight." Her hair was matted to her scalp; her face seemed larger. Emerson thought he could see the woman emerging in those delicate features.

He nodded. "And the storm hasn't even hit full yet." He turned toward the bay and watched the whitecaps for a while. The *Seraphim* was over forty years old but still tight. It was quite protected here in the inlet, but in a surge his anchors might not hold; they could be thrust out into the bay at night, during the height of the storm. "Better we try to cross while there's still daylight. Bay's going to be rough. You pilot—just keep her in the inlet until I haul up the anchor."

The inn seemed empty. Mark walked through the dim lobby and looked in the dining room. A young waiter stood at one of the taped picture windows, staring out at the bay through a pair of binoculars.

"Where's Emerson?" Mark asked.

The boy was startled and he put the binoculars down on the windowsill. He was a college boy, blond, strong, but he looked lost. The tag on his uniform read "Kevin." "Nobody knows where the Floods are—and a lot of the staff have left on the ferry!"

Mark grabbed Kevin by the arm. He was lean but muscular, and he glared at Mark in fear. "Do you want to get on the ferry?"

After a moment Kevin shook his head.

"All right then, I want you to go up to the last house on Orange Street." He paused until the boy nodded his head. "Anne Flood is in the apartment above the garage. Tell her to bring my aunt back to the inn with you." He let go of the kid's arm. "Now move."

Kevin looked relieved to have a clear sense of purpose as he left the dining room.

A waitress came in through the kitchen doors. She was also blond, and very tanned. She didn't have on a name tag.

"Hi."

"Hi there."

"Any news about Rachel?"

"What do you mean?"

"Emerson was looking for her this morning, and a couple of guests were looking for their son. They're still here somewhere—the only guests left except for those two policemen."

Mark stared down at the cove for a moment. "The *Seraphim* is out— any word from Emerson?"

She shook her head.

"How about Randall?"

She shook her head again. "People rarely see Randall." She ventured a smile. "The staff call them 'Randall Sightings.'"

"Sightings, that's good. What about Cyrus?"

"Took a charter full of those TV people to Chatham—because of the storm." She looked out the taped window toward the cove. "But he's back because the *Angel Gabriel's* tied up down at the pier."

"Tell me about the storm."

"We have the Coast Guard Station on the shortwave in the kitchen. No one's going out on the bay. The storm's coming in fast. It's not a hurricane, but it has hurricane-force winds. Is that possible? They're now saying it might be the storm of the century. But they always say that, don't they?"

"Usually," he said. "You don't have a name tag?"

"I'm Karen."

"Karen, the ferry's leaving soon."

"I know." She looked away from the cove.

"You can evacuate if you want."

"I work for the Floods," she said.

"I'm sure Anne Flood would say the same thing—in fact, she might demand that you leave the island."

Karen smiled. "You're Ms. Flood's 'guest.'"

"Word always did get around this inn fast."

She nodded, but then said, "No, I'm staying. It's just weird how so many are leaving. Those people down on the pier have been standing in line hours waiting. All the cooks have left. I'm making some soup, getting out the candles, oil lamps, flashlights, that sort of thing."

"Good."

"There's plenty to do."

"Right."

"I'll be in the kitchen."

"Keep an ear to that shortwave."

"Okay." She pushed through the swinging door to the kitchen.

Mark picked up the binoculars on the windowsill and scanned the bay. He could not see far beyond the jetties—gray, windswept chop crashing on the rocks—but from here he could take in a fair portion of Angel's Head, particularly the coastline running south. Everything on the island was moving, trees, bushes, marsh grass; some houses had plywood nailed over their picture windows. Down at Plummer's Marsh the tidal creeks had been flooded and wide expanses of the marsh were submerged, with only the tips of grass nodding above the water. He saw no boats.

Suddenly he lowered the binoculars and turned around; the dining room was empty, though all the tables were set with white linen and silverware. Everything looked formal yet hopeless. Aside from the wind and rain, the inn was silent. No voices of guests, no hustle of staff. This was what Anne feared. This was why she wanted a bridge.

"Ain't goin' ta hear from Emerson on no shortwave."

Cyrus's voice came from the darkness of the lobby. He entered the dining room, wearing a wet slicker, and he held a hammer in one hand. *"Seraphim's* radio's busted. Emerson's got it tore down in the Boat House and he's been waiting on parts to arrive." He crossed the dining room and stood before Mark. "You notice the bees?"

"The bees?"

"They're everywhere." Cyrus pulled a bottle of Scotch from his pocket. His slicker squeaked when he moved, and water dripped on the hardwood floor. "It's the wind—it's wrecking their hives. There's this family that was staying at the inn. They got in line for the ferry first thing this morning, and they got this boy, maybe ten years old, and he must have got stung by a bee. Right on the head somewhere, and I guess he's allergic, 'cause his skull was swelling up. His face was getting really red. And they don't know what to do! They don't want to leave their place in line to go look for Doc Walter, who's going to be God knows where on a day like this, but all morning their son's head's swelling up like it's about to *burst."* He took a long pull on the bottle of Scotch.

"Bees?"

"Fucking tourists, you know, are the stupidest people in the world."

"You're talking about the bees?"

"I'm talking about any damn thing I want—"

Mark turned back toward the windows and resumed scanning the bay.

"You know what I'm talking about." Cyrus drank more Scotch from the bottle, a considerable amount of Scotch in several deep gulps. "You ever wonder just how long 'not ever' is? Is it fifteen years? Nope. Longer than that, and you know that's a long time. Only thing longer than 'not ever' is 'not ever *again.'* It's a long time. So long, I almost forget how it feels. How's it feel, Emmons?"

"Shut up, Cyrus."

"She could be some fuck when she was drunk. But I sort of liked it when she was on those pills there. They'd tend to smooth her out so you could just do what you want." He paused a moment and inhaled slowly. "You know, *anything* you want."

Mark lowered the binoculars and turned to Cyrus, who held the bottle of Scotch in one hand and a hammer in the other.

"I know why you came back, Emmons."

"Do you?"

"You were running from your life."

"Least I had a life."

"Just like Bedrosian there."

"Only I didn't arrive on a schooner."

"But you came back for the same things."

"What things, Cyrus?"

"The inn."

"Not so."

"And the innkeeper."

"There was no plan. I'm not big on plans."

"You think you get one and you get the other. Like a package deal."

"That's not what you got," Mark said.

"You don't know what I got."

"You think the Floods owe you."

"I stayed, Emmons. You don't believe in debts being owed, rights being earned. Nothing owed, nothing earned. You just come out here and take— you're a mainlander." He drank more Scotch, then nodded. "The inn really went downhill after you and Bedrosian left—all the shit about the bridge."

"You're still against the bridge."

"When the choice is between progress and erosion, salt water people always opt for erosion. We understand rust. I happen to like it that way. It's the way it's been on this island for centuries. I'm against what a bridge would do to us. We wouldn't be any different than you mainlanders. We'd be just like these idiot tourists we get. People think they can come out here and escape, but you can't escape. She believed she could escape, sail away from it all."

"Cyrus—" Mark began.

"There's only one way off this island. Ask Bedrosian. Ask Samuel Cross. Only one way off this island."

Rachel's clothes were soaked through and she was trying to control the chills that shook her. Eric stood beside her, staring out at the bay with the intensity of a watchdog. Emerson was at the wheel now; he'd eased the *Seraphim* out into the bay, and she was running with the wind, so that the hull continually side-slipped and pitched forward and back erratically as swells moved beneath her from stern to bow. Rachel was reminded of a gyroscope teetering out of control. The hull shuddered with the slap of each wave. According to the compass, they were headed due west, but they could see no sign of Angel's Head or the mainland.

"So Rachel," Emerson said without looking toward her, "what exactly was this sojourn about?"

"Sojourn," she muttered for Eric's benefit. "When he's upset, he throws words like *sojourn* at you."

Emerson slapped the mahogany frame of the windshield. "I did *not* ask for *flippancy.*"

She said nothing. Something was locking up tight inside her chest.

"You took a skiff out without letting anyone know. And I assume you—the two of you—were gone all night." He turned his head slightly toward Eric. "Young man, your parents are extremely concerned."

After a moment, Eric said, "I know, sir."

"Rachel," Emerson said, "tell me *why.*"

"That outboard quit on us."

"I understand that—don't tell me what I know, child. Tell me why Nauset, *why* in the *middle* of the night?"

"It seemed urgent."

"Urgent?"

"I wanted to talk to Eddie."

"Eddie?"

Her grandfather leaned over to the hatch. Rachel looked in too: the crew sat on the bunks and stood in the galley; their arms were outstretched to brace themselves. Down there the waves hissed as they passed beneath the hull, the vibration of the diesel engine sent chatters throughout the cabin. Eddie sat by the galley sink, which contained a thick beige fluid.

"Eddie, we're all out in this," Emerson said, "because my granddaughter wanted to talk to you. Why is that?" Emerson had been dealing with seasick passengers for decades, but he'd never seen anyone as green as Eddie; and there was that remorse, that pleading in his staring eyes as though he would truly welcome being put out of his misery. "Come on, Eddie. Talk to me."

Eddie suddenly turned and leaned over the galley sink. The other crew members looked away like frightened children.

"All *right,*" Emerson said, straightening up and staring out the windshield again. "It'll have to wait till we make the island."

Twenty-five

WITH THE BINOCULARS MARK WATCHED BEN SNOW'S STATION wagon come down through the village. It wasn't what locals call islander driving—nothing over twenty miles an hour or higher than second gear, whichever comes first. This car moved swiftly, even fishtailing slightly as it swerved into the parking lot above the cove; then a tight one-eighty so it could back up to the pier. All the passengers were aboard the ferry, and Mark assumed that someone from the exclusive Cranberry Cove Estates had called upon the local constabulary to earn his stipend and get their house guests on the ferry at the last minute.

Ben got out of his car, then Kevin, the waiter Mark had sent after Anne and Aunt Mae. Doc Walter's car now entered the parking lot and pulled up next to the station wagon; he climbed out hastily and spoke to Ben—there was clearly an urgency in all their gestures, and at one point Ben appeared to be calling up to one of the crewmen on the ferry's deck. After a moment a couple of crewmen came down to the pier. Mark noticed someone sitting in the passenger seat of Doc Walter's car, but he couldn't see who it was through the reflection on the windshield. Ben opened the rear of the wagon, and he and the crewmen began easing a stretcher out onto the pier. There was movement on the ferry as tourists crowded in windows and came out on the deck to see. The body on the stretcher was covered with a gray wool blanket. Mark caught only a glimpse of the head, but because the crewmen blocked a clear view he couldn't tell if it was a man or a woman. Doc Walter accompanied the stretcher onto the ferry, and as soon as the gangplank was pulled in the ferry's lines were dropped and she moved slowly across the cove.

Mark put down the binoculars and rushed into the kitchen. He found a slicker on a peg, pulled it on, and went out the back door. The wind was so strong it pushed at his back, forcing him to run down the slippery path.

When he reached the pier, he saw that it was Aunt Mae sitting in Doc Walter's car.

"What happened?" Mark shouted into the wind.

Ben Snow said to Kevin, "Better drive Mae up to the inn."

The boy glanced at Mark, then climbed in behind the wheel of Doc Walter's car. Aunt Mae tapped on her window. Her eyes were bright, her cheeks flushed. She smiled at him, and he realized she was trying to be brave. For him—so that he would also be brave. The car pulled away and, standing upright, Mark suddenly felt lightheaded. His stomach was painfully hollow, and his knees weren't entirely firm. *"Anne?"* he heard himself ask.

"Let's get out of this!" Ben took Mark by the arm and they ran up to the Boat House porch. Cyrus was there, unlocking the door. His face was red—he also must have just run down from the inn—and his eyes had the focused hardness of someone whose worst expectations have finally been realized. He led them inside the Boat House.

"That boy you sent to your apartment," Ben said to Mark, "he found Anne in the bed—"

"Is she alive?" Cyrus asked.

"Barely. She's in a coma. Overdose: the kid found her surrounded by all these pills, he went to your aunt's house and they called me and Doc Walter. He pumped Anne's stomach—I've never seen such an assortment of pills."

"Do you think she'll live?" Cyrus demanded.

"I don't know," Ben said.

Cyrus walked over to the window and peered out at the harbor a moment. Turning to Mark, he said, "She was in your bed." His eyes grew large, as though he were just now hitting upon the solution to a nagging problem, and he came over to Mark. "What was she doing in your bed?"

"I think you can figure it out," Mark said.

"And after you were done with her—"

"Done with her?"

"You forced all those pills down her throat."

"But why would I do that, Cyrus?"

"Because she was in your bed!"

"You seem more upset about that than the fact that she's in a coma."

Cyrus's fist caught Mark on the left cheek, moving him backwards until he hit the glass display counter. Cyrus lunged for Mark and the glass broke under their weight and they fell amidst shards, fishing lures, hooks, reels, boning knives. They were locked in a bear hug with Cyrus on top. Their slickers squeaked loudly. There were voices—more people were in the Boat House now—and the door had been opened, allowing wind and rain inside. Mark hit Cyrus on the side of the face, only to feel a sharp piercing sensation in one of his knuckles.

They were quickly separated. Page and Ben managed to pull Cyrus off Mark. McNeil held Mark's arm tightly as he let him get to his feet. Page kicked the door closed, shutting out the wind and rain. Cyrus had a lure called a popper hooked into his cheek—a long blue and white plastic cylinder dangling hooks and feathers. He didn't seem to notice as he glared at Mark.

"It wasn't an attempted suicide," Ben said.

Now Cyrus tried to turn on Ben, and they shuffled about the creaking, hardwood floor as though doing some crude dance step.

Page found a fish sapper among the debris on the floor and raised it as if to hit Cyrus. "You know what this can do to cartilage and bone?"

Cyrus nodded his head and became still.

McNeil loosened his grip on Mark, though he continued to stand close behind him. "Someone made her take the pills?" Mark asked.

Ben nodded his head. "Doc Walter was certain that someone had forced those pills down her throat—there were bruises on her neck and jaw, and her lips were swollen."

Page came over to Mark. He still held the short, wooden bat, and it occurred to Mark that this man had eyes as flat and lifeless as some fish. "When we left your place," he said, "we both said 'She's on something.' What happened after we left?"

"We argued—"

There were quick footsteps out on the porch steps, then the door was thrust open. Randall ducked inside and stopped, startled to find anyone in the Boat House. He looked at Cyrus, then at Mark. He opened his mouth as if to speak, but his lower lip only trembled, as his face became more contorted with fear and inconsolable grief. His hands came up in a gesture of futility, then he quickly stepped outside, ran down the porch, and out into the storm.

The bay was getting rougher. Emerson was having difficulty keeping the bow from swinging off course. Dead ahead the water seemed to be exploding, shooting up around the wheelhouse windows and pouring down on the glass so that it was difficult to see. Looking toward the stern, Rachel saw a wave curl above the transom and swamp the deck. The boat lurched and heaved, and as she turned she was thrown forward, her forehead striking the windshield. She regained her balance and stared at the glass, stunned. She didn't realize glass could be that hard, that it would not just break. Then her knees buckled and she felt herself going down—while at the same time the deck of the wheelhouse seemed to rise swiftly. She was thrown to her right and she slammed into Emerson. As they both fell the hull leaned so hard to the starboard that cabinets burst open, spilling their contents of tools, fishing gear, and nautical charts.

Rachel opened her eyes and everything was moving. Emerson was lying on his side beneath the wheel. Something was missing—the vibration of the engine was not coming up through the deck. When he got to his feet, Emerson turned the ignition key. Nothing. He adjusted the choke and tried again: still nothing. A large wave struck the bow of the boat, throwing Rachel against the bulkhead. Pain shot through her shoulder and down her back. The boat was foundering, lying broadside to the chop.

Standing up she couldn't see Eric—then she saw him through the open hatch. The crew was holding him on a bunk. Beneath, the keel was groaning and cracking under the force of the sea.

They all followed Randall up to the inn—running uphill into the wind was slow and cumbersome in their raingear. McNeil took the lead, negotiating the muddy path with a fullback's low center of gravity. Mark followed close behind, and he could hear the others farther down the hill, slipping and cursing as they were buffeted by the gusting wind.

When they got inside the inn everything—the lobby, the dining room, the bar—was dark. They tried light switches, but the electricity was out. Looking down on the village, Mark could see that the entire island was cast in darkness. He followed the others into the bar, where McNeil turned and grabbed the front of his slicker.

"Why did he run?"

"I don't know!"

"You're protecting him." McNeil pushed Mark back against the end of the bar. "What happened in your apartment after we left?"

Mark looked down the bar. Page and Ben Snow were slumped on stools, still trying to catch their breath. Cyrus was behind the bar, holding a bottle of Scotch in his fist. He had removed the popper and his cheek was bleeding.

"You argued," McNeil said.

"Yes."

"Randall showed up," McNeil said. "You could see it in his eyes—he *knew* what happened to his sister."

"No." Mark pulled himself free of McNeil's firm grip, then unbuttoned his slicker. "I can't believe—Anne and I argued. About something that happened *years* ago—between *us*. About her pills—I threw them against the wall. That's why they were all over the place. And she told me that she had caused Randall's head injury, not Bedrosian. She had been carrying that guilt all these years, and then—" He looked down the bar again. The other men stared back in silence. "Randall was there, he was out on the roof. He heard what she said, and he ran off. He's always running off—he's a boy, don't you understand? He's scared and confused—"

Page came down to the end of the bar. He'd regained his breath. "We've got to find him," he said to his partner.

"I'll take the east wing. Snow," McNeil said, smiling slightly, "think you can keep these people here?" He and Page went out into the lobby and climbed the stairs.

Rachel stood at the wheel, waiting for the signal from Emerson, who was now lying on the stern deck, his head and arms lowered into the engine compartment. Eric had braced himself with outstretched arms and he stared out at the waves. The crew below were groaning, and there was the constant rattle and clang of loose gear. Emerson's arm finally came up out of the engine compartment. Rachel turned the ignition key. Nothing happened.

Twenty-six

THE INN WAS NOT UNLIKE A BOAT, ITS WALLS AND TIMBERS giving to the wind as a hull gives to the waves. The storm created a violent music throughout the inn, and beneath its melody rose a chorus of human invention: voices and the clatter of pots and pans coming from the kitchen. Mark was curious, and when he moved toward the swinging door, Ben Snow got off his stool. "Relax," Mark said, "I just want to see—" He pushed open the swinging door and was greeted by the smell of ham cooking.

Snow followed him into the kitchen, where Aunt Mae was giving orders to the few remaining staff members. There were several kerosene storm lanterns on the counters and tables, and when Aunt Mae looked up her cheeks were red with heat from the oven. In the dim yellow lamplight, Mark felt as though he'd stepped back into the nineteenth century.

There was also a couple in the kitchen, who Ben greeted as Mr. and Mrs. Grier. Their son was lost in the storm with Rachel. They appeared distraught yet grateful that Aunt Mae was keeping them occupied; they were helping to cut vegetables—broccoli, carrots, scallions. Mrs. Grier said to Mark, "Your aunt here has everyone working. It's the best thing to do in such a storm—work. And we've decided that the children are—" she glanced up at her husband.

"They're fine," Mr. Grier said enthusiastically. "They're holed up somewhere until the storm blows over. Probably having a real adventure—"

"Absolutely," Aunt Mae said. "This always happens with storms like this. People out on the water find shelter and wait it out. Then they come in when it starts clearing. Always excited. Always tired. Always hungry." She leaned over the stove again. "Here, Ben—grab a potholder and let's have a look at this ham."

Pleased with this duty, Ben obediently went to the oven door and donned a couple of potholder gloves. When he opened the oven, he said, "You think it's done?"

"Not yet, but it could use a good basting," Mae said as the Griers and the rest of the staff gathered around. Ben leaned over and reached into the stove, and they all sighed as though witnessing the birth of some unique creation. Only Mae was able to look upon the ham with a critical eye, and she announced, "Another hour and we can glaze it."

There was a shelf of canned goods next to Mark, and when he saw the cans of black olives he quickly jammed one into the pocket of his slicker; then he slipped out the door, crossed the lobby, and took the wide central staircase two steps at a time. The second floor was nearly pitch dark, the only light the faint glow coming from empty rooms with their doors open. Soft oblongs of pearl light. He walked slowly down the hall; the floor was carpeted and he could barely hear his own footsteps. He knew where Randall would most likely go—the roof—and he hoped to get there before Page and McNeil. When he reached the stairs at the end of the hall, he climbed up to the third floor, which was so dark he walked with his hands outstretched. And he listened: nothing but the wind and rain outside. Until he heard a sound, a carpet-muffled creak—it came from farther down the hall.

He walked toward the sound. In the pale light of an open door he saw movement as someone stepped into the room. He began to jog down the hall, until he hit a piece of furniture—probably one of the small antique tables that could be found throughout the inn—and fell to the carpet, clutching his right kneecap. The pain flooded his leg, but he realized that there was suddenly a cool breeze moving over him and he got up and limped into the room.

This was at the end of the wing, one of the large hexagonal rooms in the turret. There were bowed windows on all sides, and the one facing east was open, the curtains snapping in the wind. Mark went to the window and leaned out into the rain. He could see across the slate roof of the main building, its peaks and valleys, the row of brick chimneys. In the distance the whitecapped bay stretched beneath roiling clouds. It would be pitch dark within the hour. He saw something that startled him: a shoe—a deck shoe, sitting in the rain-filled gutter. Looking down to the ground, Mark also saw a pair of pants lying in the sand, and a tan shirt with epaulets was hanging on the fence that bordered the flagstone patio. It was as though Randall had disintegrated, flown apart and blown away like smoke. It was, he realized, what had happened to Randall's mind—the old Randall— years ago. But looking up toward the roof peak, he saw Randall, sitting with his back against the third chimney, his legs pulled up so his arms were wrapped around his knees.

He was naked. He sat motionless, beaten by the rain.

Mark heard footsteps coming up the stairs. He climbed out the window and clambered up the roof. The wet slate was very slick, and his tennis shoes squeaked as he moved along the peak. His right knee throbbed and his ankles ached from compensating for the pitch of the roof. When he was above the third chimney, he sat on the peak. Randall was about thirty feet below him; he stared straight ahead, and his skin looked extremely pale, raw and vulnerable next to slate and brick.

"Come inside, Randall," he said.

Randall lay his head back against the brick and gazed up into the sky. Below him and to the right Mark saw McNeil working his way out along the gutter; and Page stood in the turret window.

"You know what they think, don't you?" Mark threw his head back too and he closed his eyes against the rain. It felt good on his face. It seemed to renew his skin, fill up his pores. He felt unformed, embryonic. Yet it was Randall who was seated naked in the fetal position. "They think I made you do all this." Lowering his head he opened his eyes and saw that Randall was now staring at him. "They think I drove you to this."

"Anne cut my head," Randall said.

"I know."

"Everyone said it was Bedrosian."

"I know."

"He was going to take her away on the *Northern Lady*. Her and Rachel."

"I don't think that would have happened, Randall. Your sister had figured out that Bedrosian hadn't really changed. He was the same as when—" this seemed difficult to say, and he had no idea what it would mean to Randall, "when we were young."

Randall didn't react at all.

McNeil was now directly below the chimney and he was about to creep up the roof toward Randall. Mark raised his hand and McNeil kept still. Randall continued to stare up at Mark on the peak; he either didn't know or didn't care that McNeil was behind him.

"Bedrosian had to die," Randall said. "I thought about it. I thought about it a lot, you know. People think I'm stupid, but I'm not. I know there are things I don't remember. I know we were young, but it's like it didn't happen to me."

"I know."

"So I don't remember like they do. I knew what needed to be done and I thought about all sorts of ways to do it. I couldn't make up my mind." Randall grinned briefly at this. He repeated in a deep, demonic voice: "*I. Couldn't. Make. Up. My. Mind.*" He shook his head. "There was his boat, though. I knew it had to be on his boat. I thought a lot about how to get him out on a cruise and—I mean, people simply fall overboard and drown, you know."

"I know."

"But I love the ocean."

"I know."

Randall stood up. Naked and wet, his back against weathered brickwork. The human body was not built to endure the erosion of the elements. Its purpose was to house the intellect, the spirit of the individual. A brief time. An ephemeral life.

Emerson lay on the deck of the *Seraphim,* his hands pushing at the wires in the distributor cap.

It's here, Sarah, and I would welcome it if it weren't for the others, for the children.

I know.

This is no time for the children.

I know.

The inn will always survive such storms, but without Rachel what does it matter?

I know.

You lost hope and committed suicide. I have often thought to join you, but for Rachel. I can't bear this—both of us. I can accept anything else. But this child, she is our hope.

I know.

Perhaps there is no hope. Perhaps it doesn't matter?

Once more he raised his hand, and this time the diesel started up with a roar. Emerson got to his knees, slid the hatch back in place, then made his way forward to the wheelhouse.

Both Rachel and Eric were at the wheel, steering the boat west and out of the pounding beam sea. Emerson took over from them just as the vessel approached the back of a particularly large wave. The hull rose up on the swell, broke through the crest, then descended swiftly—causing cries of panic from the men below—then her prow dove under, sending plumes of water high in the air and raining down on the wheelhouse. She rose up on the back of the next wave, until she dropped over the crest and again crashed into white water.

Randall continued to stand with his back against the chimney, his nakedness pelted by rain, but his head now turned toward the bay.

"You *thought* about killing Bedrosian," Mark said. He nearly had to shout because of the wind. Randall looked up at him again. "You thought about it so hard maybe you've wondered if it wasn't you. Everyone's mind plays tricks on them. You wanted to but someone else did too. Maybe they read your mind? Maybe they saw the way you looked at Bedrosian, and they realized they could make it *look* like you had done it: gutting him, putting his heart in the shed where your mother died."

Randall shook his head. He turned around and stood to the side of the chimney. His shoulders were relaxed, his back firm and straight; it was the moment of poise before the high diver runs out to the edge of the board and leaps out into space.

McNeil began scrambling up the roof, but something changed and he stopped, his eyes on Randall's face. Slowly McNeil looked around and stared out at the bay.

And Mark saw it too. The *Seraphim* plowing through the whitecaps about a half mile out from the jetties. He scooted down the face of the roof, using his hands and feet, then stood next to Randall. He wanted to grab hold of him, push him back behind the chimney, but Randall's nakedness seemed untouchable. They watched the boat cross the bay. Finally, Mark took off his slicker and put it around Randall's shoulders. Thrusting his hands in a front pocket, Randall took out the can of black olives. Looking at the can, he said, "We could use an opener, Mark."

Twenty-seven

THE WINDOWS IN THE BAR WERE NOW SHUTTERED AND THE room was lit only by candles and kerosene lanterns. It seemed as though everyone left on the island had made their way to the inn. Mae Bough had taken charge of the kitchen, and the staff—the few who had not fled the island—served a ham dinner. Rachel sat with Emerson, Eric, and his parents; little was said while they ate. She wondered if she was in shock, yet she had never felt so clear and alert as she studied the people in the room: the two policeman; Maxine Bulikoff and the spare old woman everyone simply called Chastity; and Samuel's crew eating at a large round table at the center of the room. Cyrus moved swiftly behind the bar, filling orders. His cheek was bandaged and he avoided the far end of the bar, where Mark Emmons sat drinking beer. And Randall—Randall stood by Mark, gazing up at the ceiling beams as though he could decode the wind. So strange: just a few days ago the inn was overrun with tourists, creating the impression that it was the place to be; but now Rachel imagined that tonight's storm was the end of the world, and they were the last human beings to survive. The thought made her heart race.

Emerson didn't eat, he just drank. He considered the position of his glass and bottle of Scotch as though it were a difficult chess problem. Yet some obligation was being fulfilled as he managed to exchange occasional pleasantries with Eric's parents. Eric looked chastised, and he avoided Rachel's stare. Everyone seemed to be waiting—for the storm to end, for a phone call from the hospital in Hyannis.

When they had come up from the *Seraphim* they were told about her mother. At first Emerson wept, muttering "Not again." Then he began drinking, and that calmed him down. Rachel didn't react. No tears or hysteria. She was, in fact, quite hungry. Oddly, she never felt closer to her mother— she remembered sitting on her mother's balcony, her mother's arm about her. "Your life goes on," her mother had said. "It's all anyone can do." Rachel knew that she and this old inn would endure the storm, largely because of her mother's perseverance. Floods had endured here for generations, and that was all that mattered now.

She was not in shock.

She was a Flood.

When their dinner plates had been cleared, Emerson poured more wine into the Grier's glasses. "I've taken care of the bill for your stay," he said.

"That's not necessary," Hal Grier said.

"If these children hadn't run off like that, you would've been on the ferry this morning."

"It's a wonder no one was hurt," Ginny Grier said with quiet vehemence. She looked at Eric, then Rachel. "Whatever possessed you two to take that boat out in the middle of the night—" She stopped as her husband placed a hand on her wrist.

"We've already been through this," Hal said.

After a moment she removed her hand from her husband's grip, and said, "Eric, you do know better."

Emerson touched his fingers to his brow and, staring at his glass, said, "You're implying that my granddaughter doesn't know better?"

"My son knows better than to run off with the—"

Emerson picked up his glass, drank a fair portion of its contents, and then looked directly at the woman. "Yes?"

She was shaking now. She got up and started across the bar toward the lobby; then she stopped and glared back at the table, until Eric obediently rose from his chair. He turned to Rachel, his eyes full of fear—they seemed to plead with her to understand. He started to say something, then looked at his father. Lowering his eyes to the lantern in the center of the table, he said, "I'm sorry about running off like that. I guess it was a bad idea." He glanced at Rachel quickly, then excused himself, and followed his mother.

Hal stood up and opened his billfold.

"It's on the house," Emerson said.

Laying a ten-dollar bill on the table, he said, "For the waitress."

Emerson reached for the bottle of Scotch. "Better take a lantern with you."

Hal nodded and he picked up the lantern in the center of the table. "What this island needs is—"

"A bridge," Emerson said, "so people like you can get off quickly when a storm hits." He didn't raise his eyes, but only listened to Hal Grier follow his wife and son out into the lobby. In the near dark he poured some more Scotch, soaking the tablecloth.

"There was a reason, Grapes."

"I know. You told me: Eddie."

"You sound like you don't believe me."

"I've always believed you, Rachel—"

"This time you sound doubtful," she said quietly.

"Trust is everything, Rachel. You've always been able to trust me, haven't you? Running off with a boy, at your age, is not a terrible thing."

"It's not what you think."

"Isn't it? Just don't be in such a hurry. There will be plenty of boys. The boy may have just had the adventure of his life. I doubt he'll ever try anything like that again, even if he has a chance." Emerson picked up his glass, then put it down. "But this isn't really just about boys, is it?" Rachel shook her head. "One day you will probably leave this island, Rachel. But you have plenty of time. And remember this: once you leave, it will be very hard to return."

Rachel appeared to be stunned. She leaned back in her chair and closed her eyes. Her hand was on the table, pale, slender, graceful. Her mother's hand. Emerson placed his hand over hers, and as he squeezed he could feel the warmth of her fingers.

Mark had been watching Page and McNeil confer quietly throughout dinner, and now he wasn't surprised when they got up from their table and came to the bar. "Randall," Page said, "is there something you want to tell us about the night Bedrosian was killed?"

Randall shook his head.

Emerson came to the bar. "What're you saying?"

"When we were on the roof earlier," McNeil said, "I couldn't hear everything Randall said to Emmons, but he did say that Bedrosian had to die."

Emerson glanced at Randall, who stared at the floor.

Page continued, "Your daughter had plans to leave Angel's Head this fall, to sail south with Bedrosian on the *Northern Lady*. Randall learned about this, and he was upset. Extremely upset. He killed Bedrosian—possibly with some coercion from someone else who loved your daughter." He glanced at Mark.

Emerson said, "You think Randall went out to that schooner, cleaned that bastard, cut out his heart, and put it in the shed out back here?"

"As a gift," McNeil said. "For his sister. That shed has special significance to this family, right?"

"I think a jury will understand," Page added, "provided you help us out."

Randall continued to stare at the floor.

Mark said, "What does it matter if he knew Anne and Bedrosian were going to leave Angel's Head? That's not proof."

McNeil considered Randall, not without sympathy. "The lab has provided us with other evidence implicating you, Randall. The fishing knife used to kill Bedrosian—it was yours. We've found Bedrosian's blood type in the wood handle."

Page turned to Emerson. "Sir, we can't do anything until after this storm passes. But when it does, I suggest we all cross to the mainland. Get yourself a good lawyer. Have Randall make a statement. I have no doubt that—"

"Just Bedrosian?" Mark said. "What about Samuel Cross? Are you saying Randall killed him too?"

"We don't know for certain," Page said. "What about it, Randall? Didn't Samuel find out that you killed Bedrosian? Or maybe you told him. He's been so good to you, you and the crew out there at the Rescue Station. Weren't you confused and scared after what you did to Bedrosian, so you naturally told Samuel about it?" Randall shook his head slowly, but Page continued. He spoke slowly, with the patience of a salesman trying to explain some insurance policy. "And wasn't Samuel his usual understanding self? Didn't he suggest exactly what we're suggesting—that you tell them what happened. Didn't Samuel tell you that was the right thing to do, the honorable thing? Didn't he assure you that you wouldn't have to go to jail or anything, only see some doctors who might help you? Randall, anybody can understand how you felt about Bedrosian. For years you thought he had something to do with your accident—everybody on the island believed that, and the law has never been able to touch him—then he shows up here, in this big, beautiful schooner, and he threatens to take your sister and Rachel away."

Randall looked at Page and McNeil for the first time. He spoke slowly, uncertainly. "Bedrosian didn't hurt me."

"He didn't?" Page said.

"Who did?" Emerson said.

Randall stared at the floor again.

204

"You know. Tell me." Emerson leaned toward his son, looking as though he couldn't decide whether to hit him or embrace him.

Finally Mark said, "It was Anne. She told me today, and Randall overheard."

Emerson turned away from Randall, raised his fists and brought them down on the mahogany bar. He stared at his hands in disbelief, as though they had betrayed him, as though they had intentionally caused the pain that now swelled through them.

Rachel couldn't remember ever seeing her grandfather so angry. She felt responsible. For his anger. For her mother. She wondered if she wasn't in shock after all.

She got up from the table and walked over to Cyrus, who was now seated at the end of the bar. "You were in the shed that night," she said. "The night the heart was put there."

Cyrus had both hands wrapped around a bottle of beer. He might have been trying to conjure up spirits in its green glass. "What if I was?"

"How do you know that?" McNeil asked her. "You see him?"

Rachel shook her head. "But he was there."

Cyrus said, "I go in that shed every night."

"What time?" Page asked.

"Depends," Cyrus said.

"What time of night?"

"Fairly late. After closing."

"Why?" McNeil asked.

"Inventory. I go in there to check inventory."

"You see anything that night?" Page asked.

"You mean like a heart?"

"Yes, like a heart."

"No, I didn't. But I don't suppose that means for certain it wasn't there, does it?"

"No, it doesn't."

"I mean it could be overlooked," Cyrus said.

"Especially if the light isn't on," Rachel said.

Cyrus stared at her and once again she realized that what had always frightened her most was his lack of response. It always seemed to create the possibility of harm.

The phone rang. Emerson walked down to the end of the bar and answered it. Rachel watched his back as he held the receiver to his ear.

"Can you take inventory in the dark?" McNeil asked.

"Who says I didn't turn on the light?"

Neither detective spoke.

"Who says? Someone see me go in there in the dark?"

Page said, "Did you see him, Rachel?"

She shook her head. She hadn't taken her eyes off her grandfather's back. He was so still—his anger seemed to have become concentrated into absolute stillness.

"Perhaps it was Samuel?" Mark Emmons said to Cyrus. Rachel looked at this man. Her mother had been found comatose in his apartment. She wasn't really surprised. He looked like the kind of man her mother would want to fuck. "Perhaps he saw you and after the heart was found, he went to you and told you to turn yourself in. Page is right about Samuel—he wouldn't go to the authorities first. No, first he'd go to the offender. He believed that you would realize it was better to give yourself up."

Cyrus merely stared at Mark Emmons.

"That's why he was killed?" McNeil asked. "So he couldn't say he saw you go in the shed to take inventory with the light off?"

"We'll never know," Cyrus said. "Samuel's dead, so you'll never prove anything."

"Samuel didn't tell me," Rachel said.

They all turned to her. She went over to the table where the crew sat with Eddie. He seemed frightened, even guilty. "What did you see, Eddie?" she asked.

Eddie stared around the room, but finally he looked at Rachel, as if she could provide the one thing he needed to get through this ordeal. "I had worked with Randall, some boatwork over to the marina, and was going to stay with Randall for the night like I always do. Then we'd head back out to Nauset next day. When I was coming up the hill from the village I saw Cyrus ahead of me. He was carrying something in one hand, carrying it carefully. He went inside the shed—into the darkness. He didn't turn the light on. I didn't think much of it that night. But the next day when I saw Samuel I mentioned it. Samuel didn't seem to care—he was hungover. But after the heart was found, he asked me again. I was sure I saw Cyrus that night, and he didn't turn on the light when he entered the shed."

"When you told Samuel," Page asked, "what did he do?"

"He just said it was good that I told him. He understood that I—I was afraid. He said that I should never tell anyone, that he'd handle it."

"Even after he was killed?" McNeil asked. "You didn't tell?"

Eddie looked at Rachel. "I wanted to but—" He didn't finish.

She turned back to the bar. Mark Emmons watched her for a moment, then he said to Cyrus, "Samuel went to you, didn't he? He told you to go to the police yourself."

Cyrus got off his bar stool. "Doesn't prove nothing," he said, pulling on his slicker. "Doesn't prove nothing and you know it."

"Didn't he?" Mark said. "Didn't he do exactly what Page said: tell you it would be better to turn yourself in, to assume responsibility? And if you didn't, then he would go to the police. Wasn't he giving you a chance to redeem yourself?"

Cyrus buttoned the slicker up to his throat.

Emerson hung up the phone, turned around, and looked at them. There was the slightest lull in the wind outside, and suddenly the timbers and walls of the old inn were quiet. There came from the lobby the gentle, repetitious pat of dripping water.

Twenty-eight

MARK SAW IT IN CYRUS'S EYES. DEFIANCE—EVEN VICTORY. HE was right: Eddie seeing him go into the shed wasn't real proof that he'd killed Bedrosian. Then they both watched Emerson, who had hung up the phone and was coming down the bar.

"Anne's going to make it," Emerson said, speaking directly to Rachel. "They're going to keep her overnight, but she's going to be all right."

Mark turned to Cyrus again. Now there was something else in his eyes: sudden fear. Cornered fear. "She'll testify, Cyrus. You followed Randall out to my apartment, and after I left you went in and forced those pills down her throat—in my apartment. The police had just been there—they'd have to arrest me. She was probably half out of it already—hardly put up any resistance. You told me that's the way you like it, remember? She'll testify and you'll do time. Ever seen the inside of a jail? A real jail—a prison—not the little drunk tank Ben Snow's got."

Cyrus now appeared to swell with rage, and he moved toward Rachel without hesitation—and quickly he pulled his fishing knife from the sheath on his belt. The sight of the long blade seemed to freeze everyone. He reached out with his other hand and grabbed Rachel by the hair. She screamed as Cyrus pulled her to him. He placed the knife blade flat against the side of her cheek, and she became quiet.

"You think you can run me off this island?" he said.

"Cyrus," Mark said. "Just leave the girl alone."

"You can have it," he said. "All of it, bridge and all." He smiled suddenly, and for a moment the fist holding the knife beat against his breast. "Know what I have here?" He yanked on the girl's hair, making her wince. "The future. Not some plan to build a bridge. Not some old satchel of deeds. The future!"

Randall rushed toward them, and with one sweeping motion of his

209

arm Cyrus drew the blade across Randall's chest—his T-shirt split open and blood poured from the diagonal wound. Falling to one knee, Randall clutched his chest, but the blood kept coming, running out between his fingers, soaking his shirt, his pants, and pooling on the floor.

Cyrus laid the knife against Rachel's cheek again. The girl stood absolutely still now, staring at Mark, her eyes large and moist. Cyrus tugged on her hair, causing her to cry out, and began backing up toward the door. Using the hand that held the knife, he pushed down on the latch and shouldered the door open—the blast of wind lifted a pile of bar napkins into the air and they swirled down to the floor like snow. He pulled Rachel out into the storm and kicked the door shut.

Mark was the first to the door. He got it open and went out into the storm. He couldn't see twenty feet into the dark. McNeil came out behind him. Page was telling the others to stay inside.

Then the door was pulled shut and there were just the three of them standing in the wind and rain. Page and McNeil had guns drawn now, held before them, pointed at the sky. The rain was so hard their clothes had immediately collapsed against their skin.

"Wait inside with the others!" Page shouted.

Mark shook his head as he kept peering into the dark, looking for some sign of movement.

Page grabbed Mark's arm, but he yanked it loose. McNeil stepped between them and shouted, "All right! I'm going straight out!" Looking at Page, he said, "You work along the back of the inn that way, and you—"

Mark leaned close to Page, right up to his wet face, and shouted, "Can't you put those damned things away?"

"Go *back!*" Page shouted. "Go back *inside!*"

"*The hell I will!*"

Mark left the protection of the wall. With every step away from the inn the wind got stronger. He leaned forward and headed downhill, toward the cove. As he neared the shed, something flew out of the dark and struck him on the right shoulder. Looking down at the sand, he saw it was part of a roof shingle, jagged where it had been torn off by the wind. The shed had been stripped of most of its shingles, and the aluminum frame of a beach chair lay twisted against the door. Mark leaned against the side of the shed a moment to get out of the wind. He looked back toward the inn. Cyrus could be in there, hiding in any of the dark halls or empty rooms.

No. Like most islanders, Cyrus would be drawn to water. Just as he's drawn to the past. Rachel and the bridge—he called them the future. They're a threat to the past. Cyrus believes he's doing something necessary: protecting the past, just as water protects the island.

Mark stepped out from behind the shed and continued down the hill, shielding his eyes with his forearm. When he reached the bottom of the hill, he crossed the parking lot, its potholes filled with rainwater, and went up onto the porch of the Boat House. The door was open, creaking on a dry hinge. There was light coming from the workbench in the back room.

He stepped inside. Rain rattled against the roof like gravel. Floorboards groaned as he crossed the front room. He watched the door to the back room, looking for some movement, some shifting of shadows, but there was none. Stepping into the doorway, there was a loud clatter to his right. Turning, he saw a cat sitting on the workbench—it was licking its paw, which was stuck with a feathered lure. When Mark took a step toward it, the cat jumped to the floor and ran by him into the front room. The lure had come loose, lying on the workbench, blood covering the tip of the hook.

Mark looked at the workbench—strands of water glistened in the lamplight. *Cyrus.* The workbench was clear, all tools neatly hung on the pegboard above it, a mark of Emerson's Yankee habits. Mark studied the rows of pliers, screwdrivers, wrenches, hammers, wondering what Cyrus had been looking for. Some tool that could be used as a weapon? Why a weapon when he had a knife? When he had Rachel? Mark reached out and put his fingertips in the water. Under the lamplight his own hands were raw, the skin puckered, as though they'd been submerged. At the bottom of the pegboard was a row of keys. Boat keys, with worn plastic name tags above them: *Patsy M., Much Obliged, Irish Wake, Saline Solution.* Under the tag marked *Angel Gabriel,* the keys were missing.

Rachel's scalp ached but she would not cry. It was like someone was trying to peel the skin off her head. Cyrus had dragged her by the hair all the way down to the Boat House, then out to the pier, his knife still flat against her cheek. The pressure of the steel against her skin said *Not a sound, not one word.* And his knuckles in her hair felt like rocks. She could feel clumps of hair tear loose, leaving a searing pain in her scalp.

The *Angel Gabriel* rocked wildly in its berth. They climbed aboard and Cyrus forced Rachel down into the cabin, then shut and locked the hatch. It was dark and there was nothing but the motion of the boat, its lines straining, its rubber tires groaning against the pilings. She spread her arms out and braced herself against cabinets. Then the diesel turned over, sending a vibration up through the hull.

"Cyrus!" she shouted. "We can't go out in *this!*"

All she heard overhead was the sound of his footsteps, moving up to the bow, then back toward the stern. The gears engaged and she felt the boat slowly back out of the berth.

Moments later she heard a thump, up toward the bow. At first she thought it was just something loose on the deck, but when it was followed by several lighter thumps, she knew someone had jumped on the deck just as the *Angel Gabriel* had pulled away from the pier.

As the boat swung up into the wind Mark lay down on the deck, holding tightly to the chrome rail. The running lights came on, casting the deck in red and green, but then they were switched off, probably because they reduced Cyrus's visibility. The boat plowed through the chop, moving across the cove toward the jetties.

Mark pulled himself on his stomach along the port side of the cabin. Ahead of him he could see rain-swept decking, and looking astern across the cove he could see that the village was completely blacked out. Several boats had washed up on the shore and were leaning against each other or against shacks at the marina. The only boat still tethered to its mooring in the cove was the *Northern Lady.* One of her masts had been toppled by the gale.

Mark's progress along the deck was a matter of inches—waves repeatedly washed over him—but he continued to work his way back toward the wheelhouse. Then he heard a tapping on the porthole ahead of him. Pulling himself up to it he could barely see Rachel's face behind the glass. She opened the porthole.

"He's going out of the cove?" she said. "We'll never—"

"Shh!" Mark put one hand in the porthole and touched her face. "Are you all right?" She grabbed his wrist with her hand and nodded her head. "Listen: I need you to divert his attention."

"But I'm locked in here."

"Anything. Just make some noise." Mark withdrew his hand and, reaching forward, continued to pull himself along the deck, pausing as another cold wash of water swept over him.

Rachel began pounding her fists on the hatch, but it only hurt her hands. She stopped and looked around the cabin. Her eyes had adjusted to the dark now and she could see dull reflections: the tiny aluminum sink, the cabinet latches, chrome edging along the galley counter. And above the sink, a chrome cylinder: the fire extinguisher. She removed it from its harness and slammed its bottom end against the hatch. After several blows, she felt some give in the wood, and she could hear Cyrus shouting at her. Once he kicked the hatch and she stopped.

Dropping the fire extinguisher, she quickly pulled the cushions off the benches, and raised the hinged seats. Underneath were life preservers and coils of rope. Clipped to the bulkhead there was a fire ax.

With one swing Rachel broke through the wood hatch, showering her forearms with splinters.

When Mark reached the wheelhouse door he got to his knees and looked through the glass. Cyrus stood on the far side, hunched over the wheel. He was shouting at Rachel as she pounded on the hatch. When the head of an ax broke through the wood, Mark stood up, opened the door, and went into the wheelhouse.

"You can't go out through the jetties!" Mark shouted.

Cyrus turned and looked at him but kept both hands on the wheel. His wet, contorted face was illuminated by the dim light of the gauge panel. "You don't think so?"

"It won't work, Cyrus—none of it worked. You're right, this is about the future. But killing all of them won't stop it—" Mark looked out the windshield. "You'll never make it across the bay now!"

"Acrost—where? To the *mainland?*" Cyrus leaned close to the windshield. "No mainland for me. I'll find another island. They want to build bridges and destroy this one? There's other islands."

The ax blade came through the hatch again, breaking out the center panel. As Rachel began to climb through the opening, Mark took the ax from her and shouted, "Stay below!"

A wave struck the hull broadside, throwing Mark against the back of the wheelhouse, and Rachel sprawled across the deck. As she got to her feet Cyrus wrapped one arm around her chest, holding his knife blade in front of her face. He steered with his other arm, but was having trouble keeping the boat on course.

"Drop it!" Cyrus shouted.

Mark dropped the ax.

Rachel squirmed and shouted, causing Cyrus to let go of the wheel. The boat was slapped by another wave that jerked it to the starboard. The pitch of the hull sent the three of them sprawling against the back of the wheelhouse. For a moment Mark felt the handle of the ax under him, but then it was gone. Cyrus punched him in the mouth, throwing him against the bulkhead. Then Cyrus was on his knees, holding up the knife. As he lunged, Mark rolled to his left. They grappled on the deck, their arms entangled, and Mark felt the blade of the knife slide along his left cheek, just above the jawbone. It was a long, clean cut, and his skin felt cool, until the warmth of the blood poured out and down his neck. He threw several punches, two seeming to connect, causing Cyrus to groan. The *Angel Gabriel* was taking the waves broadside now, and the boat rocked so that they were finally pulled apart.

"*The jetties!*" Rachel screamed.

Mark got to his feet and, looking out the windshield, he could see the jetty rocks dead ahead. A wave struck and he was thrown to the deck again. Turning, he saw Cyrus, crawling toward Rachel now, the fishing knife in his right hand. The ax was under Mark's side. He picked it up, raised it, and swung down with everything he had—it made a deep, clean cut in the deck. He'd missed.

But Cyrus was stopped—the ax had pinned the bottom of his slicker to the deck. He reached behind him and began pulling on the ax handle. It was too deeply embedded in the deck. He began tugging at the slicker, but the material would not rip away from the blade. Then his hands frantically began undoing buttons.

Mark got to his feet, took hold of Rachel's forearm, and pulled her out the wheelhouse door. The jetty rocks weren't twenty yards away. He led her to the stern of the boat and together they jumped off the transom. In the moment before he entered the water Mark saw the faint outline of the inn, swept by relentless sheets of rain. There were no lights anywhere. Through the rain he could see the line of the two hills forming the angel's wings, but its head was now a gnarled, black configuration of storm cloud.

Emerson had been helping to wrap Randall's knife wound when the wind carried the sound of the *Angel Gabriel's* diesel up to the inn. He and Randall led the crew down to the pier. Across the cove they could hear the plaintive sounds of cracking wood, and they all stood on the pier, listening, gazing into the darkness. Everyone came down to the pier—Max, Chastity, Mae, Page, and McNeil, fishermen and villagers—and they all stared out at the black cove.

There came an explosion, and flames shot high into the darkness. On the pier Angelians cried and shouted, their voices raised against the wind.

Randall squatted on the pier and the crew encircled him, shielding him from the storm.

Emerson walked out to the end of the pier. He held his face directly into the wind and rain as long as he could endure it; then he came back slowly, seeing that the others had not moved—they had become a kind of tableau of grief. He paused to check the lines that held the *Seraphim* to the pilings. She bounced and groaned in her berth, but she sat poised in the water. Standing at the edge of the pier, he looked out at the jetties once again. After several minutes the flames were gone. There was nothing but black again; no way of telling where sky and water met, just the limitless storm.

He was listening, listening for a voice, but he heard none.

When he was about to turn back, to insist that everyone return to the inn, he noticed something in the water. He ran to the end of the pier and saw two heads bobbing in the chop. Mark was pulling Rachel behind him. He looked exhausted, she looked asleep. With great effort his arm came up out of the water and he grabbed a rung of the ladder. Emerson got to his knees and reached down to lend a hand.

Twenty-nine

LYING ON HIS BACK, MARK CAN SEE HIS BREATH. HE THINKS
winter.

He is alone in bed now, but he can hear their voices coming up through
the heat grate in the floor. There is the smell of pancakes and coffee.

He gets up and dresses quickly in the cold room. Out the frosted window he can see that the new snow has drifted high against the east wall of
the Boat House, almost as though it is some white wave that rose up overnight with the intention of pushing the shingled building onto its side.
Nearer to the inn he can see the oblong depression in the snow where the
shed used to be, and he wonders why they didn't take it down sooner. It
had been Emerson's idea, to tear it down before winter set in, but since he
died in November the smallest tasks have taken on overwhelming proportions.

But I finally got round to it yesterday.
'Bout time.
We'll do more through the winter.
Good.
Repair.
Yes.
Maintenance.
Better. Maintenance avoids repair.
Yes. We can't sit around reworking the past.
No, you can't.
*But I often—I often catch glimpses of you about the inn. Walking up from the
Boat House, a string of fish dangling from your hand. That will not be forgotten. You
will not be abandoned.*

There is nothing but the sound of wind against glass panes.

Mark goes down to the kitchen. Kindling is in the stove—boards from the shed—snapping and hissing. Anne is seated at the table with Rachel. She turns and smiles up at him, something rare since the morning when they found Emerson slumped in the Boat House. He pours himself a mug of coffee and refills Anne's cup.

Rachel holds a glass of orange juice in one hand, flips the pages of the latest edition of *The Current* with the other. She doesn't once look up from her reading—she has developed the ability to become totally absorbed, to acknowledge adults only when she's ready, which often infuriates her mother—but suddenly she reads aloud, "'Angel's Head possesses traditions that are as old and conflicting as the constantly shifting currents of Pleasant Bay; and her inhabitants are determined to preserve her sense of history, without putting her future in jeopardy—Angelians have a clear sense of their relation to their place, to the land, to the water. Like the sealife that surrounds them, they adapt, they endure.'" She makes a face, the one with the crooked eyebrows and twisted lips, and drops the magazine on the table. "Under your byline it now says you're Associate Editor."

"Means more work, same pay—at least I'm not still a freelancer," Mark says, "and I'm covering Angel's Head and the Cape again."

He looks down at the magazine—he's seen the pages in pasteup, but they always look different to him once they're printed. To increase circulation, Max has introduced a new format, and they're going to a monthly, with color and more in-depth stories. On the page opposite his article there's a photograph that was taken from the end of the south jetty, looking across the cove toward the village; it was taken in the summer when boats were moored, the water and sky were the purest blues imaginable. Though everything in the photo is familiar, it still seems strange, even foreign. Mark studies the edges of the photo, imagining what lay just beyond those borders. "I don't really like photographs of places I know," he says. "I always look for what's missing."

"Where does the phrase 'free lance' come from?" Rachel asks.

For a moment he strokes his new, graying beard. The knife scar running down his cheek is no longer visible, but his fingers are drawn to the soft ridge of new flesh. "That's a good question," he says. "I don't know."

Rachel places both hands behind her head suddenly, pouting her lips provocatively. "It sounds—sexual, don't you think?"

Anne looks at her daughter, and for a moment Mark isn't sure whether she'll scold the girl or ask her forgiveness. Finally Anne simply shakes her head and glances toward him with a slight grin on her face.

"Tide's low at ten oh-eight this morning," Mark says.

"Think today's the day?" Rachel asks.

"After last night's storm, it's worth a look."

Both Rachel and Anne gaze across the kitchen at him. Their eyes are wide, blue, the striations clear and seemingly infinite.

I see in their eyes all the tides, all the seasons of Floods.

Yes.

The new snow is up to Rachel's knees in some places. They begin to walk, down the hill and through the village, which is quiet except for the sound of snow shovels scraping against the brick sidewalk. In front of Twomey's Hardware Geoff Twomey is clearing a path from the front door to the curb. He pauses in his labor and rests both arms on top of the handle of his shovel. Mark says good morning and Geoff nods and mutters a greeting. He watches them pass, his eyes avoiding Rachel, except for a quick, fearful glance. Rachel gazes back at him and crosses her eyes. Geoff's face flushes, then he smiles.

Yes, today is the day.

They walk several blocks through the village, until Anne finally says Rachel's name, her voice calm and deep. The girl nods, as though she too has been anticipating this conversation.

"It's long enough after Grapes is gone," Anne says, "and we need to talk about other matters. The inn—and our living arrangement there."

Rachel stares up at him. "You're staying with us, Associate Editor, you're staying as a permanent guest."

Anne says, "We were thinking also about as a husband and—"

Rachel looks back down at the snow. "Will this make you a father, too?"

"Yes," Anne says. "Next summer."

"My father?"

Anne doesn't answer.

Mark raises his gaze and follows the flight of a seagull across the clear winter sky. "If that's what you want," he says. "It would be fine with me."

Rachel keeps plowing ahead, swinging her arms with effort.

You walk like a Flood.

"I know," she says. Her mother and Mark are watching her now, and she says quietly, "Sometimes I swear I hear Grapes's voice."

Mark is about to say I do too—he wants to say something, do something, touch her, give her some sign. In recent weeks they've all been tentative, settling in for winter. He is no longer a summer guest—they have started a life together. And this is the first time Rachel has shown not just acceptance, but approval.

Behind them comes the sound of a horse-drawn sleigh. Doc Walter and his wife Amanda ride through the village and stop—the chestnut mare snorts plumes of steam from her nostrils, her leather harness creaks softly. "Headed down to Plummer's?" Doc Walter asks.

Anne squints up at the old couple, then nods.

"We've plenty of room," Amanda says.

"I don't mind the exercise," Anne says. But Rachel is already climbing into the rear seat, and Anne appears relieved at the idea of a ride.

Mark says, "We can always walk home."

They climb into the sleigh and cover themselves with an old quilt. Doc Walter speaks to his mare and she begins walking; for such a cumbersome vehicle, it is remarkable how smoothly the sleigh's runners glide through the snow. The air is frigid on Mark's face above his beard. Anne leans against him, and beneath the blanket her hand seeks his coat pocket. He works off his glove and takes her hand, which is surprisingly warm. They travel down the east coast of the island. Jagged ice formations stretch hundreds of yards offshore; beyond the ice the water is a deep blue. Across the bay the dunes of Nauset are white with snow.

When the sleigh reaches the southern tip of the island, Rachel stands up before they come to a complete halt. A small crowd of villagers has already arrived—Mae Bough, Dorothea Cross's cousin Chastity, several of Samuel's crew. Most have walked. Maxine came on skis with her dogs. A few rode horses. Everyone is staring out across Plummer's Marsh. The blizzard has completed what had begun after the storm last summer. Increasingly through the fall and winter Blacke's Channel was shifting, its current turning south so that at low tide a sandbar began to expose itself, running off this southern tip of the island. Mark fished here often throughout the fall, and by Thanksgiving he noticed another bar surfacing, working its way out from Grummond's Neck. Over the weeks the two spits of sand advanced toward each other, seeming to gain a few more yards and to widen with each new high tide. And now under this bright January sun the bar finally extends all the way across to Grummond's Neck; with this one storm—which came on the first night of the full moon—the migration of sand is done. Blacke's Channel is diverted. Angel's Head is connected to the mainland by a wide spit of sand.

"It makes the whole notion of deeds and ownership seem trivial," Anne says. "The ocean creates this land at will."

"I wonder if it's like before," Mark says, stepping down from the sleigh. "Like when your ancestors saw it."

"Today feels timeless," Anne says. "It could be the eighteen-nineties."

"How long will the bar last?" Rachel asks.

"A while," Anne says. "That's all I can tell you. A while."

They walk along the edge of the marsh. The snow isn't deep here and they move with considerable alacrity, until Mark stops.

"Aren't you coming?" Rachel asks.

"Yes, but you lead," he says.

She looks at him as though he's given her a gift.

Rachel is first out on the bar. She walks ahead of the other Angelians. Turning around she looks back toward the island. It is white snow, brown sand, black branches of bare trees, and green of scrub pine; and it rises up off the wide, glistening blue water in a way that suddenly makes her afraid to go any farther, as though the island might recede from view, might simply disappear and become inaccessible. She even takes a step back toward the island, but as she does she hears clapping. She turns and looks toward the mainland, several hundred yards away. There is a man standing on top of a dune, clapping his hands, the sound coming clear through the cold, still air.

Randall, clapping.

Rachel begins dancing toward him, her head high, her arms outstretched, her feet slapping against the smooth wet sand at the water's edge, and as she dances she hears voices around her as the other Angelians begin clapping and hooting and hollering, creating a music she will always remember from when they first walked acrost the bay.